KT-174-669

Praise for Veronica Henry

'It's a glamorous and absorbing read, a well-written romp with a cast of believable, empathetic characters whom you'll be fascinated by from the start'
Daily Mail

'The book is first-class chick-lit and a great beach read'   *Sunday Express*

'Compulsive reading'   *Woman & Home*

'A perfect summer delight'   *Sun*

'Warm and brilliantly written'   *Heat*

'Beautifully written and dreamily descriptive, this delightful read will make you laugh, sob … and pack up the car for a trip to the Cornish Coast'   *Closer*

'A fast-paced gossipy read, set in glamorous locations, with sumptuous descriptions and lively dialogue'
Telegraph & Argus

'A great summer read. Veronica Henry's creation of a clever web of characters, each with their own story to tell, makes this a real page-turner'
Cornwall Today

'This sweet book would be a great beach companion'
Star

Veronica Henry worked as a scriptwriter for *The Archers*, *Heartbeat* and *Holby City*, amongst many others, before turning to fiction. She lives with her family on the coast in North Devon. Visit her website at www.veronicahenry.co.uk or follow her on Twitter @veronica_henry

By Veronica Henry

Wild Oats
An Eligible Bachelor
Love on the Rocks
Marriage and Other Games
The Beach Hut
The Birthday Party
The Long Weekend
A Night on the Orient Express
The Beach Hut Next Door

THE HONEYCOTE NOVELS
Honeycote
Making Hay
Just a Family Affair

The Beach Hut Next Door

Veronica Henry

BAINTE DEN STOC

WITHDRAWN FROM DLR LIBRARIES STOCK

An Orion paperback

First published in Great Britain in 2014
by Orion Books,
This paperback edition published in 2014
by Orion Books,
an imprint of the Orion Publishing Group Ltd,
Orion House, 5 Upper St Martin's Lane,
London WC2H 9EA

An Hachette UK company

1 3 5 7 9 10 8 6 4 2

Copyright © Veronica Henry 2014

The moral right of Veronica Henry to be identified as the author
of this work has been asserted in accordance with
the Copyright, Designs and Patents Act 1988.

All rights reserved. No part of this publication may be
reproduced, stored in a retrieval system, or transmitted,
in any form or by any means, electronic, mechanical,
photocopying, recording or otherwise, without the prior
permission of the copyright owner.

All the characters in this book are fictitious,
and any resemblance to actual persons, living
or dead, is purely coincidental.

A CIP catalogue record for this book
is available from the British Library.

ISBN 978-1-4091-4673-5

Typeset at The Spartan Press Ltd,
Lymington, Hants

Printed and bound in Great Britain by Clays Ltd,
St Ives plc

The Orion Publishing Group's policy is to use papers that
are natural, renewable and recyclable products and
made from wood grown in sustainable forests. The logging
and manufacturing processes are expected to conform to
the environmental regulations of the country of origin.

www.orionbooks.co.uk

The
Beach Hut
Next Door

DUN LAOGHAIRE-RATHDOWN LIBRARIES	
DLR20001034855	
BERTRAMS	28/07/2014
	£7.99
CA	

Summer appeared from nowhere that year in Everdene. Most people had given up hope of ever seeing it again, after two years of endless grey and wet with barely any respite. But suddenly the sun burst back onto the scene with unapologetic ebullience, throwing her golden rays with abandon onto the three miles of beach, turning the sand from sludgy beige to roseate gold. There was the touch of the show-off about her: the girl who knows she is the belle of the ball; the girl who relishes being the centre of attention.

Some, with typically British pessimism, said the glorious sunshine would never last, but those with a beach hut at Everdene exchanged secretive, gleeful smiles as day after day broke cloudless and bright.

Fifty-seven huts, painted in ice-cream colours, some immaculate, some dilapidated; some tiny, with barely room for a bucket and spade; others sprawling and substantial. You couldn't walk past them and not want to be inside one; to share the heavenly luxury of falling asleep and waking up with the sandy shore on your doorstep, and the sea itself only a few feet beyond that.

For the people lucky enough to have one, this was the summer of their dreams – a summer of hazy days and balmy nights, of the kind read about in books; of the kind recalled in distant memories. A summer of picnic baskets and bicycle rides and ripe strawberries. Freckles and ice cream and stolen afternoon naps.

And love. Love blossomed and unfurled. The heat healed rifts and forged bonds and mended broken hearts, reaching across miles and spanning decades. Love in many different guises. Sometimes the love had waited patiently to re-emerge, blinking, into the sunlight. Other times it sprang up unexpectedly and surprised itself.

It was undoubtedly the sun that had coaxed love out of hiding, though, a golden, glittering orb that stayed fixed in the sky for weeks on end, only standing aside occasionally for the rain to moisten the parched earth.

Nobody wanted it to end.

The
Winter Before

ELODIE

The woman stood at the top of the steps. She knew, without counting, that there were twelve. Right now they were treacherously silver with morning frost. They ran from the terrace at the back of The Grey House down to the sweeping lawns, which in turn led down to the sea via a secret path. It wasn't a terribly well-kept secret, as secrets go, but it certainly gave off an air of mystery, its entrance hidden amidst clumps of marram grass, twisting its way down the cliff to the beach that was just starting to reveal a crescent of pinkish sand as the tide receded.

It was called The Grey House because it was built of the local grey stone, but it was in no way as cold or forbidding as its name might suggest, even on this dreary, indeterminate morning. On the contrary, it was soft and mellow in the morning mist, snuggled in amongst the twisted monkey puzzle trees, the oldest of a very few houses overlooking the bay. There were plenty of windows to break up the facade, and a set of French doors that led out onto the terrace, and above that a wrought-iron balcony that made the most of the panoramic view.

'We don't expect it to stay on the market long,' the estate agent warned her. 'Not now it's gone online.'

Elodie ignored him. Her eye was on a fat rabbit at the

far end of the lawn, nibbling on the first tender shoots in the herbaceous border. Well, what had once been an herbaceous border. It was choked with weeds that allowed only the most audacious of plants to push their way through. She recalled a time when that would never have been allowed. Two gardeners had kept the grounds manicured. Not into municipal, soulless precision – they had allowed nature to have her head up to a point – but into the joyful abundance of an English country garden at its best. Or the best it could be, given its exposure to the sea.

It was going to take some serious landscaping to get it back to its former glory. The lawn was ruined, speckled with moss and bare patches. She could see, in her mind's eye, a croquet ball rolling across the grass once again. She thought she heard the joyful cry of a child, but it was a seagull, slicing through the air with determination. She gave a shiver. There was no sound more evocative of the seaside. And summer.

That summer. More than fifty years ago now. Yet what struck her more than anything was the fact that it was the good memories that came flooding back to her, rather than the reminder of what came after. She had been right to come back. It wasn't the house, after all, that had done the harm. It was the people in it.

'I'll have it,' she said.

The agent blinked. 'You haven't seen inside.'

Elodie flapped the details at the view. 'When you look at that, the inside's almost irrelevant, wouldn't you say?' She didn't tell him that she already knew every last inch of the house; that she had imagined it sitting up and taking notice as she'd swept in through the stone pillars and up the drive. That she had sensed its relief as she emerged from her car. A ludicrous notion, of course. Fanciful. But it was her imagination that had got her where she was.

'It's a magnificent property. The most coveted position in Everdene. This was the first house to be built here, so it's in the prime position.'

'Yes. I've read the details.' Elodie knew more about the house than even the details revealed. That it had been built by a doting father for his convalescent daughter. That she had died, despite the sea air, and that the house had languished empty for half a century. That it had been home to a battalion of soldiers during the war, when they had practised manoeuvres on Everdene beach in preparation for the D-Day landings.

That once they had left, it had lain empty again, until—

The agent interrupted her thoughts. 'Are you ... proceedable?'

Proceedable. It was one of those estate agent euphemisms that basically meant: have you got the cash?

Elodie looked at him. Her eyes were as grey as the stone of the house, only at this moment not nearly as forgiving. 'I wouldn't waste your time if I weren't,' she told him.

He nodded. 'I can assure you, that's not the case for everyone. But I do apologize.' If he could get this one tied up, that was next month's wages paid. 'Are we talking asking price?'

Elodie didn't answer. Her mind drifted, to a day when the sun had baked the pink sand so fiercely you could barely stand on it and a motorbike roared through the frill of surf at the tide's edge. She could feel her outrage as if it were yesterday. She could see the rider's eyes dance as he came to a halt five feet in front of her – there were no

7

safety measures in those days; no helmets required – and smell the hot, oily exhaust. How dare he invade their privacy; the Lewis stronghold? Everyone knew this was their stretch of beach; no one dared venture onto it unless invited. It was an unspoken lore.

'Oi!' She'd marched up to him. 'What do you think you're doing? This is a private beach.'

'Actually,' he said. 'It's not. There's no such thing. Haven't you read the Magna Carta?'

Elodie had – well, some of it – but she wasn't going to let herself be intimidated by history.

'Bugger the Magna Carta,' she said. 'No one comes here unless they are invited.'

'Ah,' came the reply. 'Well, I have been.'

Elodie wished she were wearing something more fetching than her old school swimming costume with the life-saving badges sewn on. Normally, she never cared what she was wearing on the beach but she suddenly felt underdressed.

The stranger smiled at her.

'Your father has asked us for the weekend. My parents are coming down by car but I can't stand it when they squabble over the map-reading so I made my own way.'

'Oh.' The wind was taken out of Elodie's sails some-what. Her father had mentioned the visitors at breakfast. The Jukes, she thought they were called.

That was the whole point of The Grey House, after all. The never-ending stream of summer guests – friends, relations, business associates, hangers-on – that swarmed through its walls during July and August, when the Lewis family decamped en masse from Worcestershire to Devon, staff and all. Elodie never bothered to keep track of exactly

8

who was who or why they were there. She was socially adept and gregarious, equally comfortable joining in or doing her own thing, depending on the circumstances; as happy organizing a game of rounders on the beach for the youngsters or mixing cocktails before dinner for the grown-ups.

This guest, she decided, was much more likely to require a gin and tonic than a glass of squash. The cigarette he pulled out of a gold case stored in his trouser pocket confirmed this. He proffered one and she shook her head. She wanted to get back to the house as quickly as possible. He snapped the case shut, put it back in his pocket, put the cigarette in his mouth and looked at her.

And in that moment, she knew this man – who wasn't that much older than she was, a month short of nineteen – was going to shape her future.

If she had known then what she knew now, would she have walked away? She took in a deep breath at the memory of the first time his gaze met hers; the flicker of something strange and new and terrifying yet irresistible. A feeling that had made her feel concomitantly vulnerable and powerful, because she had looked in his eyes and seen surprise; shock even. Elodie tried to push the image away.

Today, the sea lapped the shore beneath The Grey House in the same rhythm as it had that day, and the dunes were as soft as ever they were. The only visible change from this vantage point was the row of brightly coloured huts that had ventured further down the beach. Back in the day there had been no more than a dozen, home to an exclusive but hedonistic crowd intent on merriment over the summer months. Now she could see at least another twenty.

'Does the hut still come with the property?' she asked.

The hut belonging to The Grey House had been the last one in the row then, allowing the Lewis family to spread themselves out as far down the beach as they liked. Now it was smack bang in the middle.

'I believe so,' said the agent. 'Although it's been rented out for the summer of late. It provides quite a good income.'

'Good,' said Elodie. There was no point unless she had the whole package. The Grey House was nothing without its beach hut.

'So – do we have a deal?'

'We do. How quickly can we tie things up?'

'The owner had to go into a home a month or so ago. She's very fragile. We're going to have to arrange house clearance on her behalf before proceeding, but if there's no chain involved on your side we're looking at … six weeks? Assuming no snags.'

Elodie looked away, gazing out at the horizon, chewing the inside of her cheek. There was a lump in her throat suddenly. She took in a couple of deep breaths to dispel it before she spoke again.

'Good. As quickly as possible. There'll be no snags.'

'Are you absolutely certain you don't want to see inside?'

Elodie nodded. She was quite sure. She wanted to be on her own the first time she went in. She had no idea how she would handle it, but she certainly didn't want a stranger gauging her reaction or feeling the need to hand her a handkerchief. Privacy was paramount to Elodie. She didn't share easily. Once she had, and that had taught her a lesson: never give any of yourself away.

Until, of course, the time was right.

VINCE

Vince planted his feet wide on the deck to maintain his balance while he shovelled the last of the bacon roll into his mouth and checked his mobile phone for the last time before they went out. It was going to be rough out there today and he felt the same twinge of unease he always did, because although the forecast said it wouldn't go above gale force 6, you couldn't be sure. You could never be sure. He cast a look at the skyline. The clouds above the harbour were slate grey but not as threatening as they might be – a certain lightening around the edges hinted they might go away by mid-morning given an incentive.

The water was sludgy and choppy, slapping against the harbour wall and the sides of the fishing vessel. The other boats clustered around were mostly day boats; there was nothing flashy or grand in Tawcombe. The seas around the little town were too challenging for most fair-weather sailors, and there were no smart restaurants or bars to lure the gin-palace brigade. Vince liked it that way. He didn't want tourists pushing up the mooring fees or pricing out the locals, turning Tawcombe into a chichi playground, abandoned at the first hint of autumn then turned into a ghost town for the next six months.

The two lads he'd taken on at the beginning of the

summer were setting the pots ready. They were good lads. Fearless, hardworking and as loyal as you could hope for; ex-Marines who'd given up military life for something that was, at times, just as tough and physical and decidedly less glamorous. Yellow oilskins and blue plastic gloves didn't have the pulling appeal of a uniform, somehow.

There was no sign of Chris. Of course not. Given that he'd ended up in a lock-in at the George and Dragon last night. The barmaid there had texted Vince at about eleven. He had a network of people around the town who gave him the heads-up on Chris's whereabouts and condition. Not that he could do anything about it, but he still felt responsible. He always felt responsible. For what had happened. For what might still happen. It was a curse. He would have given anything to wake up and not feel the burden on his shoulders, weighing him down like an albatross.

He swallowed the last morsel of bacon and stuck his phone back in his pocket with a sigh. There'd been no more reports, so presumably Chris was sleeping it off somewhere. It was lucky Vince didn't have anything else planned for today, but then he was used to dropping everything at the last minute to step in as skipper.

He wasn't supposed to be hands-on any more. He and Chris had agreed, when they'd taken on the two Marines, that Vince would concentrate on expansion so they could afford the extra wages. It was his role to find bars and pubs and restaurants to supply, and to organize delivery, and run the business generally: advertising and administration and endless paperwork, organizing the maintenance of the boat, liaising with the foreign agents whose lorries swept into the harbour three nights a week to pick up any excess catch; overseeing the shop – well, if you could call it a shop; it was a glorified market stall – that opened at weekends and throughout the summer. It was all Vince could do to keep up with it, now they had expanded, but he always had to be ready to step in and, quite literally, take over at the helm.

If Chris weren't his brother, he'd be seriously considering a written warning.

The sign on their lock-up still said Maskell and Sons. It stood amidst a row of dilapidated buildings on the quay – a raggle-taggle row of storage units, sheds and warehouses that reeked of fish and salt and diesel. They'd just had a proper roof put on, instead of the wriggly tin that had been there since forever, and put heating in, and divided the inside into an office, a storage area containing the tanks which held over a metric tonne of lobster at any one time, and the open-fronted booth where they sold their catch. They'd wanted to be sensible with the insurance money. It would be all too easy to fritter it.

Nevertheless, Vince couldn't bring himself to get the signwriter to change the sign to Maskell Bros, even though that was what was on their headed notepaper now.

The boat had nearly reached open water, passing the last of the unforgiving cliffs that made up this part of the coast. The ozone-rich breeze ruffled Vince's shoulder-length hair, bleached almost white by the sun and the salt. Only his semi-permanent stubble gave away his true hair colour, an indeterminate brown. He shaved it off once a week, on a Saturday night, because after six days he couldn't bear the itching. His face was tanned to a light brown by the elements, and in the midst of it ice-blue eyes analysed everything with a thoughtful, perspicacious gaze.

Someone once said Vince's eyes spoke more than he did.

He felt his phone buzz in his pocket. He thought about ignoring it. Now they were on their way, there was nothing much he could do if it was Chris either grovelling or demanding a lift from wherever it was he'd ended up.

Curiosity got the better of him and he pulled out his phone.

It wasn't Chris. It was his mate, Murphy. He often phoned at this time, when he stopped off for his morning latte and almond croissant in Chiswick High Street. Their worlds, which had once been the same, were now a universe apart.

'Vince. It's Murph, man. Meet me in Everdene tonight.'

'On a Monday? At this time of year?' Vince was puzzled.

'I've had a tip-off. I've got a proposition for you.'

'Why does that make my heart sink?'

'Come on – where's your entrepreneurial spirit?'

'I'm a fisherman, Murph. Not Alan Sugar.'

'Don't give me that. You haven't kept that business going without having your head screwed on. Most people would have gone under by now. Come on – six o'clock in the Ship Aground. You know you want to.'

Vince smiled to himself.

Murphy could talk anyone into anything. It was part of his charm. He was so utterly plausible and convincing. A born salesman. Even Vince, who was by nature cautious, even cynical, could already feel himself beguiled by Murphy's enthusiasm, just as he had been at school.

They were Tawcombe boys, the two of them. They spent their youth bunking off school, kicking around the

14

harbour or grabbing the bus to Everdene or Mariscombe, the nearest beaches, where they'd spend the day surfing then finish off by building a campfire. They'd been carefree times, thought Vince. Neither of them had had a thought for the future and what it might bring.

Of course, Vince's future had already been mapped out for him. He'd known from birth that he would join his father in the fishing business. It was unspoken. There was simply no point in him thinking about going to college or having any other kind of career. He was born to it. It was as simple as that.

His acceptance of his fate had driven Murphy insane: he saw it as lack of ambition. Murphy couldn't wait to get out and see the big wide world. His mum and dad weren't indigenous to Tawcombe like Vince's. They'd moved down from Birmingham after the IRA pub bombings, when there was a wave of anti-Irish sentiment in the city and it all got too much for them. They'd bought the run-down café by the bus station, where Vince had bought his bacon roll that morning, thinking it would be a better life for them and their five children, and it was. Murphy had been a fat, laughing baby in a pram who became a fixture in the café, spoiled and cosseted by every customer who walked through the door.

His name was Sean, but everyone called him by his last name, because it suited him better. And he and Vince had been firm friends since the day they first met at primary school, where Murphy made a profit selling blackjacks he'd stolen from one of the jars behind the counter at the café, and Vince tried to buy the lot off him in return for a ride on his BMX.

Vince had admired Murphy's entrepreneurial spirit even

then. And Murphy had admired Vince's quiet practicality; his skill with tools and engines and knives and knots; his knowledge of wildlife and the sea. And, as they grew older, his magnetic pull where women were concerned. Murphy was no slouch in the looks department, with his close-cropped black curls and his green eyes and his Celtic freckles, but there was something about Vince that women found irresistible. Maybe it was Vince's total self-containment and his apparent lack of interest? Murphy could never feign that as long as he lived. He was border-line obsessed with women and could never disguise it. He just couldn't help himself. He still couldn't. Even now, when the two of them went out to the Ship Aground in Everdene, Murphy would be chatting up girls until closing time, even though he was happily married with two daughters of his own. Vince wondered how many times he had picked up the pieces over the years. Or calmed some sobbing female who had been the victim of one of Murphy's flirtatious overtures. Not that they ever came to anything. If he'd been a girl, Murphy would have been called a prick-tease.

'You can't play with people for your own amusement,' Vince told him repeatedly. 'Or to feed that bloody ego of yours. And it's not fair on Anna.'

Anna. Vince's heart always missed a beat whenever he thought of her. Vince didn't think he had ever met anyone as serene and beautiful and calm. With her silver-blonde hair and her milk-white skin, she was as pale as moonlight, her eyes large and lambent in her face.

Anna was a piano teacher. She gave lessons on the baby grand in the bay window of their living room in Chiswick. She was booked solidly, with an endless waiting list.

Mothers and fathers fought between themselves to bring their darling ones to her lessons, and were so entranced by Anna they often found long-dead ambition rekindling and a sudden burning desire to play Chopin or Debussy.

Vince loved the Murphy house. It was filled with music and candlelight and laughter. Everything was pale and beautiful, like Anna. Bleached wood, voile curtains, lace tablecloths. He imagined heaven a bit like this. Murphy himself was the only thing that didn't seem to fit there. Even their daughters were mini versions of Anna, drifting like moonbeams around the house, pensive and other-worldly. Amongst the three of them, Murphy crackled with pent-up energy, restless and wired. But then, Vince told himself, opposites attract. He himself, with his calm introspection, was probably too like Anna to capture her interest. She just laughed at Murphy, who she called Smurph and never took too seriously.

Their symbiosis intrigued him, and he wondered if there was a girl somewhere for him who would balance him out in the way Anna balanced out Murphy. He was never short of offers, but no one intrigued him the way she did. Although he suspected that together they would sink into nothingness. There would be no traction, no momentum. They would drift.

Whenever he went to visit them, he didn't want to leave.

'You should come and live up here for a while,' Murphy had told him a few years ago. 'Everyone should live in London at some point in their life.'

'And do what?' asked Vince. 'Not much call for a lobster fisherman in Chiswick.'

That was back in the day, when he could have left if he'd really wanted to. Now, he reflected, as the boat chugged out into open water and he steered it towards Lundy, towards the deep, cold water where their bounty lurked, he had no chance. His life had certainty and rhythm, but no hope of escape.

Though maybe whatever it was Murphy was going to propose would provide a distraction at the very least. After all, his last great idea had been a stroke of genius. Murphy, who had his finger on some mysterious pulse that gave him the heads-up on everything from VIP Glastonbury tickets to shares that defied all trading records, had been offered two beach huts, side by side, on Everdene Sands, for a steal. And being a friend, he'd offered Vince one, instead of selling it on at a substantial profit. Vince was eternally grateful that he had given him the opportunity, not because the huts were now worth double, but because his hut had provided him with the sanctuary he needed. It was an escape, a refuge, a home from home; somewhere he could forget the past and his responsibilities.

So he wasn't going to ignore whatever Murphy had up his sleeve.

'Six o'clock it is,' he said, and hung up. Vince didn't waste words. Besides, once the boat had rounded the promontory, they would lose signal. He would be incommunicado for the rest of the day.

At six that night, showered and dressed in faded jeans and a soft grey sweatshirt, an olive-green beanie pulled down over his damp hair, Vince strolled into the Ship Aground. Murphy was perched on a high stool at the bar. His uniform was much the same, only his sweatshirt was Abercrombie & Fitch and his beanie was cashmere. Had it been the height of summer, the two of them would have attracted infinite female interest, but the bar sported only a smattering of drinkers. The pub stayed resolutely open throughout the winter for the sake of the locals, who would otherwise have nowhere to meet or drink. The owner didn't mind that he rarely met his overheads over the hibernal months. He more than made up for it in summer.

The two friends clasped hands as Vince took the stool next to Murphy.

'How's it going?'

'It's good,' said Murphy. 'But it's going to get better. You know Marianne's?'

'The restaurant?'

'She's had enough. She's shutting down. She's given me first refusal on the lease.'

Marianne's was a rather tired French restaurant that had been in Everdene for as long as anyone could remember. Its eponymous owner was a legend, but an ageing one. Come every winter she threatened to close and move back to France. Only this time, it seemed she meant it.

'Have you taken it?'

'Too right. Leases like that don't come up round here very often. And I've got a plan.'

'Course you have.' Vince smiled. When did his friend not have a plan? It was one of the things he loved best about him.

Murphy slid the elastic band off a rolled-up set of drawings.

'This, my friend, is the venture we have been waiting for.'

He spread out the paper, which was smothered in sketches and scribbles and mathematical equations – the inner workings of Murphy's mind; a tangle of hieroglyphics and images that Vince had learned to decipher over the years.

'We strip the building out completely. Take it right back to the bare walls. Re-plaster; wallop it out. Then, we put in an open-plan kitchen separated from the restaurant by a zinc counter. Out the front we have rubber flooring and long tables with benches and stainless steel shelving. All very industrial chic.'

'OK.' Vince nodded. He could totally visualize it. 'But I'm not sure where I come in.'

'Ah. That's the beauty of it. The USP.'

'Really?' Vince had never seen himself as a restaurateur.

Murphy grinned. 'We're just going to serve seafood. Lobster, crab, mussels and prawns. With skinny fries on the side. That's it. Red or white wine, no choice. Big baskets of home-made bread to dip in extra virgin olive oil while you wait for your catch to be cooked.' Murphy sat back and smiled. 'Simple. Are you in? Fifty-fifty.'

'You want me to invest?'

'Vince – I'm in total awe of what you do. You know that. I love that your business has been handed down, and it's traditional and sustainable and all that shit. But I think you need to – pardon the pun – widen your net. Take a chance. Get out of your comfort zone.'

'Hey. Listen. I've been out of my comfort zone. I still am. It's not that great.'

Murphy looked a little shamefaced. 'No, I realize that. I didn't mean that kind of out-of-your-comfort-zone. I meant something stimulating. And profitable!'

He leaned across the table. His eyes were shining, green and glassy as the marbles they used to roll on the pavement. 'Vince, I wouldn't ask you if this wasn't a winner.

And if I didn't think you were the right guy. I have other people who would invest. I think this project is perfect for you. You get to supply the main ingredients. The publicity will be great, because it has that artisan, hands-on, handed-down-through-the-generations story behind it that the press all slaver over.'

Vince looked at Murphy, trying to assess how objective his pitch really was. Yeah, they were mates. Yes, it was a good match. But he knew Murphy knew he still had money, even after the improvements they had made. Money he hadn't touched because he considered it blood money: his father's insurance payout. It sat festering in his current account. He couldn't even be bothered to put it in a high-interest account, even though the manager at the bank kept pestering him to move it.

As if he could read his thoughts, Murphy grinned. 'This isn't because I know you've got the cash. It's because ever since the day I clocked you in that schoolyard and you tried to do a deal with me on those blackjacks, I've wanted to do business with you. But I've had to wait nearly thirty years for the right project to come along.'

Murphy unrolled another piece of paper. On it was a logo: The Lobster Shack, and a lobster motif, in bright coral on turquoise. It was perfect.

Vince took a swig from his glass because he knew that silence was the killer when you were doing a deal, and that the less he said the more Murphy would say, and he wanted it all out there before he shook hands on it.

'Everdene belongs to us, Vince. It always has done and it always will. And I want people to flock here because of us. I want people to plan a weekend around this place. I want a waiting list as long as your arm. Customers being turned away on a Saturday night. I know that will happen. It's all there. It's all to play for. But I don't want to do it without you. There's no point in doing it without you.'

Vince could feel in his bones that it was a good idea. It was just the sort of joint Everdene needed: relaxed, casual, buzzy. A foodie haven that wasn't pretentious but had all the buzzwords. And if they didn't do it, someone else would move in. Murphy was right. Everdene belonged to them.

'Why the hell not?' he said, and held out his hand for Murphy to shake.

'Right decision,' Murphy pumped his hand hard. 'Man, we are going to clean up.'

As he left the Ship Aground, Vince decided to sleep in the hut that night. Murphy was driving back up to Chiswick, and Vince knew if he went back home to Tawcombe he would be straight on a downer. Either Chris would be there, and he would find his state depressing, or he wouldn't, and Vince would worry until he heard the door go. He still wasn't sure at what point Chris's drinking had turned from normal laddish over-indulgence to dysfunctional; nor did he know what to do about it. Nothing he said seemed to make a difference: threats, concern, ultimatums. They all went unheeded.

It was cold and dark and windy on the beach, but Vince didn't care. Once inside the hut, he snapped on the side lamps and lit the wood-burner – it would warm the place up quickly. Soon it was surprisingly cosy, while the wind whipped itself into a frenzy outside. Sometimes it blew so hard he worried the entire hut would blow away, but after half an hour it was as warm as toast inside and

Vince snuggled into his bunk, wrapping himself up in a nest of blankets. The wind had died down, and all he could hear was the relentless sea pounding the sand.

The sea. They had such a conflicted relationship. It provided everything he had. It was his daily life. But it had taken away the one person he had looked up to and admired. Every day he looked out at the water and cursed it. Yet they were inextricably bound. He couldn't imagine life without it.

And tonight it was the sound of the sea that soothed him to sleep. Vince was excited by his new venture with Murphy, but there was a crack in the plan he couldn't hide from: a little worm of a flaw that he also knew was part of what had attracted him to the venture. It would inevitably bring him into contact with Anna, and he knew he would spend his days and nights wondering if and when he would next see her. And when he did, it would be the sweet torture it always was.

Anna. His curse. His obsession. His infatuation. As he lay there, he finally admitted to himself that she was the only thing that mattered to him. He was addicted to the possibility of her and there was nothing he could do about it.

JENNA

Jenna had never wanted anything quite so much in her entire life.

The want took her by the throat; it felt tight, like a silken rope. She swallowed, aware that she shouldn't show too much interest. She knew the rules of negotiation.

She walked carefully around the object of her desire. It was tatty and unloved, but she could immediately visualize it brought to life. Next to her, she could smell Weasel's signature scent of Bell's and Embassy mingled with the sweat of anticipation. He was watching her every reaction, sucking on the last inch of his cigarette, his beady eyes narrowed.

They were in his lock-up, an old warehouse on the harbour at Tawcombe. She was astonished by the amount of clutter: boxes of trainers, surfboards, crates of booze, car parts, a row of decapitated shop dummies. God only knew where it had all come from or where it was headed. The key with Weasel was not to ask questions. Or, at least, only to ask the questions that were pertinent to your particular deal.

'Hold on.' Weasel chucked his cigarette on the floor without bothering to put it out, and climbed inside the van. Jenna watched him through the sliding window, above which was written 'Go on – you know you want to' in brown cursive writing. To the right of the window was an ancient menu with faded photographs of lurid, additive-encrusted ice creams.

Weasel pressed a button by the dashboard and 'Greensleeves' played out, slightly discordant and jangly and incredibly loud in the confines of the warehouse. It was the clincher.

Weasel gave a proud smile, like a toddler who has done something particularly clever for its adoring mother.

Jenna nodded, indicating defeat.

'How much?'

'To you, darling – fifteen hundred.'

'There's no MOT. Or tax.'

'Exactly. If there was, you'd be looking at twice that. Take it to my mate and it'll sail through. Guaranteed.'

Jenna wondered, if that was the case, why Weasel hadn't organized it for himself and got the higher price, but she didn't ask.

Weasel was the Arthur Daley of Tawcombe. Which was saying something, because Tawcombe wasn't short of people trying to swindle you. Somehow, though, Weasel was the top dog. Jenna spent most of her life trying to avoid him and his ilk these days, but this was just too tempting.

Weasel had come looking for her, because he knew she would want it, and he was right.

'I fort of you,' he told her, 'as soon as I saw it. You were the Ice-Cream Girl, after all.'

'I was,' said Jenna, cautious. She had indeed spent considerable time hawking ice cream to the great and good of Tawcombe, from a booth down near the front, until her boss had done the dirty on her and shut up shop without paying her. Even now, people told her how much they missed her. Everyone, it seemed, loved ice cream.

Which was why she knew this was an opportunity she couldn't afford to turn down. She would never have enough money for a proper place in town to sell from, but a vintage ice-cream van? That was within her reach. It was perfect in its simplicity. She had the contacts, the knowledge and a supplier: a dairy farmer who made thirty-two flavours of delicious Devon ice cream. She could get a pitch on the beach at Everdene; take the van round the campsites – the possibilities were endless.

She felt a tingle of excitement inside her that was like nothing she had felt for a long time. A shoot of optimism. The enticement of a challenge. The chance for a new beginning.

'Twelve hundred,' she said to Weasel.

He gave a leery sniff.

'Sweetheart, I can get two grand no problem if I take it to auction up country.'

'Fine. Do that then.' Jenna shrugged and went to walk away. 'See ya.'

She'd nearly reached the door when Weasel called her back.

'Fifteen hundred. Cash. By the weekend.'

'Done.'

She held out her hand and took Weasel's grimy one. Not that a handshake with him was worth anything. But she was pretty sure he wasn't going to find another buyer too quickly. The thing with Weasel was that he was lazy. He wouldn't want to be bothered. So she was confident she had a deal.

The only snag was where the hell was she going to get

thirteen hundred quid from in the next three days? Jenna didn't know, but she didn't care either. She wasn't going to let this opportunity slip through her fingers. She wanted this little baby really badly. It was going to be her future. It was going to make her feel good about herself again.

Her life had changed dramatically over the past year, since she had met Craig. There were things in her past Jenna wasn't proud of. She had been able to justify some of them up to a point, because there was no doubt she'd been dealt a rough hand. Growing up in a deprived town like Tawcombe was tough. Oh, it looked all too pretty on the surface, with its picturesque little harbour nestled amidst the dramatic coastline and the impressive architecture, but underneath the facade there was little economic infrastructure and a lot of unemployment. And with that, disillusionment all too often blotted out by alcohol and drugs, for what else was there to do?

Jenna could easily have found herself going down that route. Some of her family already had. But Craig had saved her just as she was about to cross the line. He'd intervened, her knight in shining surf shorts. She gave a little shiver as she thought of his toned body and his strength. His strength, both inner and outer, that had helped her see there was a better way.

There was a better way, but it had still been tough. It still was tough. Craig had been working as a policeman up country, but had managed to get a transfer to Bamford, the nearest large town. He was away a lot at the moment, on training courses, and did a lot of night shifts. And they were still living with her mother, because he hadn't sold his flat yet – once he had they were going to buy somewhere. Well, he was. Jenna was very conscious that she had nothing to contribute, and that made her feel useless and like some sort of sponger. While her family drove her insane, with their rowing and arguing and the constant drama and the dogs barking.

And in the meantime, she was finding it impossible to get a proper job, with proper money, because most of the work down here was minimum wage and seasonal and she had no qualifications. In the summer season she sang, doing cover nights twice a week at the George and Dragon in Tawcombe and the Ship Aground in Everdene, but the pay wasn't fantastic. People seemed to think you should sing for the love of it, never mind that you were packing the place out and helping their tills ring. And in the winter, there was no one to listen – some locals, maybe, but there weren't enough of them to make it worthwhile anyone paying her.

The ice-cream van was the answer to her dreams. She could get it done up easily enough – sometimes it was handy knowing everyone who was anyone in Tawcombe. She just needed to get her hands on the money.

One thing she was sure of. She wasn't going to ask Craig for it. He had done so much for her already. And she wanted to prove herself to him. She wanted to prove that she wasn't the low life she had been when he first met her, nicking money on the beach. If he hadn't seen something good inside her, if he hadn't believed in her, she'd have been up before the magistrate, she'd have a criminal record – like almost everyone else in her family – and she'd be in with even less chance of a new start.

Jenna thought she was probably the first person in her family to go and see the bank manager. They dealt strictly in cash. They didn't have a mortgage or a credit card between them. They had a morbid fear of anyone official, so the bank was somewhere to be avoided like the plague. But she'd already committed the ultimate cardinal sin by going out with a copper, so she thought she'd give it a go.

She made an appointment with the high street branch. She put on a black polka dot skirt, a polo-neck and a pair of high boots, finishing off the ensemble with a pair of black glasses from the supermarket, hoping she looked both respectable and entrepreneurial. She put her business plan in a clear folder, and tried to remember everything she had ever gleaned from watching *Dragons' Den* and *The Apprentice*.

She was left waiting for twenty minutes before being ushered into a glass cube with a round table and plastic chairs by a man in a cheap grey suit. Her details were called up onto the computer. Her stomach churned while the manager surveyed the figures.

'I'm sorry,' he said finally. 'But you're too high a risk for us. Your credit rating is very poor. You don't have a regular wage, or any collateral.'

'So that's a no?' said Jenna. She felt slightly sick.

'Yes.'

She stood up. She felt humiliated but, more than that, she felt angry.

'So here I am, trying to better myself, and you're not prepared to invest in me?'

'I'm afraid that's how it works.'

'So I just go back to where I was? Scumming about with the rest of them?'

'I'm very sorry. But we can't take the risk.'

Jenna picked up her paperwork. She felt sick with

frustration. She'd been foolish to think that playing it straight was the way forward. Her family would laugh at her if they knew.

And she couldn't tell Craig, because Craig would immediately offer to lend her the money, or, worse, give it to her, and the whole point of this was to prove, both to him and herself, that she was worth more, that she was capable, that she wasn't just a thieving nobody.

As she left, she turned to the manager.

'So, when I sort the money for myself, and go on to make a killing, you won't be wanting me to bank the profits here, right?'

The manager held his hands up in a helpless shrug. 'Listen, if it was up to me ...'

'I know, I know. The computer says no,' said Jenna. 'Thanks for your time. Not.'

She walked back up the high street and towards home. She passed a bin and shoved her business plan inside it, watching a half-eaten burger spill its entrails onto the carefully calculated figures. What was the point? Her dream was shattered. It was so frustrating, when she could picture it all so clearly. It was made for her, that van, but the chances of her getting her hands on it were so remote.

There were loan sharks, of course. They wouldn't be mealy mouthed about her credit rating. Their exorbitant rates of interest soaked that up. It would take her two minutes to contact one of them; they roamed the estate where she lived with her family, enabling instant gratification and impulse purchases.

She looked at the high street – the run-down shops, the bookies and the pubs where the underbelly of Tawcombe ran amok. This was her world, and she couldn't see a way out, not without hanging onto Craig's coat-tails. Maybe that didn't matter? She knew he wouldn't mind. But she had wanted to feel proud of herself. At the moment she felt worthless. She didn't feel as if she deserved his attention. All sorts of horrible possibilities were wandering through her head, including compromising herself with Weasel. She sighed. She must be desperate to even give that head room.

She walked towards the harbour, pulling her jacket around her to shield herself from the wind. The tide was out, and the boats that had been left in the water over winter were wedged into the grey sludge. In a few hours the scene would change completely as the harbour filled up again. It was compelling. One of the reasons people were so drawn to Tawcombe. It was a never-ending story.

She turned along the back of the George and Dragon, which looked out over the sea. In the height of summer, you couldn't move on the terrace for heaving bodies. Now, it was empty and desolate, the furniture stacked away. She decided she'd go in for a drink and see who was about. She didn't want to go home yet. She couldn't think at home. There was always too much going on, the telly thundering and the dogs wanting attention.

Inside, there were only three customers. One interacting with the fruit machine, one doing the *Sun* crossword and one sitting at the bar.

'Hey, Chris.' Jenna perched onto the stool next to his.

A pair of bloodshot eyes slid round to her, peering out from under a shaggy fringe. His hand was curled around a pint of lager. Jenna knew it would probably be his sixth or seventh, and he wouldn't stop until gone midnight. He was part of the furniture in the George, although he might move on to another pub further down the pier later if he got bored.

She liked Chris. Everyone did. But there was nothing anyone could do about the way he was living his life. There was something broken inside him and no one knew what to do about it. It had been terrible to watch, his descent into self-destruction over the past twelve months, but it was starting to become part of the rhythm of Tawcombe; a given. People had stopped commenting and just accepted that was how he was and that he wasn't going to change.

Chris gave her one of his sleepy smiles and raised a finger to the barman to get Jenna whatever she wanted to drink. He was infinitely generous. His slate was the biggest in town and he always settled it, every Friday, not seeming to care that he was subsidizing the drinking habits of most of the slackers in Tawcombe. It was easy to take advantage of him, but he didn't care. 'What else am I going to spend it on?' he would ask.

Jenna got out her purse. 'I'm good, thanks,' she told him. She was going to pay her own way. She asked for a hot chocolate. She wanted the comfort of sugar, not alcohol.

'So what's going on?' Chris leaned his head in one hand and rested his elbow on the bar, looking at her. He hadn't shaved, and his hair was wildly overgrown, but he was still compellingly attractive – the boozing hadn't raddled his fine features and his killer smile; the dark-blue eyes with the black rings round the iris might be bloodshot, but they still drew you in. He was always interested in people and what they were doing. He would help you weave your dream until four o'clock in the morning. He just wasn't very good at weaving his own.

Hordes of women had tried to help him. He'd had no shortage of them queuing up at the beginning, thinking they could save the handsome fisherman with the tragic past from himself. But, in the end, none of them could cope with the car crash that was Chris after about seven o'clock in the evening. A shambling, incoherent wreck who slid from charming to obnoxious in the melting of an ice cube; who would get himself mixed up in fights with bellicose out-of-towners who didn't know not to antagonize him and thought he was an easy target; who would turn over tables and then stumble home, veering from one side of the road to the other like the ball in a pinball machine. If it weren't for the fact that Chris kept the tills ringing over the winter months, he would be banned from every pub in town.

Jenna fiddled with a beer mat. 'Weasel has just shown me the future. I'm trying to get my head round it.'

'Weasel?' Chris made a face. 'I don't want any part of a future with Weasel in it. I wouldn't piss on him if he was on fire.'

Weasel was a necessary evil in Tawcombe, but he wasn't popular.

'He's got an old ice-cream van for sale,' Jenna told him. 'He wants thirteen hundred quid for it. I was going to buy it and do it up. And sell ice cream. Obviously.'

'Cool.' Chris grinned at his lame attempt at a joke.

'Ha ha.' She started tearing the beer mat up, peeling the paper off in little strips. 'There's no way I can get the money. He wants it by the weekend. I just went to the bank and they pretty much laughed at me.'

Her hot chocolate arrived. She spooned the cream off the top. Chris ordered another pint. She frowned.

'You've only just finished that one.'

Chris gave her a look. 'Don't start.'

She shrugged. 'Listen, it's none of my business. But you know what? I know you've been through it, but you're luckier than a lot of people in this town.'

Before it happened, Chris had been totally together. A party animal, yes, but not a car crash. He and his brother Vince were the most eligible boys in town, working hard and playing hard. And then tragedy had struck.

Jenna could remember the day clearly. It was the sort of day that brought a community together. She could remember the feeling it gave her: that horrible realization that fate could intervene just whenever it liked; a realization that drove an icy skewer of fear into your heart. Although there were people who said that it had been reckless for them to take the boat out when the forecast was so bad. That it wasn't fate; it was foolhardiness.

The Maskells had wanted to get the lobster pots in before the weather broke. If they left them out in the storms, the lines might break and get lost. And the conditions were set to be bad for nearly a week, so it was anyone's guess when they would be able to get out again. They couldn't afford to lose a catch.

The storm had taken them unawares while they were out at sea, hurling itself in hours earlier than forecast. Huge swells had appeared from nowhere, combined with lashing rain and high winds. They were pulling the lines in when Vince and Chris's dad was washed overboard. One moment he was there; the next he had been sucked into the sea, a tiny little figure tossed out into the maelstrom.

By the time the lifeboat got out to them it was too late. The brothers couldn't have done anything without risking their own lives. There was no point in going in after him.

Jenna remembered everyone waiting at the harbour for the boat to be brought back in. Hunched figures waiting in the relentless downpour for news, hands shoved in pockets, heads bowed. Even now, she could feel them all willing the Maskells home to safety, a combination of prayer from the believers and hope from the non, but, it seemed, they didn't have the power.

The boys came back but their dad never did.

As the news filtered through, people avoided each other's eyes on the harbour front, shuffling their way into the pub to drink a farewell to John Maskell. The worst fear of a seaside town had been realized. They had lost one of their own. And then, over the next few months, they watched Chris drown himself, not in the sea but in drink, floundering helplessly from one day to the next, no one seemingly able to reach out a hand and help him, not his brother Vince or anyone else. It was as much of a waste as John Maskell's death, only more painful to watch. Until it became normal, until everyone accepted that was just the way Chris was going to be, forever after.

And here he was, lagered up at two o'clock in the afternoon, deadbeat and defiant, because at this time of year they didn't take the boat out much, so there was nothing else for him to do.

'Lucky?' he said to Jenna, his eyes narrowed. 'How so?' He picked up the pint the barman had poured him and drank defiantly.

Jenna sensed she had strayed into dangerous territory.

'I just don't know why you drink the way you do.'

'I drink because it's the only thing that stops me feeling guilty.'

'But it was an accident. It wasn't your fault.'

Chris shook his head. Jenna had the feeling her words had been echoed a million times before.

'I should have been able to save him. I should have been quicker. I should have been the one pulling in the line. It should have been me that went over ...'

'Chris – you have to stop torturing yourself. Thinking like that isn't going to bring him back.'

'I should have gone in after him.'

'Oh yeah? You know the rules, Chris. No one but a fool goes in to rescue someone in those conditions. Both of you would have drowned.'

'Yeah, well – maybe that would have been a good thing.'

'I'm sure Vince wouldn't think so.'

'I bet he'd rather I'd drowned than dad. I can see it in his eyes. Why wasn't I the one pulling in the line? Why didn't I go overboard?'

'You're talking crap. Self-pitying crap. It was an accident – how many times do I have to say it?'

'Whatever. He's never going to come back, either way. And that's why this helps.' He held up his glass. 'When I wake up in the morning the first thing I see is him falling out of that boat. And until I get my first drink, the image doesn't leave me. The first drink makes the edges of the picture go blurry. By the second one it starts to fade. The third one makes it disappear altogether. And then I don't have to think about it at all for the rest of the day. Until I wake up the next morning.'

'And it starts all over again.'

'You've got it.'

'But you're wasting your life.'

'I haven't got a bloody life.'

Jenna wasn't sure where the anger came from. Whether it was her recent humiliation, or a genuine sense of waste, or a combination of both. She slammed down her cup, the watery brown liquid sloshing over the edge.

'You could have,' she told him. 'You could have if you stopped blaming yourself and feeling sorry for yourself and wallowing in it all. I mean, what's the point? It's like *Groundhog Day*. Chris gets up. Maybe he gets on the boat to help Vince. Maybe he doesn't. Then he drinks himself into oblivion, and pisses off everyone in the pub. Gets into a fight or pulls some bird whose name he can't remember the next morning.'

'Yep,' agreed Chris. 'That's pretty much how I roll.'

'But you've got loads going for you.' Jenna leaned into him; looked into his eyes in the hope of getting through. 'You've got more going for you than most people in this godforsaken town. You've got a bloody business that makes money, for a start. Have you got any idea how hard it is for most people here? They'd give their eye teeth for an opportunity like you've got.'

Chris glared at her. 'My dad drowned, Jenna. Right in front of my eyes. There was nothing I could do about it. Don't you lecture me when you don't know what it's like to live with that.' His eyes burned bright with rage.

'I might not know what it's like but I do know that drinking yourself to death isn't going to make any difference. It's not going to bring him back. It's not going to make things better. And, apart from anything, what do you think your dad would think if he knew? Do you think he'd think: great, that was worth dying for?'

She knew her words were harsh, but at this stage there was no point in holding back. Maybe no one had ever got through to Chris before. Maybe she wouldn't now, but she was damned if she was going to let him wallow and defend himself to her.

He looked furious. He gripped his glass even more tightly.

'Fuck off and save someone else, Pollyanna,' he said.

Jenna shrugged. 'You know I'm right. I *am* right. But you're too much of a coward to do anything about it. It's much easier to slosh about in seventeen pints of lager than get help. You're just on a massive self-pity trip. Poor little me. Well, Vince went through it too and I don't see him on self-destruct.'

'Vince is different.'

'Vince isn't a self-indulgent tosser.' She widened her eyes at him. 'Yep. That's what I said. Because that's what you are, Chris. You're a total waste of space. If you had anything about you, you'd get out there and make your dad proud. You'd create something in his memory. Instead of making yourself a laughing stock for the whole town to roll their eyes at. John Maskell's son, the drunken loser.'

Chris held his glass to his mouth and drank deep, holding her gaze, then slammed his glass down on the bar top.

Jenna felt as if she had run out of steam. 'Sorry,' she said eventually. 'But that's what I'm seeing and I find it upsetting.'

Chris got off his bar stool. Even at this hour of the afternoon he swayed slightly. He leaned in towards Jenna.

'I'll leave you to it, then, if you find it so upsetting.'

There was menace in his tone. Jenna gave a wry smile and a small shrug. Chris turned and swaggered out of the pub. She felt sad as she watched him go. He had so much to offer. He would make any girl in the world happy. But he was destroying everything he had: his looks, his living, his relationships, his reputation. His health, no doubt.

The landlord caught her eye.

'That went well,' he said.

'Someone had to tell him.' She looked at him witheringly. 'Although I suppose you wouldn't. It would put a right hole in your profits.'

Jenna slumped into a decline that evening, which carried on for the next few days. She knew she would have to snap out of it before Craig came back at the weekend, because she didn't want to put a downer on things. He worked hard, and he lived for his time at the beach hut with her. And she lived to see him. She just wished she could sort out something that gave her life meaning in between. Not to mention some money. Craig was incredibly generous, but Jenna wanted to pay her own way.

On Friday afternoon, she still hadn't come up with a solution. She stared at the bedroom ceiling, looking for inspiration in the cracked Artex. She could feel the Tawcombe torpor seeping into her bones; it sapped you of your energy and drive; sucked any ambition you might have right out of you. She'd felt it before. It was soul-destroying. She was damned if she was going to let it get her again.

She rolled off the bed, jumped to her feet and ran out of the door. She wasn't going to stop and think. She was acting on impulse, fuelled by rage and frustration and the injustice. It took her fifteen minutes to get to the bank, and by the time she arrived she was red-faced and dishevelled. This time, she wasn't dressed to impress. She was in jeans and a hoodie and trainers. She didn't care. She marched up to the first cashier to become vacant.

'I want to see the manager,' she said. 'The actual branch manager, not one of his gofers. And I want to see him now.' She paused. 'Or her. And, actually, I hope it is a her, because she'll probably have more sense.'

The cashiers could tell by the tone of her voice, and the volume of it, that it was in their interests to do what she said. They quite often had disruptions, and usually they called Security. But, miraculously, within five minutes Jenna was seated in a slightly larger glass cubicle than the one she'd been directed to earlier in the week, and an upbeat, businesslike woman marched in and shook her hand before sitting down.

'Well? What can I do for you?'

Jenna took a deep breath. 'It's your responsibility to take a chance on me,' she said. 'The man who saw me earlier in the week didn't even look at my business plan. He just crunched a few numbers on the computer and said no. What kind of bank are you, if you can't see a good idea when you're hit over the head with it? If you're not prepared to take risks?'

'Well, we tend to take *calculated* risks ... We can't just go throwing money out at random to anyone who wanders in here, I'm afraid. We have a checklist. If you don't meet the criteria ...'

'But that's so short-sighted. My plan is as watertight as they come. I know this area. I know the market. I know I can make it work. I might not have a good credit rating but I've got experience. I made my last boss loads

40

of money. It wasn't my fault he threw it all away at the bookies. If it had been me, if it had been my business, it wouldn't have gone under. It's just common sense. Common sense and hard graft.'

'So where is your plan? Let me have a look.'

Jenna hesitated. 'I chucked it in the bin.'

The woman raised an eyebrow.

'But I can talk you through it. I can remember every detail. It's a no-brainer. And it's not as if I'm asking for millions. Five grand. That's all.'

The woman held up her hand. 'Slow down. Start at the beginning. Explain to me just what it is you want to do.'

Jenna shut her eyes. This was her only chance. 'I've been offered a vintage ice-cream van. Thirteen hundred quid. And I need some money to do it up and buy some stock . . .'

Half an hour later, Jenna walked out of the bank having signed a loan agreement. Five thousand pounds would be in her account the next day.

'You better not let me down,' the manager told her. 'I've put my job on the line for this.'

'You can have free ice cream for life,' smiled Jenna.

'I don't want ice cream. I just want you to make your repayments.'

'You won't regret it.' Jenna thought it probably wasn't on to hug your bank manager, so she resisted the urge.

She did want to celebrate, though, and share her news with someone, so she made her way down to the George and Dragon. She was surprised to find no sign of Chris.

'I haven't seen him for two days,' the landlord told her gloomily. 'My profits are plummeting.'

Jenna felt unsettled. She knew she'd been pretty harsh. What if Chris had buckled under her diatribe? He must be fragile, after all, and she'd given it to him with both barrels. Then just left him to it. She'd been so absorbed in her own affairs she hadn't thought of the consequences. Feeling slightly sick, she hurried up the hill to Fore Street where Vince and Chris still lived in the house they had grown up in. It was a narrow, cobbled street lined with crooked fisherman's cottages, picturesque but run-down, more attractive in the height of summer when the windowsills sported geraniums than in the gloomy light of winter.

She banged on the door, imagining the worst: Chris, slumped on the sofa with a bottle of whisky in one hand, unkempt, unshaven, possibly even unconscious. And possibly even … she didn't want to think about it. She cursed her strong opinions and her outspokenness. As much as they had just done her a favour, she feared their other consequences.

As she waited for an answer, she wondered why she couldn't keep her opinions to herself and mind her own business.

She was wrong-footed, therefore, when Chris answered the door vertical, if a little pale, but definitely having shaved, his skin looking pink and clean as a newborn piglet.

'Oh!' she squeaked.

'Hi,' he replied.

'I was worried. The landlord at the George said you hadn't been in. So I thought you might be …'

'Lying in a drunken stupor and a puddle of wee?'

Jenna shrugged and nodded.

Chris leaned against the doorjamb, smiling proudly. His jumper rode up and she caught a flash of his washboard stomach.

'I haven't had a drink since the night before last.'

Jenna blinked. 'Seriously?'

'Seriously. After I saw you in the George I went up the road and got totally bladdered in the Town Tavern. The worst bender ever. Believe it or not. Threw up so much my eyeballs nearly came out…'

Jenna winced. 'Too much information…'

'I'm not kidding. Then I woke up yesterday and I thought: Jenna's right. She's totally nailed it. Drinking myself to death is pointless. It's not fair on Vince, more than anything. I keep letting him down. And if we lost the business, Dad would never forgive me…' He looked subdued, and she saw, despite the pink newness of his shaven skin, that there were dark rings under his blue eyes; darker than the rings around his irises. 'So that's it. I'm on the wagon. From now on, not another drink will touch my lips.'

Jenna could see that under the bravado he was trembling; whether from the emotion or the need for a drink, she couldn't tell. Probably both. She touched his arm.

'Chris, that's amazing. That's so brave.'

He shook his head. 'I know I've got a long way to go. I don't trust myself yet. I don't know how long I'll be able to last. But if I can do one day without drinking, then maybe I can do two. And if I fall off the wagon, I can get back on it again. He gulped, slightly overwhelmed by his outburst.

'If you ever want to talk about it,' said Jenna. 'If you need a mate, you know where I am.'

He gave her a grateful smile. Yet again, she thought how gorgeous he was; how the girls would be queuing up.

'You've already done enough,' he told her. 'I'm going to have to find myself stuff to do. Maybe start surfing again. Get a dog, maybe...'

She held up the bank's paperwork. 'I got my loan,' she told him. 'For the ice-cream van.'

'Awesome.'

'And now I need to find someone to help me do it up.' She grinned up at him. She knew he was handy: the Maskell brothers did all their own repairs and building work and kept their boats in working order.

Chris took the bait quite willingly.

'Hey, listen. Look no further. I need a project to keep me out of the pub. That'll do nicely.'

'Well, I know how good you are with your hands.'

Jenna wasn't flirting. She'd known Chris since forever.

'We can take it down to the boatyard. You can keep it there for the time being.'

'Great. Cos if I take it back to mine, some bright spark will take it for a joy ride.'

'Do you want me to come with you and try and knock Weasel down?'

'Do you know what? I can handle Weasel. And now I've got the money I can negotiate.'

'Spoilsport.'

Jenna felt a burst of excitement. Her recent victory still tasted sweet, and she felt so proud of Chris. Not to mention relief that her outburst hadn't tipped him over the edge.

She put her arms round his neck. 'You're going to be OK. You know that?'

Chris patted her back. 'I hope so. I feel like shit, if I'm honest. I've been held together by Beck's for the past six months at least. I'm not sure my body can take it.'

'Just call me,' said Jenna, 'if you ever think you're going to cave in.'

'I'm not caving in,' said Chris. 'Come on. Let me come with you to Weasel's. Please. I could do with someone to take my frustrations out on.'

'Go on, then,' said Jenna. 'If you can knock him down to twelve, I'll split the difference with you.'

Just over a month later, Jenna was dozing in bed early one morning. In her sleep, she could hear the chimes of 'Greensleeves'; at first from a distance, then coming nearer and nearer, slightly out of tune – a nostalgic sound that conjured up images of children running from afar, clutching a few coins in their hands, eager to queue up at the window and survey the price list before choosing.

The next thing she knew, her brother was banging on her bedroom door.

'Here – there's a bloke outside for you.'

She scrambled out of bed and downstairs to open the door.

Outside, on the pavement, was her ice-cream van. Fully renovated, the paintwork gleaming, painted in cream and pink stripes with 'The Ice Cream Girl' emblazoned along the top of the window. At the wheel was Chris, grinning from ear to ear.

He got out and handed her the keys.

'MOT sorted, tax sorted, new tyres, resprayed …'

He gave a little bow.

'Oh my God, she's beautiful,' breathed Jenna. 'More beautiful than I could ever have imagined.'

She could picture the van resting at the top of the beach, her paintwork gleaming, a long queue of people snaking from the window while she scooped out ball after ball of ice cream to cool them down. It would be hard work, she knew that – she would have to find as many opportunities as she could to make a decent profit – but Jenna wasn't afraid of hard work.

She threw her arms around Chris's neck and squeezed him. 'You are amazing,' she told him.

'Well. Enjoy her. And I want the first ice cream, when the day comes.' He turned to go.

'Hold on – let me give you a lift back at least.' Jenna lived on the outskirts of town and it was a good walk back in.

'It's OK. I'm going to run. Part of the new fitness regime. Gonna get myself back into shape.' He patted his already flat stomach with a grin and started to jog along the road.

Jenna watched him go. She prayed that he would find the strength to stay on track. He'd been a wreck for a long time. But she would keep an eye on him, from afar.

She turned back to the van. She climbed inside, pressed the button and listened to the jangle that would herald her arrival. She threw back her head and laughed with joy.

She spent the day in a frenzy of excitement, unable to wait for Craig to come home so she could show him. She unpacked all the dresses that she had stowed away when she moved back to her mother's, disillusioned: the ones that had been her trademark when she sold ice cream from the booth on the front – fifties halter-necks with circular skirts in bright colours, splattered with flowers and cherries and hearts. She'd wear a different one every day again, she decided.

And when Craig arrived back from his course that evening, she couldn't stop laughing when she saw his face.

'What on earth is that?' he asked, looking at the van parked on the road outside. No one would dare touch it now they knew he was home.

'This,' said Jenna proudly, 'is going to make me my fortune this summer.'

Craig looked at her for a moment, puzzled. She could see he wanted to ask where she had got the money to buy it, but didn't quite like to.

'I went to the bank,' she said, 'and forced them to give me a loan. I wouldn't leave until they coughed up.'

She took him by the hand.

'Come inside,' she commanded him. And inside the van, she wound her arms around his neck and kissed him, for if it wasn't for Craig, goodness knows where she would be, but certainly not where she was now. And the future was even brighter. She could feel it in her heart.

The Ice Cream Girl was back. All she had to wait for was the summer.

That
Summer

ELODIE

There was nothing more thrilling than being handed the key to a new house. Nothing to beat the sensation of sliding the key into the lock and pushing open the front door, wondering what you would find, breathing in the stillness, knowing that now you could do what you liked; that you could make it yours.

As she held the cold metal in her hand, Elodie thought of the times she had gone through this ritual over the years. Five or six, she calculated, each time with an incremental rise in property value. She was, after all, her father's daughter more than her mother's, and she had inherited his business acumen rather than her mother's spendthrift tendencies. Not that she didn't like spending money. On the contrary, she had already spent several thousand in her mind before she'd even got to the front door, putting up a new set of gates and re-landscaping the drive and pulling down the awful flat-roofed garage someone had stuck up.

The difference between the money Elodie spent and the money her mother had been used to spending was that Elodie worked on the basis that you had to speculate to accumulate. Anything she spent was an investment, or an enhancement to her investment. And it was her own money that she was spending. Her mother, as far as she knew, hadn't done a day's work in her life. Her mother had been a professional wife. A role for which, Elodie realized now, she herself had been groomed. An over-priced girls' boarding school that taught you how to make rum babas but sapped you of any ambition; a job with daddy; no mention of anything intellectually strenuous…

In some ways, thank goodness things had turned out how they did, or she would just be a carbon copy of her mother.

The front door hadn't altered. Oak, with large metal studs, a latch with a twisted ring for a handle, and a mortice lock that opened surprisingly easily. As she stepped inside, the ghosts all came fluttering forwards to meet her. She knew perfectly well they were only in her mind, but they were just as real. And the smell. How was it that the particular smell of a house never changed? The Grey House scent was a familiar mixture of seaside dampness and wood and something else that unlocked the flicker of a memory but wouldn't be pinned down. The trace of someone's perfume, perhaps?

She stepped into the hall. The staircase rose to her right, curving upwards, its bannister as inviting as it ever had been. How many times had she slid down it as a child? How many times had she walked down the stairs from her bedroom, carrying a book or her bathing things or an empty glass or cup? And what of the last time she had walked down those stairs, her head held high and her heart thumping at the thought of what was to come, her father's hand in hers? The final descent. Even now, the emotion made her chest feel tight.

She walked through the hall, through a shard of dust motes spinning in the midday sun, ignoring the doors to the dining room and the morning room and the corridor that led down to the kitchen and scullery and heading straight for the drawing room. As soon as she opened the door, the light from the French windows blinded her, the light that bounced off the infinite sea; the sea that was the reason for the house being built. And she could hear it, too, the roar that never ceased, for the waves here never abated; the comforting susurrus that used to reassure her whenever she woke in the night, lulling her back to sleep with its gentle rhythm.

The room had barely changed. Its shelves were empty of the books and ornaments she had grown up with; the wooden floor was scarred where the furniture had stood. The yellow curtains were still there, faded and thick with dust. They hung limp and tattered, as if too tired to carry on their job. The chandelier, too, was crusted in grime. But it was still a room to take the breath away, with its perfect proportions, the full-width French windows leading out onto the garden, and the staggering view beyond.

Elodie stood in the doorway. She felt an incredible calm settle upon her. She had done the right thing, she felt sure. There was no other place on earth to make her feel like this. She walked across the floorboards, her footsteps echoing in the emptiness. She twisted the metal knob that undid the lock of the French windows. Even now she could remember the extra push you needed to unlatch it. As she stepped outside, the wind ruffled her hair, playfully rearranging her Sassoon-style bob, as if to say this is no place for your city chic, madam.

She had so many plans. Landscapers, builders, decorators: she had them all lined up. There was a strict schedule to adhere to if she was going to meet her deadline. The beauty of it was that it was all here. She didn't want to change a thing. All she wanted was for it to be restored to its former glory. Except for the hideous garage, there was to be no smashing down of walls, no restructuring, no ripping out of the kind that was so fashionable in magazines and on television. After all, you couldn't improve on perfection. She wanted the house to be just as it had been, the last time she was happy. So that she could be happy again. It was just within her reach. She could feel it.

But first, there was something she had to do. Someone she had to see. How easy it would be not to. How easy it would be to forge ahead with her plans regardless, and leave that particular door closed for ever, never knowing what lay behind it. Forgiveness, Elodie knew, was the way to make her soul, and therefore her happiness, complete. Because without forgiveness, she couldn't forget, and unless she could forget...

She pulled the card out of her handbag. It had taken a bit of dissembling to get it. The address for all the conveyancing had been care of the solicitor, so that had given her no clue. But if there was one thing Elodie had inherited from her distaff side, it was the ability to give off the air of being someone. And when Elodie chose to pretend to be someone, she was hard to resist, especially if you were a gullible and rather bored estate agent in a small seaside town. He'd been easily foxed by airy hints of a bunch of thank-you flowers for the vendor.

'I know how hard it must have been for her to give up the house. And I want to reassure her it's in good hands,' Elodie had gushed, wide-eyed with sincerity. Moments later, she'd had the address of the nursing home in her hand.

And it wasn't a lie. Not really.

July 1962

Lillie Lewis was the mistress of ceremonies at The Grey House. Of that there was no question. It was her playground and her guests were her playthings. More than one person had compared her to Marie Antoinette, and not just because she was French.

Every year she decamped to Everdene for the summer, and had free rein and a limitless budget to entertain whomsoever she liked. Her husband Desmond came down at the weekends, for the factory he owned, which churned out jam and money in equal measure, couldn't stop just because the sun was out. On the contrary, this was its busiest time, when strawberries and raspberries and apricots burst their skins and begged to be transformed into sweet, sticky preserves. The air around the factory smelt intoxicating in summer – to anyone who didn't actually live near it, that is. After a while, you longed to go to sleep without the scent of hot sugared fruit invading your sleep. It got into your nostrils, your hair, your dreams.

There was money in jam. Oh yes. More than even Lillie Lewis, not known for her pecuniary restraint, could burn through (although she could drive a hard bargain, as those who dealt with her knew). And there were some – many, in fact – who observed afterwards that money is no substitute for attention.

Lillie far preferred summer at The Grey House to the rest of the year in the Lewis's ugly, sprawling Gothic monstrosity in Worcestershire; a former lunatic asylum which Desmond felt had the stature and grandeur he needed to prove his social

55

standing. For, like many people who made a lot of money very quickly, he felt the need to prove his wealth over and over again, as if it might disappear if he didn't ram it down people's throats. It had been a pleasant surprise to him, his ability to turn a profit, but it became something of an addiction – an obsession, almost.

The Grey House had been Lillie's choice; an impulse purchase she had seen in Country Life. It hadn't taken her two minutes to persuade her husband that a summer home was the ultimate proof of your success. She relished her guests' delight in the setting, overlooking Everdene Sands, the most glorious bay on the north Devon coast. The house slept twelve comfortably, but as many as you liked if you weren't worried about bunking up, which children, especially, weren't. Tents, bunks and hammocks abounded, all in the spirit of summer fun. Four or five families would descend at a time, some related to the Lewis's, some not. Some whom Lillie barely knew, but had taken a fancy to at a point-to-point or a dance. She collected people. And then she entertained them. As a hostess, she was unbeatable. No need was left untended; she asked nothing of her guests but for them to do just as they pleased.

She would appear at midday, in a pink silk peignoir, all décolletage and déshabillé, then smoke her way through three cups of very strong coffee, opening her post, only paying any real attention to missives from fashion houses announcing their new collections, which she would annotate with a fountain pen, putting exclamation marks next to anything she really liked so her dressmaker could copy them. She rarely ate: the occasional piece of ham or triangle of bread, but her disinterest in food was evident.

At midday, she poured her first glass of champagne, a glass

that stayed topped up to three quarters full for the rest of the day and from which she took tiny, delicate sips, as if it were the bubbles in the champagne keeping her oxygenated. She drank about a glass an hour, so was never drunk.

She bathed at one, was dressed and coiffed by two, then wrote letters until three. By then she deemed herself awake enough to start communicating with the rest of the world, and the whirlwind of organization for the evening's social events would begin. Meanwhile, her guests would have made the most of the facilities at The Grey House – the huge drawing room overlooking the garden in which were laid out the day's papers and the latest magazines, the tennis court, the terrace for sunbathing, the beach hut and, of course, the wide blue ocean beyond. Grown-ups relaxed in the knowledge that the children roamed in packs and looked after each other, all under the vaguely watchful eye of the Lewis's good-natured and obliging only daughter, Elodie.

And although she had no interest in food herself, Lillie understood the importance of a good table for guests. So she sat with a towering pile of cookery books, making lists of recipes for the kitchen staff. Mousses and fricassees and terrines and jellies and blancmanges: anything with visual impact that took hours to prepare. Her favourite was a show-stopping fish mousse in the shape of a salmon, decorated with piped mayonnaise and wafer-thin slices of cucumber, wedges of lemon, curls of parsley and served with melba toast.

Lillie would smile at her guests' gasps of admiration, as if she had applied all the cucumber herself, and would chain-smoke at the end of the table while she watched them devour it. After dinner there would be dancing in the drawing room with the latest records sent down from a shop in Carnaby Street, or moonlit croquet, or charades.

Lillie's guest list was drawn up with military precision at the end of June and followed up with handwritten letters of invitation on lilac notepaper. Occasionally, just occasionally, Desmond asked her to invite a business associate or customer and his (invariably his) family. Lillie could hardly refuse, because no doubt the associate or customer had in some way contributed to the Lewis wealth, but it annoyed her because it upset the equilibrium.

This had been exactly the case with the Jukes. Desmond had asked her, at very short notice, to include them in the upcoming weekend, and Lillie was irked, because that particular Saturday's dinner was centred around the Kavanaghs, who had bought the manor house in the next village, and Lillie wanted all her attention to go on making them feel special. As local royalty she didn't want them to be overshadowed, but Desmond pulled rank, which he rarely did, because the Jukes were instrumental in his plan for world domination.

The Jukes owned a chain of upmarket grocery stores in strategic locations that Desmond had his eye on as a possible acquisition. It didn't do to have all your eggs in one basket, or indeed all your jam in one jar, and he was eager to diversify. The Jukes had fallen on hard times since the founder had passed away six years ago. It was evident to anyone with half an eye for business that they now didn't have a clue about running the shops. Desmond was keen to swoop in and take over – a substantial investment and his entrepreneurial eye would mean a soar in profits, he felt sure. But the Jukes needed convincing this was the way forward first.

'They can't read a spreadsheet between them,' Desmond told Lillie, 'so they don't know they are in trouble. I need to

charm them; show them the way forward – and make sure they don't go to anyone else for investment.'

He'd been to each of the shops and assessed their profitability. Ill-stocked shelves, dilatory staff, minimal advertising, dreary window displays – the shops were sliding backwards into the post-war austerity everyone else was charging away from. And Desmond knew retail. After all, his wares were readily available all over the country. There was barely a home that didn't have a pot, or even two or three, of Lewis jam on its shelves. From castle to council house, it was classless; universally popular.

But as Desmond had pointed out, where do you go after jam? He was tired of experimenting with flavours – and anyway the money was in the popular; for him there was little point in experimenting with peculiar fruit varieties in an attempt to brainwash the nation. No, his ambitions lay elsewhere.

So the plan was to lure the Jukes down for the weekend so Desmond could butter them up and steer them into a deal of some sort. And although she was disgruntled that her carefully balanced guest list had been tampered with, Lillie loved nothing better than a challenge and the chance to charm. One of her favourite things was to watch people melt under her ministrations. As narcissists go, she was a beguiling one who managed to make people think it was all about them, not her.

'I hope they're not dull,' she warned Desmond. 'Dull would just be dreadful.'

But, being a man, he couldn't give her a great description. The Jukes, according to Desmond, were aristocratic but impecunious – and likely to be even more so unless they took advantage of his timely intervention. 'They're about our age, with a son about Elodie's age – and he's the one due to inherit, so we need to butter him up too.'

Lillie rolled her eyes. 'Well, there's no point in asking Elodie's assistance.' Elodie didn't have a scrap of guile. 'In fact, it's probably better not to tell her anything.'

The day the Jukes were due to arrive Lillie put the finishing touches to the menu plan – oysters (being French, she was convinced that there was no social occasion that couldn't be ameliorated by a platter of oysters), beef wellington and an elaborate cherry-filled gateau smothered in swirls of cream. She sent the menu down to Mrs Marsh, the housekeeper, then she put her mind to what to wear. As she flipped through her rail of dresses, Lillie imagined a stuffy couple rigid with tweed and florid of face, like most people who lived in the English countryside seemed to be. It wouldn't be hard to dazzle them, she thought, but nevertheless she put her mind to it. She wondered where Elodie was, and thought about giving her sartorial guidance but, actually, it was too hot to have that battle. And Elodie wasn't really part of the battle plan. She would fit in wherever. She always did.

Elodie was, at that moment, charging up the cliff path, running through her wardrobe in her mind, trying to remember which of her decent clothes she'd brought down from Worcestershire and wondering how long it would take the new arrival to follow her directions back to the house on his motorbike: he would never be able to get to the house by way of the beach, so she'd given him detailed instructions which took him the long way round, via the village church. She just hoped it was long enough to get changed into something respectable and do her hair.

Her mother was always on at her to pay more attention

to how she presented herself. Elodie didn't give a stuff what she had on most of the time, as long as she was comfortable, spending most of the summer in shorts and her old school aertex and a pair of battered plimsolls. She knew this was a source of frustration to Lillie, who was rigid about being properly dressed for every occasion, but you could take the woman out of Paris, thought Elodie, but you couldn't take Paris out of the woman.

Having a beautiful mother when you yourself weren't could have been a heavy cross to bear, but Elodie had spirit and a spark about her that was ultimately more pleasing to the casual observer than her mother's Gallic perfection. She'd never been intimidated by her mother's looks, and didn't care that people probably compared them unfavourably. Her mind wasn't exactly on higher things, but Elodie was cheerful and optimistic and interested – interested in everything and everyone – which gave her a more grounded view to life. Lillie, by comparison, was fragile and an air of simmering neurosis clung to her as surely as her scent.

There was nothing fragile about Elodie. She was solid. Besides, although she wasn't delicate and ravishing like Lillie, her rather hooded sludge-grey eyes smiled, as did her full mouth which delivered wit and encouragement and things that people wanted to hear, because more than anything Elodie was nice.

Suddenly, however, she saw herself through the eyes of Jolyon Jukes and imagined him being slightly less than impressed by what he had seen: a gangly nineteen year old, unkempt and unsophisticated. And something primal in her told her it was very important that his second impression should be a better one. By the time he got to The Grey House, she determined to be gliding down the staircase, soigné and serene, in time to lead him through to the drawing room and offer him a cocktail.

Thereby playing the role her mother had been grooming her for since the dawn of time. Lillie had known, of course she had known, that this moment would come. Elodie, in her headstrong way, had resisted. Not that there was any animosity between them. Elodie wasn't the type to invite animosity: Lillie was only ever exasperated with her daughter, and possibly slightly mystified by her lack of vanity. She never gave up presenting her with the very latest in skin creams and cosmetics. She brought her with her to the hairdresser and made him work his magic on Elodie's thick, dark curls. She had dresses and coats made up for her and shoes delivered, but they rarely saw the light of day. Desmond just laughed, and told his wife she was wasting her time and his money. Lillie pouted and stamped her foot with the frustration of it all. 'One day she will understand,' she declared.

And, suddenly, Elodie did. It was sudden and startling and urgent, the feeling. No one had ever made her feel that way before.

She'd always been perfectly comfortable in the company of men. She held her own at the dinner table with her parents' friends. She had male friends of her own with whom she played tennis and went to dances. She'd had several fumbling skirmishes after too much fruit punch, which she'd found more amusing than enjoyable, and certainly not upsetting – she wasn't squeamish – but she couldn't say she was longing for the next encounter; to embroil herself in the next kiss. They were all much of a muchness to her, men, and certainly not a source of fascination.

Jolyon Jukes, however, was different. Golden hair, dark eyes, tanned skin, but best of all a ready smile, he was confident without being cocky. The hairs on her arms had rippled as his gaze swept over her. His voice was light and dry and teasing; and there was a challenge in his eyes that Elodie couldn't resist. She wasn't entirely sure what that challenge was yet, but it had sparked something in her. Adrenaline fuelled her onwards, up the steps of the terrace, through the French windows, in through the drawing room, into the hall and up the stairs to her bedroom. Her heart carried on pounding even when she had regained her breath. She flew into the bathroom, splashed cold water on her face to tone down the redness, dampened a flannel and rubbed it under her arms and onto the back of her neck to wipe off the worst of the perspiration. She dragged a comb through her hair, still salty from this morning's dip in the sea, and tried to pat it into some sort of style.

It was a most peculiar and particular kind of panic.

Elodie ran into her mother's bedroom and sat at the kidney-shaped dressing table. Her fingers fumbled amidst the make-up in the right-hand drawer. She pulled out lipstick and powder and a wand of mascara. Moments later, an alien with frosted-pink lips stared back at her. There was no time to take it off and start again. She snatched up a bottle of Ma Griffe and dabbed it on her wrists, rubbing them together.

'Elodie? Darling?' Her mother was behind her, her perfect eyebrows raised in question.

Elodie didn't flinch at being caught. Lillie wouldn't mind her ransacking her things.

'I've just met Jolyon Jukes,' Elodie told her. Lillie looked blank. 'The Jukes' son? They're coming to stay this weekend.'

'Oh.' Lillie widened her eyes with interest. 'And is he something else?'

'He's ... something. Certainly.' Elodie looked at her mother behind her in the mirror. She shrugged but her eyes were sparkling.

Lillie gave a laugh of delight. 'You see!' she said.

'But look at me. I look ridiculous.'

Lillie came forward. 'Not pink, my darling. Never pink with your complexion.' She fished in the drawer for a different colour. 'Rouge.'

She demonstrated that Elodie should purse her lips. Her daughter did, and moments later the pink was removed and a carmine slash replaced it.

'Hold still and shut your eyes.' Lillie traced a sweep of black eyeliner over each of Elodie's eyelids. She picked up a comb and teased a few curls, backcombing them into place.

Elodie gazed at her reflection, intrigued. She was still in there, somewhere, but she wasn't quite sure how to make this new incarnation behave. She stood up.

'What should I wear?'

Lillie flicked her eyes over her daughter. 'White linen. Cool. Crisp. Chic.'

Virginal, thought Elodie, and her stomach tumbled.

Lillie reached out and picked up a pearl necklace hooked over the side of her dressing table mirror. She slipped them over her daughter's head. Elodie felt their coolness settle on her collarbone.

'White linen,' she repeated obediently. Her mother kissed her forehead. Outside, they heard the deep rumble of a motorbike coming up the drive. They looked at each other for a moment.

'That's him.' Elodie felt her heart thump.

'I'll let him in,' said Lillie. 'Go.'

Five minutes later, Elodie examined herself in the bedroom mirror she usually never gave a second glance. Her dress was round-necked and short-sleeved and because she had grown taller since they had bought it, on a trip to London two years ago, it was only just to the knee, but it had a simple elegance. She fluffed up her hair and curled the ends up with her fingertips. She looked at herself in profile, put her hand to her chest and breathed in to calm herself.

She wasn't scared, she realized with surprise. She had waited long enough for someone to make her feel like this, so she wasn't going to waste time being afraid. Anyway, what was there to be scared of? At worst she would look a fool, and that didn't bother Elodie much. She covered her face with her hands as she gave herself a last glance in the mirror. Her eyes twinkled at her, and she laughed, both at herself and with the exhilaration.

She dropped her hands to her waist, made her expression sober and locked gazes with herself. 'Good evening,' she said, in a cool, languid tone, then burst into peals of laughter, throwing back her head as she left the room.

Jeanie and Roger Jukes were not what Lillie had expected from Desmond's description. They roared up to the front of the house in a dark-green frog-eyed Sprite with the roof down. Roger was lean and louche, in a sports jacket and white trousers, and looked as if he would rather be anywhere else; Jeanie was an English rose with a cloud of white-blonde hair and a primness that was almost certainly a smokescreen. Prim girls didn't marry men like Roger, whose coal-dark eyes were all over everything.

They drifted into the house, a beguiling double act impossible to decipher. Lillie observed them through narrowed eyes as Desmond ushered them out onto the terrace. The Kavanaghs, she decided, would pale into insignificance next to the Jukes, which in some sense relieved her. Yet she felt wrong-footed.

Desmond hadn't been straight with her. He'd dismissed the Jukes; played them down. Or perhaps he genuinely couldn't see it? Even she, perspicacious and never missing a detail, could never be sure with Desmond.

'Superb,' drawled Roger, standing by the stone balustrade and taking in the view as Elodie, armed with a silver tray, handed him a coupe of champagne.

'I love the English seaside,' sighed Jeanie, her little-girl voice only just above a whisper. 'But Roger insists on the Med. He's a sun worshipper.'

'England would be fine if it was like this all the time.' Roger waved his glass at the early evening sun, shining with such bright confidence that you could hardly imagine it wasn't there every day through the summer months.

'We are very lucky,' Lillie told them. 'Me, I love the South of France, of course, but I have grown to love it here. You never know what you are going to wake up to.'

She fixed her gaze on Roger. He didn't flicker.

'So,' continued Lillie, undaunted. 'You and Desmond are in discussion about Jukes's?'

Roger looked amused. 'Oh no,' he said. 'Not me. There would be no point in him talking to me. Jeanie wears the trousers where the business is concerned. Jukes is her family name, not mine. I took it when we married.'

Jeanie's eyes were wide over her champagne. 'Such a bore. Such a responsibility. But Grandpa left me the shops. I used to go round them with him all the time when I was small, telling him what he should sell. So as recompense for my utter bossiness, I was left the lot.' She rolled her eyes. 'But they've turned out to be rather a millstone.'

'What a shame,' said Lillie, and her gaze settled on Desmond, who looked implacable.

'Well,' he said soothingly. 'I don't think you need to panic just yet. There's huge potential. You just have to come at it from a different angle.'

Lillie raised an eyebrow. Jeanie smiled. Roger drew on a cigarette, eyes narrowed.

Elodie cleared her throat.

'Peanut, anyone?' she asked, thrusting a silver bowl amidst the grown-ups. She felt something shifting amongst them: a shift in the balance of power, and it made her feel uncomfortable.

Roger scooped up a handful of nuts and dropped them into his mouth, one by one. No one said a word. At that moment, Jolyon came out onto the terrace. Now they were together, Elodie could see his dark roving eyes belonged to his father, and his fair hair was Jeanie's. He was one of those people for whom genetics had played an excellent game.

'Hello, everyone,' said Jolyon. 'Goodness, what a view.'

'Champagne?' said Elodie, proffering a glass, and his eyes settled on her and she felt relieved that there was a diversion from the awkwardness.

'I met your younger sister on the beach earlier,' said Jolyon. He was teasing her. He was definitely teasing her.

'Really?' said Elodie. 'I hope she wasn't rude. Only she can be.'

'She was perfectly charming.'

Their eyes met and Elodie felt her cheeks pinken slightly. Suddenly she wasn't sure if he was joking or not. Did he really think she was someone different? Then he smiled, showing white teeth, and the way his eyes crinkled showed her he was joking, and for the first time ever in her life, she felt rather beautiful.

As the rest of the guests arrived – the Kavanaghs, and two

*other sets of friends Lillie had made at the tennis club –
Elodie and Jolyon gravitated onto the lawn.*

'So – you work for your father?'

*Elodie made a face. 'Yes. Very unimaginative. But it
seemed like the logical thing to do.'*

*He gave a sympathetic smile. 'Same here. Well, I work for
my mother. What do you do? Secretary, I suppose?'*

*She shot him a fierce glance. She didn't like being pigeon-
holed.*

'No, actually.'

He widened his eyes at her and drew back. 'Sorry.'

'I'm in charge of marketing. And advertising.'

'Impressive.'

*She relented with a grin. It wouldn't do to be on her high
horse. 'Well, not really. Basically it means making up slogans.
And drawing pretty pictures to put on labels.' She swirled
her champagne in its glass. 'At the moment, I'm working on
Sally and Sammy Strawberry. To try and get children to eat
as much jam as possible. Each jar has a Sally or a Sammy
sticker behind the label. If you collect ten you can send off
for an enamel badge.'*

'Very clever.'

*'Actually, it is,' she told him. 'Sales have soared.' She
leaned in to him. She felt very daring. 'If you're very good,'
she said, 'I'll get you a badge of your own.'*

*He put his head to one side as he considered this, and she
was amazed how his eyes laughed even though his face was
perfectly straight.*

'I wouldn't want you abusing your power.'

*Elodie felt something rise up inside her; a joyful bubble
that was like the beginning of a laugh, but had a keener
edge, something syrupy and sharp. From the terrace, she saw*

her mother watching the two of them, an expression of approval on her face. Lillie gave her a nod. Of encouragement, she thought.

Then she realized Jolyon was watching them watch each other.

'You're not much like your mother,' he said.

'It has been said.' She rolled her eyes. 'I haven't inherited much from her at all. It's a wretched curse, having a beautiful mother. People can't help but compare.'

His eyes didn't leave her face. She found it disconcerting. 'What?' she said.

'But you're beautiful,' he said. 'Much more beautiful, to my mind.'

Elodie just laughed. Jolyon looked perturbed, as if he wanted to press the point further, but Lillie was waving at them to come in. It was time for dinner.

Lillie had done the placement with care, Elodie noticed. You could always tell her motives by where she chose to seat people. Lillie was next to Roger Jukes. Jeanie was in placement Siberia, at the bottom end of the table, in between the two tennis club husbands. Elodie could tell she knew that she'd been outcast by the way she didn't flicker as she took her seat.

She wondered who was better at the game, Jeanie or her mother. She saw her father frown as he took in the table arrangements. He was next to Mrs Kavanagh; another tennis club wife on the other side. If he thought he should be next to Jeanie, it was too late for him to say, or for the placement to change.

Jolyon was on Elodie's left. She was pleased, but she thought she probably couldn't face food. There was too much excitement in her stomach for so much as a morsel. But she could copy her mother. Not help herself to anything. Push her food around her *plate. Talk so much that no one noticed she wasn't actually eating. So many of her mother's tricks, hitherto ignored, were coming into play today. She could already imagine Lillie's triumph.*

'*So you spend all the summer here?*'

Elodie nodded. 'Always. We shut up our Worcestershire house. Well, my father rattles around in it during the week, but basically we all move down here for July and August.'

'*It's wonderful.*'

'*It's heaven. I love it.*'

Jolyon looked gloomy. 'It's the nearest we're going to get to a holiday. We used to go to Capri. But we're a bit strapped.'

Elodie let him fill up her glass with wine. 'Well, that's why you're here, isn't it?'

'*Is it?' Jolyon shrugged. 'I've stopped listening.*'

He looked weary.

'*I think the idea is we join forces,' said Elodie. 'I think my father's going to invest. Or something. But I probably shouldn't say too much.*'

'*Well, there's clearly more money in jam than shops.' Jolyon looked impressed as several platters of oysters resting on ice were set on the table.*

'*Who cares about money?' asked Elodie. 'No, please, you help yourself first. I'm not an oyster person.*'

'*It's easy to say* who cares about money *when you've got it,' Jolyon told her. 'We nearly couldn't afford the petrol to get down here.*'

Elodie looked at him. 'Well, you should all have come in one car then,' she said. 'And a more sensible one at that.'

Jolyon was speechless for a moment, then laughed. 'You speak your mind, don't you?'

'Whose mind am I supposed to speak?' Elodie retorted, but she was laughing too.

At the other end of the table she could see Lillie effervescing, as only Lillie could when she had someone who interested her in her sights. Jolyon's father was leaning back in his chair, bemused, his eyes glittering, a glass of wine in his hand. It was clear Lillie was nothing he couldn't handle. He was the kind of man who attracted female attention and thrived on it. It was all in an evening's work to him.

At the other end of the table, Jeanie was composed, as cool as the ice the oysters were resting on, as charming to the man to the right as to the left of her. It was still early on in the evening. The chatter was animated but controlled; the champagne had relaxed everyone but it was not yet time for fierce debate or ribaldry. There were several courses to get through yet.

At the head of the table sat Desmond. There was something kingly in his presence tonight, thought Elodie. She felt he was surveying his courtiers, as if each one had a role. What was hers, she wondered? She put down her glass. She'd had more to drink than usual. Reality was slipping away from her. For a moment, she felt unsettled. For the first time, she felt like a grown-up at her parents' table, rather than a child.

'Are you all right?'

She turned to find Jolyon staring at her, concerned.

'Fine. Sorry. It's just a bit hot in here, that's all.'

Elodie picked up her water glass and drank.

When dinner ended, everyone left the table together. Lillie had never subscribed to the tradition of the ladies withdrawing next door while the men were left to smoke cigars and drink port. She was nothing without the company of men, and she presumed all women were the same, so she served coffee and *digestifs for everyone in the drawing room. Lit by lamps, with the doors open out onto the sea, the atmosphere was languid and relaxed. Everyone, it seemed, was comfortable in each other's company. Any fears of a pecking order, the tyranny that rules so many dinner parties, had been rubbed out by the excellent food and wine, and they all slumped into the comfort of the sofas and armchairs while Oscar Petersen played in the background. The stresses of the working week receded into the background, and the pleasures of the weekend ahead stretched out in front of them.*

Only Elodie felt restless, but she hadn't drunk as much as the rest. She had spent the whole of dinner enraptured by Jolyon, although she had remembered not to forget her good manners, and had spoken to everyone else at the table. Now she couldn't remember a word anyone else had said, only what he had. She prowled the room, turning over the record when it came to an end, refilling the silver cigarette box, not sure where to put herself.

Where she wanted to put herself was next to Jolyon, but he was engrossed in conversation with her father. Every now and then he would look over at her, and twice he held her gaze and smiled. She had no way of telling if he felt the same way she did. Had he just been polite throughout dinner? He too had perfect manners, after all, and would have been trained in feigning undivided interest. Yet the way they had laughed at the same things, and the way he was happy to contradict and argue with her – in a teasing way, not a high-handed way – implied to her there was a mutual attraction. But Elodie was an ingénue. She really had no knowledge of the games men and women played between them.

Her mother, of course, would be able to guide her. Her mother would know the signs. But Lillie was perched on the edge of a golden velvet armchair, describing something to Roger, her hands drawing pictures in the air, her hair slipping from its chignon, her eyes alive. She was oblivious to her daughter's need for advice.

'Be bold,' Elodie told herself. 'You have to make it happen.'

Where she had got this courage from, she had no idea, but she had a staunch heart, and she still wasn't afraid. What was the point in running away from the momentous? Surely you had to do everything in your power to draw it to you?

She picked up the glass of wine she hadn't finished from dinner. She looked across to Jolyon and caught his eye. Then she turned and walked out of the French doors and onto the terrace. The night was still and warm and smelt brackish: the tide was out and the trace of drying seaweed tinged the air. The moon hung in the sky, as pale and lustrous as the largest pearl on the necklace her mother had lent her. She could feel it on her skin. She could feel everything on her skin.

Even his presence. She heard his footsteps behind her. She wasn't going to turn. She bit her lip with the anticipation, smiling to herself. He stood right behind her. She felt his hand on her waist. She breathed in, revelling in his touch, a touch that told her everything she needed to know, then leaned back until she was nestled into him.

'Shall we go for a walk?' he asked, his voice low.

'Yes.'

She put her glass down on the balustrade. Then she slipped her hand into his. Together they walked down the stone steps and across the lawn. She knew the grown-ups in the drawing room would have a perfect view of them if they chose to look out, but she didn't care. Everyone, after all, had to start somewhere. And her mother, for one, would be cheering her on.

Without a word, they made their way down the cliff path,

swishing through the marram grass, the sand beneath them giving way so their steps got faster and faster until they fell in a laughing tangle onto the beach.

It had a special magic at night. A softness, like a cashmere blanket; the sound of the waves as soothing as a lullaby; the darkness leaving all other senses heightened. They left their shoes at the bottom of the cliff path, their feet sinking into the cool damp.

'I've never felt like this before,' whispered Jolyon, and part of Elodie wanted to press him further, ask him what he had felt with other girls; find out why she was different, what it was he was feeling. Common sense told her, however, that this would be wrong, and so instead she stopped in her tracks, turned to him, went up onto her tiptoes and slid her arms around his neck.

'Neither have I,' she breathed. 'Neither have I.'

And the next thing she knew, she understood why it was that people bothered kissing.

The rest of the summer was perfection. It was as if God had snapped the final piece of the jigsaw he was doing into place. Jukes's Groceries became Lewis and Jukes. Desmond drew up a masterplan for the stores, and he and Jeanie and Jolyon spent the weeks implementing his vision, travelling to each of the stores in turn. No one was quite sure of Roger's role in all of this, but he seemed to have his own affairs to attend to.

They all reconvened at The Grey House at the weekends. Elodie found the days of the week without Jolyon endless, and lived in a fever of excitement until she heard his bike roar through the drive on a Friday lunchtime. Eventually Roger would reappear, then Jeanie and Desmond, and forty-eight hours of heavenly hedonistic eating, drinking, card-playing, tennis, bathing, fishing and cricket would begin, mingled in with Lillie's summer guest rota.

For Elodie, her relationship with Jolyon was breathtakingly simple and uncomplicated. He was just so right for her. They made each other laugh. He didn't dismiss her thoughts or opinions, but had spoken to her father about Elodie helping with the advertising side of things for the shops, and they'd had a meeting in the dining room and Elodie felt she had really contributed. There had been talk of giving her a place on the board, and although she wasn't sure entirely what this meant, she felt sure it was important.

Only Lillie seemed slightly adrift, languid in the heat, but she came back to life at the weekends, when her rightful role as hostess was restored and she set the pace, the brightest star around whom the constellations moved.

And one night, towards the end of the summer, when dusk was starting to close in earlier and earlier, the moment Elodie had been both longing for and dreading arrived. She and Jolyon had spent the afternoon in the beach hut, and as dusk fell they were drowsy with heat. They'd trailed to the water countless times to take a dip to cool themselves down, and the salt had dried on their skin. They were tangled in each other's arms, but this time, as they began to kiss, there was something more urgent between them, a sense that there was no going back. Something unspoken but agreed.

Elodie wondered how many hours she had spent in this hut over the years. Curled up with a book on a pile of cushions, sheltering from the afternoon rain as it rattled on the roof, eating toffees. Drying herself after an early morning or late afternoon swim. Sheltering from the fierce midday sun, drinking squash and chewing on egg sandwiches. Several times *she had slept here, when the house had overflowed, lugging down cushions from the sofa in the living room to construct a makeshift bed. Playing draughts or Ludo with her cousins.*

And now, the most important thing to have happened to her so far in her life was about to happen. She could feel it between them. There wasn't a cell in her body that wasn't affected. Every nerve ending, every square inch of skin, was crackling. Her blood was like mercury, balls of it running haywire through her veins.

He put up his hand and ran it through her hair, and she shivered with pleasure. His hand rested on her neck, stroking it gently, and she tipped her head back. She felt his lips on her throat, warm and gentle.

This is it, she thought. She was melting; giddy and helpless. When he brushed his hands over her breasts, running his thumbs over the thin cotton of her dress, she pushed herself towards him, longing for more.

'Are you sure?' he whispered, as his hand reached down to her thigh and pushed the hem of her dress upwards. 'I want you to be sure.'

Nothing in the world would stop her now. Nothing. 'I'm sure,' she breathed. 'I am absolutely sure.'

Outside, she could see the stars spinning round in the sky.

The cushions with the anchors on, which had been in the hut for as long as she could remember, on which she'd lain so many times, were the perfect resting place. She pulled him down onto them. Underneath, she felt grains of sand. There were always grains of sand in the hut, no matter how many times you swept it. Each one dug into her skin, but she didn't feel them. All she could feel was him.

'Tell me if it hurts,' he told her, but it didn't. Not one bit.

*

76

That New Year's Eve, Lillie threw a glittering party at The Grey House. She didn't like to leave the house empty over the winter, and this was the ideal opportunity to open it up and breathe life into it.

At midnight, Elodie and Jolyon slipped away from the revelry and down to the beach hut. They'd offered to camp in there as the house was full to the brim with guests. They went down armed with blankets and hot water bottles and Thermos flasks full of hot, sweet coffee laced with brandy.

And when the hands of her Timex watch reached midnight, and she asked Jolyon if he had any resolutions, he said, in a gloomy voice, 'Give up going to bed with single women, I suppose,' and she looked at him, frowning, puzzled, and then he laughed, and she punched his arm and then he turned to her and said, rather fiercely, 'Don't you get it?'

And she stood very still while she thought about what he might mean, but she didn't want to voice her theory in case she'd got the wrong end of the stick and she didn't want to start the New Year looking like an idiot, so she said, in rather a small voice, 'No. I don't.'

And Jolyon sighed and said 'El. Darling El. You absolute nit. I'm asking you to marry me.'

TIM AND RACHEL

The beach hut was the only thing they couldn't agree on in the settlement. Rachel had the cat. Tim had the power tools. Everything else, including money – even though there wasn't much left, even after they sold the house, which was hardly surprising – was split straight down the middle.

But when it came down to it, neither of them could bear to part with the hut. The thought of selling it was anathema, even though it would fetch a good price. They agreed they were grown-ups, and that as the divorce was as amicable as a divorce could ever be, there was a logical solution.

So against both of their solicitors' advice, they decided they would share it, post divorce. Six months each seemed tidiest, rather than every other weekend, so they didn't keep having to clear up for the other person. Anyway, Rachel preferred the spring, with its promise of new beginnings, while Tim liked the autumn water after it had been warmed by the summer sun.

So Rachel had it from January to the end of June, and Tim from July to December, and they pinpointed a weekend in the middle when they handed over and together made a list of running repairs and anything that needed to be replaced and divvied up the responsibility accordingly.

It was important to each of them to keep this ritual. Neither of them could ever quite come to terms with letting someone they had once loved out of their life, and there was something comforting about touching base every year. They both still cared deeply for each other. It wasn't lack of love that had driven them apart.

As soon as he saw Rachel, this year, Tim knew. She had a glow, of course, but she always did after spending time at the beach hut, so that was nothing new, her skin burnished to an even light caramel that contrasted with her white-blonde hair. But there was something else this time. An aura. A certain serenity.

She was wearing her hair up, and a faded green dress that Tim remembered her buying: its familiarity made his throat ache. She was packing away the last-minute bits of detritus to take with her: her favourite down pillow and her swimming things, piling them up into a cardboard box ready to take to her car.

The crockery and glasses in the kitchen area were the same ones they'd got when they first bought the hut – chunky blue-and-white striped plates they'd got in Ikea, with matching bowls and mugs that had come in a big white box, obviously marketed to students. Rachel had liked them because they were nautical; Tim had liked them because they were cheap. Surprisingly, none of them had got broken. There were still eight of each.

Their crockery had survived, but their marriage hadn't.

Looking now at the plates, with their blue lines, Tim imagined another blue line, and the joy he knew Rachel would have felt on seeing it. He couldn't identify the feeling this gave him, because it was a cocktail of emotions, some razor sharp, some duller. Shock, despair, sorrow – but also happiness on her behalf, because Tim wasn't an unkind person; far from it.

They'd never seen their own blue line. Time and again he could remember waiting, those few minutes interminable while she lurked in the bathroom then came out, face bleak. He realized now he'd never really hoped to see one; that he'd always known deep down, with some sort of sixth sense, that it wasn't to be.

As he stood there now, the hut suddenly felt very small. She couldn't quite meet his eye. She was babbling on about all sorts of inconsequential nonsense. She wasn't going to tell him, he realized. Although she would have to at some point. After all, next year it would be blindingly obvious. There would be another little being in the world. She couldn't keep that a secret. He would arrive here, and there would be tiny clothes, and baby sunscreen, and a bucket and spade … He couldn't expect her to expunge the presence before his arrival. No matter how hard she tried to hide it, there would be evidence. A sock under a chair; a sippy cup in the sink; a pack of baby wipes …

She was smiling at him, uncertain. Her awkwardness was tangible. There wasn't an elephant in the room, he thought. There was an embryo. But it was the size of an elephant. Its impact was just as big.

'Let me carry that stuff to the car for you.' He reached out his arms, anxious that she shouldn't overdo it. She hesitated, then smiled at him, grateful. He'd always been a gentleman. An opener of doors and a puller out of chairs. It was one of the things Rachel so missed about him. So few men were instinctively kind.

'I'll make us a sandwich.' She put a hand up, ruffling her hair, pulling it out of its ponytail so it fell to her shoulders, before scooping it up again and re-tying the band. It was the gesture she always made when nervous. He knew her better than he had ever known anyone, even now.

He nodded, satisfied with the deal. He trudged up the beach with the box in his arms, her car keys in his pocket, not knowing how to prioritize his emotions, even though she hadn't officially told him yet.

The sun seared down on him. It was the sort of heat that might drive you to kill, like Camus's *Outsider*. As he walked along the front of the beach huts with his cargo, he felt as if he were in a film, a close-up in a fashionably long tracking shot that followed him past endless pageants of happy family life. Fathers patting sandcastles into perfection; mothers doling out beakers of squash and peeling the wrappers off ice-creams; haphazard games of rounders fuelled by squealing and cheating; babies dozing off in buggies under the shade of a huge parasol, slick with factor 50. All of them saying to him: 'this is what it's all about'.

He had thought he would get over it. But, of course, he couldn't. What did everything count for, if you had no one to look up to you, no one that mattered? No one to inherit the good bits of you and carry them on into the next generation? And the bad bits too, he supposed. Without children, life was just one long round of self-gratification, without someone to nurture, to teach, to spoil, to share with the person you loved.

By the time he reached the car park, his mouth was dry with despair. He bought a Coke from the kiosk by the car park, gulped it down, letting the sweet coolness soothe his parched throat. Respite from his physical discomfort, perhaps, but not the raw anguish he felt further down, in his gut. A pain that dug and twisted and nipped, like a cornered rat.

He was tempted not to go back; to dump her stuff then go to his car and drive away until she had gone. He didn't want to see her. He didn't want to breathe in the essence of new life that she breathed out. They could leave the things that needed to be organized for another day. Or he could work it out for himself. None of it was complicated.

But he had to give back her car keys. Anyway, not going back would be ungracious and mean-spirited. It would make Rachel feel even more guilty than she obviously already did, and he didn't want that. He didn't want her to feel anything that might adversely affect the precious cargo she was carrying.

How bloody selfless of him, he thought, miserably.

He could still remember the day they'd been told about his useless, apathetic sperm. As humiliation went, you couldn't top it, even though Tim was repeatedly reassured it wasn't his fault; it was nothing he had done. Nor was there anything he could do about it. For nearly two years the diagnosis lay there between them. He felt useless and ashamed. He couldn't give his beloved wife the one thing she wanted. The thing she deserved.

He couldn't get her to accept that she needed to go and find someone else.

'I love you. A baby doesn't matter. It's us that matters,' she repeated, time and again, when he railed, drunker than he should be on a Friday night after a takeaway curry.

In the end, he made himself so dislikeable that she'd

had no choice but to leave him. Short of having an affair, which he couldn't bring himself to do, it was the only way he could think of to give her another chance. He drank, he brooded, he made himself and her life unbearable. He was never quite sure if she suspected his tactic, because she stood him for a lot longer than he would have stood himself. Once or twice, she tried to get them to go to counselling.

'We don't have to deal with this on our own,' she pleaded. 'We aren't the only ones. Plenty of people go through this and go on to have a happy and fulfilling life.'

'Fuck you and your bloody leaflets,' he'd snarled, and the memory of it seeped acid into his stomach. He had never wanted to hurt her. He wanted to give her the world, but he couldn't. And the pain of that ground him into a bitterness that made him impossible to live with. She wept uncontrollably as she packed up and left, and he sat on the turquoise velvet sofa they had impulse-purchased one New Year's Day sale, six years ago, and said nothing. Nothing to stop her; nothing to explain how he felt.

They sent each other tentative polite emails about the divorce. They met in fashionable coffee shops with bare brick walls and industrial lighting to finalize the details. And then, suddenly, 'they' were no more. No longer responsible for each other.

Tim could never let go of the guilt. He was still riddled with an anxiety that drained him, a fear that he'd ruined Rachel's life; that he had taken away her raison d'etre. Even when he slept, the ache of it ran underneath his dreams, persistent and debilitating. It was like a curse, and he raged against it. It wasn't that he felt he deserved to be ecstatically happy; just at peace would have been enough. But the torment wore him down.

As for having another relationship, there was no hope of that, at least not a proper one. He could never do what he'd done to Rachel to another woman. Of course, the next time he could be totally up front about it; they wouldn't need to go on that agonizing, humiliating voyage of discovery to uncover his infertility But at what point did he announce it? Should he wear a badge? Divulge it on the first date? Or even before? 'By the way, before we go any further, I've got duff sperm.' Clever use of the word 'duff'. But then, Tim was a copywriter; a player with words.

He certainly wasn't short of offers. On paper and in the flesh, he was a great proposition. More than solvent, easy on the eye, creative without being flaky, a connoisseur of coffee and wine and French cheese without being a bore about it, fit, fashionable without being a victim ... He skirted around women, longing for intimacy but fearing the inevitable conclusion that if it was going to go anywhere they would one day have to have the baby talk.

He knew, if he was his own friend, he would tell himself off for deeply unattractive self-pity and martyrdom; that there were plenty of women out there who didn't want a baby, or who couldn't have one themselves so his infertility wouldn't matter. Or what about women who had already had the children they wanted? But Tim didn't want to choose his love because she fitted in with his physical shortcomings. So he would rather go without. He had become adept at meaningless two or three night stands, after which he would let the women down gently.

He usually told them he wasn't over his ex. No girl wants to play second fiddle to the ghost of an ex-wife.

Once he'd dropped off Rachel's stuff, he started to head back to the hut. He remembered their excitement the day they'd decided to buy it. They'd spent a lazy bank holiday on the beach, picnicking and sunbathing and swimming, and on the way back to the car they'd seen the For Sale sign in the window. Rachel had sighed, 'If only.' By the time they got to the car, Tim had done the maths. 'Why not?'

They'd never actually vocalized it, but of course the purchase had been a long-term one, and each of them had envisaged family holidays there in the future. Now, for Tim at least, that vision was crushed.

He trudged back along the crescent of sand. The tide was right in, and the crowds had moved accordingly, shifting their picnic blankets and UV tents as far in as they could go. Although the sun was high in the sky, Tim felt a grey bleakness close in on him. Most people would give their right arm to have the summer ahead of them to enjoy Everdene, but it filled Tim with a sense of dread. Maybe he would just sub-let it; it would be easy enough. And better than being reminded of his broken dream every weekend ...

He tried to snap himself out of his *doleur* by drinking in the sparkling sea, thinking about the early morning surfing he could do; the mates he could ask down over the next few weeks. He stood outside the door for a moment: it was propped open to let in what little breeze there was. The huts always baked in the afternoon sun, and he could smell the heat of the bare wood.

Rachel had made a pile of sandwiches, pulled open a bag of Kettle chips and flipped him open a beer. They sat next to each other on the steps, as they had so many times over the years, and ate in silence, each pretending that it was simply too hot to talk.

Afterwards, they sat on the sagging corduroy sofa – the one the turquoise velvet bargain had replaced – with their feet on the coffee table Tim had made out of old wine-boxes, and went through the to-do list. The felt on the roof needed replacing. Tim got out his iPad to check out workmen who might be able to do it. As he searched, he realized that Rachel had fallen asleep.

He barely dared breathe as he didn't want to wake her. As she fell deeper into slumber, she sank into him until her head was on his chest. It was an unbearably familiar pose, the one they'd always ended up in on a Friday night in front of the television, after a hard week's work and a bottle of wine. Rachel would pass out after the first half hour of whatever movie they had decided to watch, and Tim would curl himself round her, protectively, watching it until the bitter end. And would then have to tell her what had happened, when she woke up in indignation as the credits rolled.

He wanted to put a hand on her stomach. He wanted to see if he could feel the baby. He knew it wouldn't be big enough yet, but he felt sure he would be able to detect some sort of energy pulsing inside her. But he fought the urge, even though he knew she would be so deeply asleep she wouldn't notice. It was too invasive. Creepy. And Tim didn't want to be a creep. Or jealous. Or over-interested. He wanted to run away from the whole situation. He had no idea how to deal with it. Not least because he didn't really know very much about the guy Rachel was seeing, who was presumably the father. They didn't touch upon their personal lives when they met. Well, they didn't touch on hers. Tim didn't have one. Or at least he felt as if he didn't. There was nothing personal about his existence.

He couldn't even remember Rachel's boyfriend's name. They weren't married, he knew that. She very sweetly made a huge effort not to mention him, and made sure he wasn't there when Tim turned up. Tim supposed his name didn't much matter; only his sperm count.

He grimaced. Self-pity again. It really was time he got over himself. But as he sat there, her head warm and heavy on him, he realized this was as intimate as he had been with anyone since the divorce. Sure, he'd had sex. But he hadn't had someone melt into him like Rachel was right now – someone who was so comfortable being near him that it felt as if they were as one...

Rachel stirred, then woke. She looked up at him, con-fused, that same end-of-movie face he remembered. What happened? she was thinking. But nothing had happened.

'You were out for the count,' Tim told her.

She sat up and wiped at her mouth, anxious she might have dribbled. 'I'm sorry, I'm just so tired,' she said, then looked straight at him. 'I'm pregnant.'

'I know.'

'I'm sorry.'

'Jesus.' Tim looked pained. 'Don't be sorry. It's great. Congratulations. I'm really pleased for you. Really.'

'Oh shit.' She put her face in her hands and dissolved into tears. 'I'm sorry. I'm all over the place. It doesn't take much to make me cry. Oh God.'

She leaned against him again. He stroked her hair away from her face, the little fine strands that had stuck to her forehead in the heat. He willed her not to say any more.

He didn't want to go through it all again, the fault thing, the blame thing.

He imagined a tiny boy with Rachel's white-blonde hair and caramel skin. A tiny boy with laughing eyes and white teeth, patting his mother's cheek. He felt a terrible creak inside him that he guessed was his heart breaking. Yet he was still alive. He was still breathing, in and out. He could still feel her head on his chest. He wondered if she'd heard the noise?

He patted her. 'It's OK, Rach. It's cool. I'm cool with it. It's what I want for you.'

'Really?' She sat up, her face blotchy with heat and tears. 'I didn't know how to tell you.'

'I'm really happy for you.' Tim looked into her eyes. 'It's wonderful.'

She sniffed and nodded.

'Listen,' he said. 'I've been thinking. The beach hut – I've kind of grown out of it. It doesn't fit into my life any more.'

'Oh.' She looked shocked.

'There's too many memories. I need to broaden my horizons. Move on.'

Her face creased with anxiety, and he itched to smooth out the fine lines on her forehead. 'I can't afford to buy you out, Tim. Not with the baby and everything … We'll have to sell it.'

'No, no – that's not what I meant.' Tim realized she'd misunderstood. 'I want you to have my half.'

'What?'

He threw his hands out in an expansive gesture. 'It should be yours. For you and the baby. To grow up in and have fun in.' He wasn't going to mention brothers and sisters, but already he could imagine them. Wonderful Rachel, with her tow-headed brood, calm and kind and funny and—

'Don't be silly,' she interrupted his thoughts. 'We can still share. Maybe we could move the dates round in the school holidays when it comes to it, but otherwise ...'

'No. I don't want to be here any more. I want you to have it.'

It was true.

'That's crazy. It must be worth a fortune. You can't just throw away your half.'

'Rach, I'm not poor. I'm earning a good wage and I've got no one else to spend it on.'

She stared at him, swallowing hard. 'Wow.'

'It would give me enormous pleasure to know that it was yours. Honestly. I wouldn't do it if I didn't feel it was the right thing to do.'

It would be too painful, to carry on sharing it with her and her new little family.

And actually, maybe this was exactly what he needed to do and should have done ages ago. Cut the ties. Maybe then he could move on, instead of being reminded when he saw her, every six months ...

Just how very much he still loved her.

'I think you should think about it,' she said. 'It's a huge decision.'

'I'll spend August here,' he said. 'Then I'll hand it over to you in September. I'll get my lawyer to sign it over to you.'

She put her hands up to her face. She was making a terrible choking sound. He tried to smile.

'It was supposed to make you happy. Not cry.'

She screwed her eyes tight shut and nodded. 'I know. But …'

He didn't want her to say anything. If she did, he would cry too. And it was as if she knew that it was all getting too much for him, because she suddenly pulled herself together, looked at her watch, re-did her ponytail again.

'I'd better go. I want to beat the weekend traffic …' She moved away from him, looking for the things she needed. Her car keys. Her big wicker bag with the gingham lining. He knew without looking what was in it. Her battered Filofax because she still loved writing things down. A paperback – something thoughtful and thought-provoking. A tube of rose-scented hand cream because her hands were always dry. Her camera. A hairbrush with half a dozen hair ties wrapped around the handle. A bandana. A tiny rattan box full of worry dolls they'd bought in a museum in New York – he couldn't remember which one now, but she'd loved them and kept them with her.

Would he ever know anyone else so well?

He kissed her goodbye, not quite letting his cheek brush hers. Moments later she was gone, and he watched her walk across the sand, carrying her flip-flops in one hand, her back straight, still walking with grace. He imagined she would still be graceful at full term. He imagined her in a year's time, walking with the baby over one shoulder, confident and resplendent in her motherhood, talking to it gently while she did something, always so unflappable, always so mindful.

Stop it, Tim, he told himself.

He walked back inside the hut. There was still a dent in

the sofa cushions where the two of them had been sitting. He patted them back into shape until there was no trace. Then he picked up his iPad and began to compile an invitation list from his email contacts. Including, he decided without hesitation, the cute girl who ran the deli up the road from him. She flirted with him when he bought his cheese on a Saturday morning. Not in an obvious way, but she always had something new for him to taste, and she'd wrap him up a tiny sliver in waxy brown paper for him to take away and try at home, and she recommended wine to drink with it. He didn't have her email but he looked up the deli website and found the info address.

No one but him need know that this was to be a farewell party; the last one he would throw at the beach hut before it became Rachel's for ever. He would make it a party never to be forgotten. The party to end all parties. He selected an icon of a palm tree from his Clip Art file and created a border, then began to fill in the words.

🌴 🌴 🌴 🌴 🌴 🌴 🌴 🌴 🌴 🌴 🌴 🌴

BEACH PARTY AT EVERDENE SANDS.
THE SUMMER STARTS HERE

🌴 🌴 🌴 🌴 🌴 🌴 🌴 🌴 🌴 🌴 🌴 🌴

My life, he thought, starts here.

KIKI

So prison, it turned out, wasn't like it was on the telly: like an episode of *Bad Girls* or *Orange is the New Black*. No script or camera could ever capture the tedium, the boredom or the fear. Not so much the fear of what might happen inside – Kiki was used to being in care, after all, and prison wasn't so different – but the fear that the experience might change you for good; that you would never be the same again. That you would lose hope, and that any good inside you might be snuffed out, and that you would be destined for a lifetime of recidivism, in and out of trouble and court and prison, in an endless, mind-numbing loop of utter uselessness, shunned by society, never able to get ahead and become respectable. Let alone respected.

So when she found herself surrounded by a cluster of people from the local council, the tourist board, the various arts charities that had funded the project and a photographer from the local newspaper – the great and the good of Everdene – Kiki couldn't quite believe it. As she took the key to the beach hut and put it in the lock, smiling for the camera, she wondered if they really had any idea of how far she had come to get here? Of course, it was a good story, and she was happy for them to use it in their PR, but seeing it in black and white and actually living it were two different things. And, of course, the true story had been glossed over and given plenty of spin so it just read as if she had been unlucky; that getting caught had been a one-off, a momentary aberration because she had fallen under the influence of someone charismatic and evil who had made her do Bad Things.

'So – tell us how you feel about your new role?' The reporter who'd been sent to cover the story smiled at her winningly. 'I mean, it's a dream come true, isn't it?'

'It is,' agreed Kiki. 'I can't believe how lucky I am to be spending the summer here. And I'm so grateful to all the bodies who made it possible. And I'm really looking forward to giving people the opportunity to paint while they are down here. Anyone can pick up a brush and create something beautiful. You just need confidence. And inspiration. And what could be more inspiring than this?'

She threw her arm out, taking in the wide expanse of Everdene Sands. The bay was looking particularly stunning, as if it knew it was going to be splashed all over the papers and had made the blue of the sea more blue, and the pink of the sand more pink, and the few clouds in the sky whiter than white.

Kiki smiled as the photographer got the money shot: Kiki opening the door of the beach hut, where she was going to be artist-in-residence for the whole summer, encouraging visitors to unleash their creativity. At the same time, Kiki was being commissioned to paint a body of work to be exhibited during the winter months, all designed to raise the profile of Everdene as a holiday destination.

She still couldn't believe she had been chosen. There had been hundreds of applicants. After all, who wouldn't want to spend the summer in a beach hut sploshing paint about? So the competition had been fierce. The application process had involved submitting a portfolio of work, supported by an artist's statement, and then a round of rigorous interviews.

Kiki had decided that the only way she was going to get through was by being up front and honest; not trying to dress herself up as someone with something deep and meaningful to say. In the end, her story had said it all. Art had, without wishing to sound melodramatic or pretentious, saved her from the gutter. She was quite upfront about that.

'If it wasn't for the painting classes in prison,' she told the journalist. 'I'd still be up to no good. I know I would. But it unlocked something inside me. It gave me hope. And—' she searched for the right word – 'passion. Passion for something other than the next high.'

The journalist nodded solemnly, as if she understood, but Kiki knew she had no real comprehension of what it was like or how far Kiki had really come. People loved to think they were down with the dark side but they didn't have a clue. Being born to a heroin addict and being taken into care at three days old was not a good start in life. Playing musical foster homes was even more traumatic and unsettling, especially when your spoilt and over-privileged mother was battling to get you back while trying to conquer her addiction. Kiki had been bounced from luxury back into care for the first twelve years of her life, as her mother desperately tried and failed to get straight for the sake of her child. She had eventually lost the battle when Kiki was thirteen, overdosing very quietly and suddenly after five months of being clean. Her devastated parents had washed their hands of the whole messy situation. They didn't want to be reminded of the fact they had somehow failed their beautiful daughter. It was far easier to banish her most visible mistake. They had hurriedly handed Kiki back to Social Services. Kiki had gone from the funeral back into care in her best dress.

It was inevitable, therefore, that she had fallen into the same black hole as her mum. Drugs had filled that hole, of course they had, and the world she had ended up in made it only too easy to lead a life of scoring, using, dealing and all the concomitant crime. She thrived on chaos and drama underpinned with violence, manipulated by men who saw a pretty and vulnerable girl who could be used and abused. And to find she had a use had given her a purpose. She had been a naive but willing victim, wild and rebellious, not really caring what happened to her, because she knew only too well that anything good could be taken away overnight, that just when you thought everything was going to be OK your world could be turned upside down. Going down for a crime she hadn't masterminded, by the time it happened, was an inevitability she accepted. An occupational hazard.

Now, as she stood on the beach, smiling for the camera, glowing in the warmth of the sun, she knew at long last that she trusted herself; that she was in control of her destiny. No one could destroy her now, or bring her down with them.

'What do you think?' the photographer thrust his camera at her to preview the pictures he'd taken. She still couldn't believe what she saw. Not a skinny, mangy creature with matted extensions and peeling false nails dressed in minimal denim and high heels, but a glowing creature in a Hawaiian dress, her hair braided in hundreds of tiny plaits piled on top of her head, her skin smooth, her eyes, once dead, as bright as the light that bounced off the sea. She looked, she realized, happy. Something she had once had no experience of. She hadn't recognized the feeling when it had crept up on her: a lightness, a warmth, a tingle that was not drug-induced and that didn't fade once the hit had worn off.

She almost hadn't gone to the workshop that afternoon. The prison often put on talks from visitors they thought would inspire the inmates. Why would she want to go and see some famous artist bang on about painting? It would have no bearing on her life either inside prison or out of it. But something about the poster drew her in. Sebastian Turner, one-time bad boy of the British art scene, had spoken to her somehow. The photo on his poster showed both vulnerability and defiance, and something deep inside Kiki connected with that bravado. She wondered what he was hiding. So much that after a nondescript lunch of something vaguely orange floating about in a beige sauce, she found her way to the art room.

When he arrived, she couldn't take her eyes off him. He was petite and pretty, but with a panther-like stealth that made him dangerously attractive in a dissolute rock-star kind of way. Dressed in skinny leather jeans and a white shirt, he obviously came from a privileged world – he spoke like the people who had surrounded her when she was younger, in a clipped, languid drawl. Kiki had left that speech pattern long behind. It didn't do to talk nice in the circles she moved in. But it reminded her so much of her mother when he began to talk that she thought she was going to cry. She moved to the back of the room so no one could see how emotional she was – it was a sign of weakness to show cracks. She pulled herself together and listened to what he had to say.

He spoke passionately about his drug abuse, about the privileged background he had nearly thrown away, about his art and how it had been a curse at first, but ultimately a blessing. As she watched him talk, she felt something inside her. Now, she recognized it as hope; a tiny little flame that, as he spoke, burned brighter. She wanted more than anything to be part of the world he spoke of. To feel what he was describing. It was like nothing she had felt before, a lure greater than any narcotic.

When he'd finished speaking, everyone in the room was given a blank canvas and a palette of paints. Normally Kiki would be gossiping and laughing with the other girls, causing as much disruption as she dared without actually being disciplined. But today, she stood in front of the easel and stared at the whiteness. It made her fingers itch and something inside her stirred. She felt like a horse in a starting gate, pawing at the ground, ready to be let loose.

Sebastian came and stood next to her. She felt his aura, felt it flow into her as she picked up her brush. Kiki, who had never felt anything with her heart or her soul, felt almost as if she had been taken over.

'What shall I paint?' she asked, hoping he wouldn't ask her to copy the boring bowl of fruit that had been placed on a table in the middle of the room.

'I want you to paint what you feel inside,' he told her, and she had looked into his bright-green eyes and felt purpose.

She didn't think about it. She just plunged her brush into the paints and attacked the canvas. She wasn't painting anything other than her feelings: rage, confusion, frustration, mostly, with a smattering of grief; a dramatic swirl of dark red and purple and navy blue with a tiny black heart lying at its centre.

When she had finished, she stood back and he came and stood beside her. He gazed at what she had done and frowned. Oh God, he thought it was awful, she thought. Of course it was. A load of blobs with no real thought attached to them smeared all over the canvas.

'Who taught you?' he asked.

'Taught me?' she laughed. 'I've never picked up a brush in my life.'

'That's amazing,' he told her. 'This is stunning.'

'Shut up.' She nudged him with her elbow.

'How did you do it? How did you know what to paint?'

She shrugged. 'I just painted what I was feeling. Like you said.'

'Wow.' He turned to look at her, his eyes serious. 'This is what every artist tries to achieve. The ability to just paint without thinking. To put your soul on the canvas. It's brilliant.'

Kiki didn't know what to say.

'You need to do something with this talent,' he told her. 'When you get out of here, write to me. I know it's probably not the done thing, but I don't care.'

He told her his address, which she committed to memory. And the day she left the prison, she sent him a postcard to tell him she was out.

It was only later that she came to realize just how very important and influential he was, and how lucky she was that he had swung it for her to get into art college, writing an effusive reference to go with her application. But as someone pointed out later, he would never have done it, put his name on the line and risked his reputation for her, if she hadn't had the potential.

At art college, she blossomed and bloomed and flourished and channelled her energy into painting huge canvasses that were brave and bold and confrontational. She hated intricacy and fuss. Her paintings made a statement: simple, almost naive, yet they left you in no doubt as to what they represented. She never hid behind detail. And like them or hate them, her art was undeniably hers, for her life had given her work something unique. And people wanted her work. She was astonished to find that she could command quite a good price. Enough for her to make a living, which was unusual for an artist these days.

She had made a point of not keeping in contact with Sebastian. She never wanted anyone to accuse her of exploiting her relationship with him. She didn't even invite him to her degree show, because she thought it would be showing off. Nor did she invite him to any of her private views or mention him in her interviews or artistic statements. It wasn't that she wasn't grateful – far from it – but he had done enough. He had given her the key that day and she never wanted him to think she was using him.

And now, as her entourage dispersed and she was left at the beach hut, she couldn't believe how far she had come. She'd turned her life around so it was unrecognizable. She sat on the steps and looked at the scenery around her, the dunes and the bay and the horizon, and the people on the beach all with their own story.

She took a small sketchpad out of her bag, and began to draw. After an hour, she was satisfied with what she had done. It wasn't her usual style, because it was small, but it still had the looseness and positivity that was her trademark.

She turned the paper over and wrote on the back.

Dear Sebastian

This is to thank you, from the bottom of my heart, for everything you did for me. If it wasn't for you, I might not be here now. I think you know better than anyone how the darkness can swallow you up. But you brought me into the light. This is a picture of where I am now, at Everdene Sands. I'm artist-in-residence for the summer, living in a beach hut. I would never, ever have believed I could be in such a good place. In that one afternoon, you turned my life around.

I just wanted you to know that, and to say thank you.

With very best wishes
Kiki

Then she slid the drawing into an envelope and wrote his address on the front, the address she had never forgotten. She wondered what he would do with her little painting – whether he would toss it to one side, or pin it on his kitchen wall. She didn't much care, as long as he appreciated just how important what he had done for her was. She hoped that she would be able to do the same for someone else this summer.

She licked the flap of the envelope and sealed it tight.

To inspire someone, she thought, was probably the greatest gift a person could give.

ELODIE

Six months after the proposal, the day before Elodie and Jolyon's wedding, The Grey House shimmered on the cliff, serene in the sunlight of a June afternoon, as if it knew how very important the next day was and that it had to prepare to look its best. Gardeners had clipped and mowed the lawn and hedges and borders; an army of staff had polished and dusted the interior. The windows shone, the furniture gleamed, not a speck of dust loitered. Vases waited for armfuls of flowers earmarked by Lillie to be cut at daybreak, and in the kitchen the shelves in the larder and fridge groaned with delicacies. Everything that could be done had been done until the day itself dawned.

The early afternoon was peaceful, and everyone was out. Some of the household had gone to the tennis club for lunch. Others had made the trek to Bamford, the nearest big town, making last-minute purchases, having haircuts or merely contemplating their existence. There was something about an impending wedding that made people look more closely at where they were in their own lives: to analyse their mistakes and resolve to make changes, for better or worse.

Elodie had managed to play everyone off against each other so that she could be on her own. She was finding being the centre of attention rather tiring: she couldn't move without someone asking her to make a decision when, actually, she knew everything was going to be perfect, whether the cake came before or after the speeches, or whether the floral arrangements in the house matched the ones in the church. She'd never been one for a great fuss, but as Lillie and Desmond's only daughter it was inevitable that the wedding was going to turn into something of a showcase – for Desmond's desire to show off his wealth, and Lillie's never-ending quest for perfection.

Elodie knew Jolyon felt the same as she did, although Roger and Jeanie seemed to have been swept up in the frenzy. A little bit of her thought they were probably playing the game out of gratitude. There was no doubt that Desmond had saved the Jukes from bankruptcy and steered them back into the black. The shops were booming, thanks to his investment of both money and time. In less than twelve months they were all turning a healthy profit. So the Jukes were making as much fuss of the wedding as the Lewis's, caught up in guest lists and present lists and any number of trips to Gieves and Hawkes for morning suits. Roger had driven to France for the champagne: twelve cases of vintage Dom Perignon. No one asked quite where he got it from because that was the sort of person Roger was. You didn't ask.

Elodie just wanted to curl up in her bedroom on her own before her life changed for ever. Not that she was going to have any second thoughts – far from it – but because she wanted to revel in it, to remember for the rest of her life just how it felt to be on the brink of marriage to the person you loved and trusted and cared for most in the world. She was so lucky to have found Jolyon. She shivered sometimes when she thought how easy it would have been for them to have missed each other. If her father had settled on some other business to expand his empire. If Jolyon had refused to come down with his parents that first weekend. If, indeed, he'd already had some other girlfriend who'd overshadowed her.

She ran up the stairs, relishing the quietness of the house. It seemed impossible to imagine that tomorrow it would be teeming with guests, caterers, flower-arrangers, hairdressers ... the travelling circus that came with a wedding.

She was puzzled when she heard voices. She was certain everyone was either out at lunch or running errands, before they all met back for a rehearsal at the church at five o'clock. She stopped at the top of the stairs while she took stock of where they were coming from: her parents' bedroom, she thought. Not burglars, surely? Burglars didn't speak in low, conversational tones while they were ransacking a house – or laugh. She felt a sharp spike of fear, nevertheless. Something told her she didn't want to investigate any further; that she wasn't going to like what she discovered. Yet her feet found themselves walking along the carpeted corridor until she stopped outside her parents' door.

She could smell them, before she actually identified them. She could smell her mother's scent and Jolyon's cologne: the cocktail of Ma Griffe and Lentheric hit her in the back of the throat and made her want to retch. She held onto the doorjamb. Maybe Lillie was helping him with his morning suit, ensuring the perfect fit? Or giving him a talk about how to make her daughter happy for the rest of her life?

She heard Lillie's laugh. The throaty, wicked one she used with men. And her low Gallic murmur: 'Darling, I know it's torture. But it's the only way. You will have every excuse to be near me, and no one will ever query what you are doing here.'

Jolyon's voice was tense. Unhappy. 'I know. I know!'

'Don't feel guilty. Elodie still has you. She has what she wants.'

'I feel … an utter heel.'

Lillie gave a dismissive French 'pffft'.

'It's all very well you dismissing how I feel.' Jolyon sounded angry. 'I love Elodie.'

'Not as much as you love me.'

Time shimmered in the corridor, the doors all shifting slightly in Elodie's eyeline.

'True,' sighed Jolyon. 'But if it wasn't true it would be so much easier.'

'Easy is boring.' Lillie's boredom threshold had always been dangerously low. 'In a year's time Elodie will have a baby. She will be as happy as can be. Then she will have another. And another. She will be more lucky than I was.' At this, Elodie imagined downcast eyes and a trembling lip. 'She will live an enchanted life here. It is the perfect place to bring up a family. In the meantime …'

The ensuing silence could only mean one thing. Eventually she heard Jolyon give a heartfelt groan.

'What else is to be done?' Lillie was getting exasperated. 'This way everyone is happy. You, me, Elodie, Desmond …'

'Oh yes, I'm sure your husband would be delighted—'

Again that French exhalation of dismissal. 'All Desmond was ever concerned about was getting his hands on your shops.'

'So this is a marriage of convenience?'

'Jolyon, Jolyon. How many times have we had this conversation? You love Elodie. You're not being forced into anything.'

His voice was choked. 'I feel as if I am.'

'Then don't go through with it. But if you don't, you're a

fool.' Lillie was running out of patience. 'This is the best way. The only way.'

Elodie clamped her hands to her ears. She had heard enough. She crept backwards along the corridor, slipped into her bedroom, pushed the door to and threw herself onto her bed.

She felt all the happiness and enchantment and excitement of the past year drain out of her, like sand out of an upturned shoe. Instead, a cold, black dread settled upon her, squeezing her heart like an iron corset until she could barely breathe. The deceit and the betrayal were too huge for her to take in. Jolyon, her dear darling Jolyon, whom she adored; whom she couldn't wait to marry, and who she thought had adored her...

And her mother.

Her own treacherous, self-serving abominable mother.

Elodie had never had any great illusions about Lillie. She had always known she liked her own way and wasn't terribly bothered how she got it. She had always known she couldn't resist proving her attractiveness to men. Yet she had always felt close to Lillie, although they were so different. She had never dreamed in a million years she would stoop this low. She had thought that a mother's unconditional love, and need to protect her child – her only child! – would take priority over her vanity and need to be adored.

She bit on her knuckles to stop herself crying out. She didn't know whose betrayal hurt the more. The two people she loved most in the world...

And her father. He wasn't complicit in their treachery – Elodie was certain he would have no idea – but all Desmond was interested in was money. Of course he'd wanted her to get married! Of course he had encouraged it at every opportunity, throwing her and Jolyon together at the earliest chance. She *thought now, looking back, it had been her father's plan from that very first weekend. The melding of two dynasties via a marriage – it was archaic. And although it wasn't official, she had been an unwitting pawn, which was arguably worse than if it had been openly arranged between them.*

She looked up. Her wedding dress hung on the wall, wrapped in cellophane on a padded hanger. It seemed to mock her, white with innocence. All that time Lillie had spent at the dressmaker with her! Making sure she had the perfect wedding dress. The hours she had spent with caterers, florists, wine merchants, scrutinising every last detail, forgetting nothing in her quest for a fairy tale.

And in one split second, the fairy tale had been blown apart.

Elodie tried to think straight. What if she hadn't chosen to come back that afternoon? How long would she have lived in ignorance of what was going on? Would she have lived out her entire married life in oblivion? Raised a family without knowing that her own mother was having an affair with her husband?

She stared at the ceiling. How long? How long had this been going on? Which of her happy memories was she allowed to keep? The moment on the beach she first met Jolyon? Their first moonlit walk? Their first moonlit kiss? How had he looked into her eyes so many times and told her that he loved her, knowing what he knew? Whose idea had it been? Who had made the first move?

She felt cold with misery and hot with fear. She curled up into a ball. She had to keep herself quiet. She mustn't make herself known. Elodie wasn't going to burst in on them and ask them to explain themselves. She didn't like drama or confrontation. And she had to ask herself why and how this had happened. She had to try and understand, before she decided what to do.

She stared at the ceiling. The room felt airless. It wouldn't be long before everyone else began to drift back. There would be tea on the terrace, then they would all head up to the church, to meet with the Reverend Peters, run through the order of service, who was to stand where, who was to hold what ... She didn't have much time to decide what to do. If anything.

Her bridesmaids, two friends from school who were arriving later this evening and staying at a local bed and breakfast, would be no help. And this wasn't the sort of dilemma you could drop on someone and expect sage advice. The only person Elodie would have trusted to give a sensible opinion was her mother. Lillie understood the subtleties and nuances of surviving adult life. Yet she was the last person on earth she could ask. She felt a sudden surge of something boil up inside her. Not hatred. Elodie didn't have it in her heart to hate anyone. Anger? Rage? She couldn't be sure because she'd never felt anything like it before.

She couldn't think about Jolyon. She just ... couldn't. Something dark and icy and cold gripped her when her mind ventured towards him, so she shut the thought of him out.

Hot and cold. She felt hot and cold. She hugged herself and shivered, yet she felt feverish. She was in shock. Mrs Marsh, she thought. Mrs Marsh would make her hot, sweet tea. But the thought of facing anyone made her stomach churn, just like the sea when the tide was on the turn, swirling into little eddies which seemed to have no sense of direction, yet had no choice in the long run about where they went.

Half an hour went by. During it she heard footsteps pass her door and go down the stairs. Whether they belonged to Jolyon or Lillie she didn't know. Or want to know.

By the time it came for everyone to gather for tea, she had a plan.

'My darling, you look beautiful.' Lillie ran her fingers over the French lace on Elodie's upper arms. The dress was so tight she could barely breathe, with its square neck and fitted waist; acres of silk satin in the skirt fell to the floor. It was heavy, almost like wearing a suit of armour. Rosebuds from the garden pinned her veil into place, and she could smell their scent, the scent outside her window in the summer that mingled with the sea breeze.

As Elodie gazed back at Lillie, she realized there were tears in her mother's eyes. What did those tears mean? Were they genuine emotion at a mother's proudest day? Was she crying out of shame at what she had done? Or because she wished that she was in Elodie's place? What was going through Lillie's head?

For a fleeting moment she was tempted to confront her. Lillie's hands were trembling slightly on the stem of her glass: she was less in control than usual. Elodie felt her stomach curdle as distaste combined with nerves and lack of food. She hadn't been able to face breakfast. She thought of Jolyon in a nearby hotel with his best man. What was he thinking and feeling? Did he wish Lillie was with him?

Eventually Lillie blinked, batting away the tears, and held her glass up to Elodie in a toast.

'To you, my darling girl. I hope you will be as happy as I have been.'

She gave a bright smile and threw back the last of the champagne as if it were a life-giving elixir.

Again, Elodie wasn't sure what to think. Was there an edge to what her mother said, or was she being genuine?

It was a terrible feeling, not to trust your own mother.

Except in matters of what to wear. She held up her jewellery box.

'Pearls or diamonds?'

'Diamonds, darling. Always. I fear pearls might be dreadfully bad luck on your wedding day.'

Elodie screwed the diamonds firmly onto her ears. It was the right choice. She looked back at her reflection and for one of the few times in her life, she felt pleased with what she saw. The chignon suited her and gave her an elegant profile; she wore more make-up than usual and it made her eyes look huge; her skin was alabaster smooth against the white of the veil.

She felt remarkably calm, all things considered. But once Elodie made her mind up about something, nothing much deterred her. She was very single-minded. And she knew just what it was she had to do. She ran through a mental checklist. Everything was planned. She had remembered every detail. There was nothing she had forgotten.

'Just another hour,' said Lilly, 'and you will be Mrs Elodie Jukes.'

'Yes,' replied Elodie, and picked up her bouquet: more white roses from the garden.

'Let's go and find your father.'

'You go,' said Elodie. 'I want a few moments on my own.'

'Don't be nervous.' Lillie put a hand over hers. 'This is your day.'

Elodie couldn't meet her eye. If she looked at her mother, she wouldn't be able to hold her nerve. She moved away, towards the window, and was grateful that Lillie didn't press the issue, but left the room. She stood, looking out at the garden, where the trestle tables were already spread with snow-white cloths.

Beyond, the sea was a sparkling sapphire blue, as perfect as if it had been chosen from a catalogue to blend in with everything else.

Her Everdene. The place that had encapsulated her childhood. A place of endless sunshine, games, laughter, happiness. A place of safety and security. And in one moment all that safety and security had been blown apart. She fingered the petals of the roses in her bouquet, velvet-soft. Their delicate scent filled the air, making her feel even more queasy.

There was a gentle knock and she turned to see her father in the doorway. He was smiling, handsome in his morning suit, another of the roses from the garden in his buttonhole. She wondered what, if anything, he suspected or knew.

He held out his arm. 'Come on,' he said. 'The car's waiting.'

It was his own Rolls-Royce they were using for the wedding car. The one he had bought four months ago, so plump were his profits, so successful had his investment in the Jukes' crumbling empire turned out to be.

For the millionth time in the past twelve hours, she wondered about her parents' marriage. Which part of it was real and which was a facade? How much did her parents really understand of each other and their needs? Had what had happened came out of calculation or accident?

She walked across the room and took his arm. He led her along the corridor to the top of the stairs. She held her head high as she walked down in her unaccustomed high heels, staring fixedly ahead.

'Nervous?' asked her father.

'A little,' she told him. In fact, she felt nothing.

They crossed the hall, opened the front door, and there was the Rolls, a driver at the wheel. He jumped out to open the door, and he and Desmond helped her into the back, making sure her dress wasn't creased. She could smell the rich cream leather of the seats as she sank into the comfort.

Her father smiled at her as he slid in next to her. 'I bought this for today, you know. I wanted the best for you, for your wedding day.'

Elodie wasn't convinced. The car was obviously just another status symbol. Yet more proof of Desmond's success for the benefit of the guests. But of course she didn't say so. She just smiled.

The car set off, crunching across the drive and out of the gates, turning left towards the village. They could have walked, but that wouldn't have been commensurate with the rest of the effort put into the wedding. Before long the car turned right into the tiny winding lane that led to the church, only just wide enough, a line of grass down the middle as if guiding them to the ceremony; the hedgerows bursting with cow parsley. Elodie remembered the times she had come down here with Mrs Marsh to collect blackberries as the summer reached its end, each fat, juicy berry plopping into the bottom of her bucket and landing with a thud.

She looked down at her bouquet, at a tiny greenfly wandering about the petals. It was as tiny and lost and aimless as she felt.

As she and her father stood in the church doorway, she felt overwhelmed by the faces turned to watch them. There seemed to be hundreds, all smiling at her arrival, their eyes dewy with the pleasure the first glimpse of a bride always gives people. It was like a roll call of her life. Aunts and uncles, cousins, friends, neighbours, people from the village; everyone who had ever been important to her and had a part in her upbringing. And in the far distance, in front of the altar, the billowing robes of the Reverend Peters, beaming at her, luring her down the aisle.

And in front of him, his back straight, his blond hair shining in the light from the stained glass, Jolyon. Her Jolyon.

Her betrayer.

She held her father's hand tight. She was trembling with emotion. With fear and the thought of what she was about to do. As the organist threw himself into 'The Arrival of the Queen of Sheba' with more gusto than skill, she glided down the red threadbare carpet that had been in the church ever since she could remember. Her mother, resplendent in grey crêpe de Chine, gave her a smile of such heartfelt fondness as she walked past the front pew that she wondered if perhaps she had dreamed it all; if perhaps yesterday had been a hallucination born of too much excitement?

Then she saw Lillie's eyes flicker towards Jolyon's back, and something in them, something hard and stony and greedy, told Elodie that no, it had not been in her imagination. And so, as she joined Jolyon at the altar, she didn't meet his eyes, instead taking in the kindly gaze of Reverend Peters, who looked slightly puzzled at her coolness. It wasn't like Elodie to be detached.

The reverend put it down to nerves and began the ceremony. He was delighted to see the little church so full, and to be presiding over the marriage of someone he was very fond of. He did so many more funerals than weddings these days, he was determined to make the most of this happy occasion.

'Dearly beloved,' he began, but Elodie suddenly stepped forward.

'Can I stop you there?' she asked.

He frowned. 'Is everything all right? Do you feel faint? Perhaps some water?'

'No,' said Elodie. 'I don't need water.'

Jolyon looked alarmed. 'What is it, El?'

Her father stepped forward from his place in the front pew and took her arm. 'Elodie...'

There was warning in his voice. Yet not surprise. And when Elodie turned to look her father in the face, she recognized that he knew. There was no consternation or confusion in his eyes. From that moment, she was on her own.

She turned to face the congregation. When she'd made her plan, she had meant to wait for the Jane Eyre moment, the 'just impediment' moment, but she knew the longer the ceremony went on, the more her resolve would weaken. How much easier it would be to put her discovery behind her and go blindly into marriage, for part of her knew that Jolyon would do anything in his power not to hurt her openly. She suspected events had overtaken him; events which had been put into play by her mother.

Mother. The very thought of the word filled her with disgust. What Lillie had done to her was the antithesis of what motherhood meant. How could anyone do that to their own flesh and blood?

Her voice rang out, quiet but true.

'There's going to be no wedding today,' she told the shocked congregation. She saw Mrs Marsh's face crumple; there was pity in her eyes but, tellingly, not surprise. Had even Mrs Marsh known, or suspected? Or was it just that the staff were so aware of the rotten state of the Lewis marriage that nothing would surprise them? Was Elodie really the only person who'd been clueless?

'I'm not going to tell you why.' She turned to Jolyon. His face was as white as her veil. He was shaking his head, then he turned to the front pew with a look of pure hatred, directed straight at Lillie.

'You told her,' he said, in a monotone.

Desmond stood up and stepped forward. 'Steady, lad.' The warning in his tone was more than evident.

Next to him, Lillie stood up. To her credit, she threw back her shoulders and prepared to take her punishment.

'Elodie,' she said. 'You misunderstand.'

'I do not,' Elodie said, 'misunderstand. There is nothing to misunderstand.'

Desmond moved to his daughter's side. 'Sweetheart, let's sort this out. I'm sure the reverend would give us a few minutes?'

He looked at Reverend Peters, who was ashen. 'Of course.'

Elodie shook her father off. 'No,' she said. 'You're as much part of this as they are. You got what you wanted.' She threw a look at Jeanie and Roger, who looked uncomprehending. 'Lewis and Jukes. That's what this is all about.'

'Elodie ...' Desmond pleaded. 'I don't know what you think, but you are wrong.'

He turned to Lillie for support, but Lillie looked away. Jolyon said nothing, mute with fear. Elodie felt nothing but distaste for his inertia and lack of chivalry. She put her arms out and held up her hands, one either side of her, to stop anyone coming close. It was as powerful as she had ever felt in her life. Yet she had never wanted power. She had only wanted love. How fragile it was, she realized now. How deceptive. Every kind of love she had ever known had been taken away from her in one moment.

No one dared intervene as she swept back up the aisle, the faces that had greeted her arrival now frozen with shock. She threw the church door open, stepped out into the graveyard *and broke into a run. It wouldn't be long before someone found their head and came after her, and she didn't want to be stopped. She fumbled with the latch on the lychgate and flew out into the road, where the taxi was waiting, as instructed, facing in the right direction.*

As she reached the car, her father came up behind her. He grabbed her wrist.

'Sweetheart. Please. If you go, then we all lose everything.'

Elodie turned. 'How could you let it happen? How could you say nothing?'

Desmond shut his eyes and shook his head. 'You don't understand. You can't understand. Everything I did, I did for us. You and me.'

By now, the driver had got out of the car and was coming to her assistance.

'Excuse me, sir,' he said to Desmond. 'Let the young lady go or I will have to call the police.'

Elodie pulled her arm away and Desmond had no choice but to let it drop. 'There is no us,' she told her father. 'There is no us any more.'

'We would have had everything. We would have had it all.'

Elodie stared at him. 'No, Daddy. I wouldn't have. Can't you see that?'

Desmond couldn't look at her. He stared at the ground. Elodie was surprised that there was so little fight in him. He seemed utterly defeated. But she didn't care, or want to hear any more of what he had to say. She pulled open the door and slid into the front seat. The driver walked round and got into the driving seat, giving her a reassuring smile as he started up the engine.

Desmond suddenly seemed to snap into action. He banged on the window. 'Elodie!'

'Go,' she told the driver. The car pulled away, smoothly and swiftly, as if the driver was used to extricating brides from their wedding ceremony. She didn't look back. She didn't want to see her father staring after her. Her greedy, duplicitous, spineless father.

In the boot would be her honeymoon suitcase, crammed with as many clothes as she could manage. And a holdall, with everything else she thought she might need: her passport, her Post Office savings book, the cash from the pot in the kitchen her mother kept topped up and which Mrs Marsh used to pay the milkman, the butcher, the window cleaner ... And some of the wedding money they'd been given by well-wishers. If it was stealing, she didn't care. There were, after all, far worse things. She'd put them all together that morning at dawn and crept out of the house. As arranged on the phone the night before, the taxi driver had met her at the top of the lane. He hadn't asked any questions, just taken the bags from her and received her instructions. The fact that Elodie was paying him more money than he made in a week ensured his silence.

As the car drove up the hill out of Everdene, she didn't turn round. She didn't want to look back at the sea that had been such a huge part of her life, or the house which had been her real home, or the hut where she had given herself to Jolyon and where he had proposed to her. She stared at the road ahead.

The driver looked sideways at her. 'Don't cry, love,' he said, concerned. 'Don't cry.'

She hadn't realized she was.

Elodie had instructed the taxi driver to take her to the next station along the branch line, because if she were to be followed the first place anyone with any common sense would go would be the station in Bamford. They crossed the moors, parched to a pale brown already by the summer sun. They stopped at a remote pub, where she changed out of her wedding dress and into a nondescript skirt and blouse. She hesitated, tempted to push the dress into the rubbish bin, never to be seen again, but she needed to be prudent from now on. She didn't know what the future might hold; she might be able to get good money for it at some point. So she folded it up neatly and put it in her suitcase.

At the tiny station in Somerset, so small there was no ticket office or guard, the driver lugged her case onto the platform for her. And when she went to pay him, he waved away her money.

'It's all right, love,' he said. He was visibly upset. 'Good luck, eh?'

She hadn't given him any details of her predicament, but he was clearly moved by it. And as he left her, Elodie had the sense that her last ally was gone, that now she was on her own. A plume of steam and a whistle heralded the arrival of the train: it swooshed in and glided to a halt, even though she was the only passenger.

She managed to find an empty carriage for the journey up. London had made the most sense when she had made her escape plan. She had little time to think of many alternatives, it would have the most opportunities, and she could be anonymous, virtually impossible to find. She sat in the corner of the carriage, by the window, and laid her cheek against the blue and cream upholstery. She felt as if there was nothing left of her; she had wilted as surely as her bridal bouquet was wilting, wherever it had fallen. She couldn't think backwards or forwards; her whole existence was contained in the compartment, airless and slightly claustrophobic. The mid-afternoon heat, combined with the fact that she had barely slept the night before, meant that she soon fell into a deep and, thankfully, dreamless sleep.

Paddington was seething with people arriving for a Saturday night in town, and people escaping the heat of the city for somewhere more pastoral. Dressed-up girls clacked along the platforms with determination; mothers herded gaggles of children; guards kept order amidst the mayhem. Doors slammed, whistles blew; the smell of Coke hung heavy in the air.

Whenever they had arrived at the station before, Lillie had whisked them to a taxi and taken them straight for lunch. Elodie realized she had only thought as far as her initial escape. She didn't really have a plan. All she had wanted to do was put as much distance between her and Everdene as she could.

She needed somewhere to take stock, to make a battle plan. She needed somewhere to take a bath. She needed something to eat. She hadn't eaten since lunchtime yesterday. She wasn't hungry, but she was sensible enough to realize that if she was going to survive, she needed fuel.

She was still in her wedding shoes – a mistake, she realised now, as her feet were starting to blister. She was hot and dusty. She couldn't think beyond the physical. She couldn't think about the Elodie inside. If she did, she would crumble. She lugged her suitcase to a black cab waiting on the platform.

The driver wound down his window.

'Browns, Mayfair,' she told him, and ignored the way he looked at her askance. It was the only hotel name she could think of: the one her father used when he was in London *on business, and where he had taken them for tea before the pantomime once. It was far grander than she really needed, but why not? After all, she thought, it was her honeymoon night. As the taxi drew up to the white stucco front in Albemarle Street, she felt comforted by its familiarity. She tried not to think that the last time she had been here, she had been with her parents.*

To her relief, the hotel had a room free. She knew there were probably a million other hotels in London, most of them cheaper, but here she felt safe, cocooned in the quiet luxury. She ran herself a bath, then ordered some plain roast chicken and the most recent copies of the Evening Standard *and* The Lady *to be sent up to her room.*

She lay for half an hour in the water, light-headed and woozy, still batting away any thoughts of what she had left behind, though it was impossible not to wonder what everyone was doing, and how they were reacting to the aftermath. Had Lillie and Jolyon confessed? Or was it blindingly obvious? How had Jeanie and Roger reacted? What would happen to all the guests? And the presents? And the food? If Elodie felt guilty about anything, it was all the hard work Mrs Marsh had put in. But then, it had hardly been her fault. She pictured arguments, threats, tantrums, tears, hysteria – who would take control of the situation? Her father, probably – he would have recovered his equilibrium by now. Lillie would be defiant. Jolyon ...

She couldn't think about him. The only way to survive this was to pretend he had never existed. To forget the warm glow she had always felt in his arms, the glow that had sparked into something even more special when they made love.

Love? That must have been an illusion. A dream state she had talked herself into, lulled by Jolyon's attentions and apparent fondness; duped by the intensity of their frequent but furtive couplings in the beach hut. He had been so very good at keeping up the facade. Elodie didn't consider herself a fool, because no girl in her right mind would ever suspect such foul play. It was unthinkable.

As the bath water cooled, and the bubbles settled to scum on the water's surface, she reflected that she could be torn apart by what had happened. She could let it destroy her confidence and her belief in people. She could howl into her cocoa every night. Or she could see it as a new beginning. An adventure. Leaving the rest of them behind to flail about in the impact. Because the more she thought about it, the more guilty they were of allowing it to happen, all of them. She wanted nothing more to do with any of it.

She clambered out of the bath and wrapped herself in a towel, just as the bellboy brought her food to the door. Dressed in her wedding nightdress, she sat in the middle of the bed, enjoying the chicken and the new potatoes and the careful spoonful of bright green peas with a sprig of mint. She was surprised she could face eating, but she knew she would feel worse if she didn't: hunger always gave her a headache.

When she'd finished, she spread out the copy of The Lady *on the bedspread. She took the tiny pencil that was by the telephone on her bedside table, and began to ring adverts. After half an hour, she had a list of six people to ring. It was too late to call now, on a Saturday night, and really she wasn't too sure if she would make much sense: the adrenaline and the travelling and last night's lack of sleep were finally catching up on her.*

She would make the calls first thing in the morning. For now, she needed to sleep. As she crawled in underneath the sheets and blankets, she mused that she was making the decisions now, and her future would stand or fall dependent on them, and not what her mother or father or fiancé dictated.

Her last thought before she fell to sleep was that she would not be the victim in all of this.

VINCE

The launch party of The Lobster Shack was the hottest ticket in town so far that summer.

By early evening it was crammed with sun-kissed and beautiful people happy to be partaking of the free jugs of margaritas that were circulating. Waiters and waitresses in white jeans and T-shirts and red aprons passed around huge plates of seafood.

The place was barely recognizable as Marianne's restaurant, which had been dark and heavy. It had been transformed into a light, bright space, all driftwood and white paint and zinc-topped counters with flashes of turquoise. A DJ was playing seventies funk: the bass-heavy riffs could be heard all the way up the street, but the music was infectious. Even if people weren't dancing, they were smiling and tapping their feet as Rock Lobster by the B52s pounded out of the speakers.

Vince thought only Murphy could have pulled it off. Only Murphy could have had the vision and the energy to turn what had been a dreary, tired space into a vibrant hotspot in so little time. Not that Vince hadn't done his bit – he'd put in hours of graft and plenty of money – but to turn something like this round took grit and determination, locking horns with the council to get a late licence, cracking the whip on the workmen and hiring the right staff.

Murphy had even commissioned Kiki, the girl who was Everdene's artist-in-residence, to design them a logo and provide them with some artwork. Six large canvasses with lobsters emblazoned in the middle, in acid-bright colours – yellow, turquoise, pink, green ... They looked perfect – they had a modern, Britpop feel to them, but also a hint of retro. The restaurant was going to sell prints, splitting the profits with Kiki.

The Lobster Shack had already been open for a fortnight, a soft opening which had gone unheralded, yet still they had been fully booked almost every night. It seemed to be just what people wanted on holiday by the sea: somewhere easy and fun and relaxed but where they knew they could eat well. His mate, Vince decided, was a genius. He felt a bit of a fraud, as if he was just along for the ride, but Murphy insisted he couldn't have done it without him.

And it had had a knock-on effect on the business. The Maskells had never sold as many lobsters. They couldn't pull them out of the water quickly enough. And Vince was incredibly proud of his brother, who had stepped up to the plate. Chris had turned up for work every morning, bright-eyed and bushy-tailed. He'd totally turned himself around. Vince was relieved – he didn't know what he would have done otherwise. You couldn't carry a drunk in a job like theirs. Even when everyone was on the ball it was treacherous, as they could all testify ...

Everyone who owned a beach hut on Everdene had been invited, and Vince saw most of his neighbours. They were going to offer a takeaway service too: lobster and crab platters loaded up with potato salad and coleslaw, so the beach hut residents were their best potential customers.

And then the door opened and he saw her. Anna. Murphy had said she was coming down for the launch, as long as the girls were happy to go to her mother's. Vince hadn't allowed himself to believe she would actually make it, but suddenly there she was, in the middle of the crowds, smiling and greeting people. She was wearing a cream T-shirt dress and gold sneakers, her pale hair in a side-plait. She came and kissed him. He breathed her in. The want never ceased. If anything, it got worse.

She played with two slim gold bracelets on her arm. A present from Murphy, no doubt.

'So this is what's been keeping him so busy for the past few months,' she said. 'I was starting to think he had another woman.'

'What do you think?' said Vince.

'Wonderful,' she told him. 'You should open one in Chiswick.'

The thought made his stomach turn over. The thought of being near her every day.

'How are the girls?' It was the only thing he could think of to say. Children were always safe subject territory. All he wanted to say was that she looked breathtaking; the most beautiful woman in the room by a mile.

She made a face. 'Not great. Lyra was complaining of tummyache when I left. I told Mum to ring me if it got any worse.'

'I'm sure she'll be fine,' said Vince.

Anna gave a vague smile. Murphy came up and squeezed her round the waist. 'You made it, babe. What do you think?'

'I think it's awesome.'

'Have you had a margarita?'

'I better not.'

Murphy frowned.

'Lyra wasn't well when I left. I might have to drive back.'

Murphy said nothing. Vince was surprised he showed no concern. On the contrary, he just walked off and grabbed a waitress, pulling another drink off her tray and making his way over to a small gaggle of guests.

Vince looked at Anna, who shrugged. 'It's always business first.'

Her voice sounded strained and Vince felt awkward. He'd never seen any real tension between them before. He wanted to console her, to slide an arm around her slender shoulders and squeeze her to him, but she gave him a brilliant smile that totally eclipsed her momentary drop in defences.

'You guys are going to make a fortune.'

'I don't know. The launch alone is costing a bomb. That's a lot of lobsters.'

'I have every faith. If Murphy can do anything, it's a business plan.'

There was an underlying implication that he couldn't do much else.

Vince supposed every marriage had its rough patch.

If he were married to Anna, he wouldn't neglect her. He wouldn't give her any opportunity to make the comments she was making.

Although he supposed it was easy to think that. What did he know about being married to someone? What did he know about anything, except catching lobsters?

*

At nine o'clock, the DJ turned the music down and the jingle of 'Greensleeves' was heard from outside. The guests all turned to see a vintage ice-cream van pull up onto the pavement outside.

Vince grinned. Another Murphy masterstroke. They had argued long and hard about whether to serve dessert. It just seemed to complicate things when they had worked so hard to keep the main menu simple. Then Murphy had hit upon the idea of using Jenna. The van could park up outside – the customers could either go out and choose their own or send the waitress for their order.

Within minutes of Jenna's arrival, there was a queue of party-goers on the pavement, eager for ice cream. Murphy met Vince's eye and winked. The DJ turned the music back up. Seafood, music, dancing, laughter, ice cream. They'd got the magic formula.

Chris was trying as hard as he could to hide his discomfort. This was the toughest test of the past few weeks so far. He'd managed to keep temptation at bay by staying as far away from the pub as he could. Work had taken care of the daytime, and he was running, doing his weights, focusing on fitness to keep the longing for a drink at bay. Once the alcohol was out of his system it was easier, but sometimes the need just jumped up and hit you. The longing for that comfort; the oblivion. And you couldn't control when it happened.

And it was hardest of all when everyone around you was indulging. The booze was flowing both freely and free tonight. How easy it would be to reach out a hand and grab a glass or a bottle from a passing waiter.

His brother had asked him if he was going to be all right earlier.

'I know it's tough,' said Vince.

Chris just shrugged. 'I have to learn to deal with it,' he replied.

Seeing Jenna turn up in her ice-cream van had given him strength. Doing it up had given him a focus in the first few weeks, and the sight of her in the window, scooping as fast as was humanly possible, was a just reward.

Yep, he could grab a margarita and revert to being the useless, drunken bum he'd once been, shambling about the place and being the laughing stock of Tawcombe. But that would be a retrograde step. And he'd be letting Vince down. If he went back under, the business would suffer, they wouldn't be able to supply the restaurant; the whole lot would come crashing down. It was his responsibility to stay sober.

But it was hard. It was a constant struggle. And there was only so much Diet Coke a man could drink.

He was going to have to go. He was going to have to leave the party, go back home. Get under the covers and go to sleep in order to escape the urge. He put his glass down on the bar and headed for the door. He wouldn't say goodbye to anyone.

He had just reached the door when he bumped into Jenna's boyfriend, Craig, coming in.

'Hey, buddy,' said Craig. 'How's it going?'

Craig knew his story. Of course he did. Jenna would have told him everything.

'I'm good,' lied Chris.

Craig looked at him. He was a copper. He could sense a lie a mile off.

'You must be really proud of Jenna,' Chris went on, hoping to distract him.

Craig nodded. 'I was getting worried about her,' he confided. 'She was starting to get depressed, you know. But this has turned her round. And I really appreciate what you did for her.'

'It's cool,' said Chris. 'It did me a favour. It got me through a tough few weeks.'

The two men shared a smile. They didn't need to articulate anything. Just an unspoken acknowledgement.

Craig touched his arm.

'Listen,' said Craig. 'I'm going surfing tomorrow if you fancy it. Jenna's going to be busy all day and I want to make the most of my time off. If you're free.'

Chris didn't say anything for a moment. He was touched. He could tell Craig knew he was struggling. And asking him to go surfing was his way of saying he knew it was tough.

He smiled. 'I'd love that.'

'Cool.' Craig nodded in approval.

They didn't need to say any more. But the exchange had given Chris the strength he needed to stay at the party. He could do this. With friends like Craig, who cared and looked out for him, he could stay on track.

At half past nine, when the place was at its fullest, Anna came in from outside, where she'd been on the phone. She went up to Vince and Murphy.

'Lyra's still complaining of tummyache. My mum's panicking. I'll have to drive home,' she sighed. 'Typical. My first weekend away without the kids for ages.' She looked at her watch. 'I'll be back home by one, I guess.'

'You sure you haven't had too much to drink?' asked Vince.

'I've only had one glass.' Anna was one of those people who didn't really need to drink. She picked up her handbag. She went to kiss Murphy. 'Baby, you're amazing. This place is amazing. I'm so proud of you.'

Murphy nodded. 'Drive safely. Hug Lyra for me.'

Anna nodded as she fished about in her bag for her keys. 'Of course. I'll text you and tell you how she is.'

She kissed Vince goodbye. 'See you soon. Look after Murphy for me.'

Vince had a mad urge to offer to drive her back to London. But of course he couldn't. He was host here and he'd had at least four beers. So he just smiled. 'Will do.'

Murphy watched his wife go. Vince couldn't read the expression in his eyes.

'You OK?'

'The bloody kids always come first.'

'Of course they do.'

'Lyra's fine. Anna's mum can manage.'

'I guess the maternal instinct is stronger than the paternal one.'

Murphy just looked at him. 'Yeah.'

He walked off. Vince felt unsettled. He didn't like Murphy's attitude to Anna's conscientiousness. But again, what did he know about marriage and parenthood?

He turned back to circulate. The artist girl who'd done the paintings came up to him. She was in a bright pink dress, her millions of braids down for once. He'd made conversation with her a few times over the windbreak that separated them: she was staying in the beach hut next door to his. What was her name? Kiki, he was pretty sure, but he didn't dare say it in case he was wrong.

'Hey,' she said to Vince. 'This is the best party ever. You must be really made up. Congratulations.'

Vince looked at her. She was very pretty indeed. She was talented. She was fun. She was single. He was pretty sure she was hitting on him. Why couldn't he respond to her? Why couldn't he smile at her and start flirting and then get her a drink, like any normal man would in this situation?

Because she wasn't Anna.

'Thanks,' he said, knowing he was being curt. 'Excuse me. I need to circulate.'

Her face fell. 'Course,' she said, nodding, and turned away. He could feel her disappointment, and he hated himself. He went to clear away some of the empty seafood plates to give himself something to do.

Chris cuffed him round the back of the head with brotherly affection. 'Hey, you've got staff to do that. Don't keep a dog and bark yourself.'

Vince smiled. 'What do you reckon?'

'It's a winner.'

Vince looked at his brother. A night like this must be hard for him. Everyone else was well on the way. 'You doing OK?'

'Never leaves you, you know. I could down six beers right now without thinking about it.'

'You're doing really well. I'm proud of you, mate.'

Chris just shrugged. 'Don't be. I've got a lot of lost time to catch up on. I was a twat for years.'

Vince slung an arm around his brother's shoulder and gave him a squeeze. This was what mattered. Sorting his life and his family out. Making the most of what their dad had left them. So he would be proud. And he thought he probably would be. The Lobster Shack wouldn't have been his dad's thing – he was strictly a pie and a pint man – but he would have been proud of what they were trying to do, nevertheless. It was a pretty good tribute.

By the end of the evening, when the last of the guests were lurching out of the door and the staff were clearing the last of the glasses, Murphy was cosied up on a banquette at the front of the restaurant with a girl. Vince didn't recognize her – which was unusual, as he knew pretty much everyone – but he recognized her type. The kind that homed in on a successful married man with a single-minded precision. She was an expert. Pretty, sexual, amoral. She was stroking the back of Murphy's hand with her finger. His eyes had glazed over and Vince knew exactly what he was thinking.

He strode over to them. 'Murph,' he said, keeping his tone mild but knowing his mate would detect the underlying warning. 'Time to go, mate.'

The girl picked up Murphy's phone and keyed her number in, then dialled it. Her own phone rang in her bag.

'There,' she said. 'Now we've got each other's numbers.'

Vince met Murphy's gaze.

'She might want a job as a waitress,' Murphy explained.

'I think we're fully staffed,' replied Vince. They weren't, but he wasn't going to give her an inch.

'You never know,' said the girl, handing Murphy his phone back. Staff walk out all the time. Just call me.'

She stood up, tossing her hair back over her shoulder, confident of Murphy's eyes on her toned body. She was slinky and dangerous. Vince didn't want her anywhere near his friend.

He walked her to the door, a firm hand in the small of her back. 'Leave him alone,' he said. 'He's happily married.'

She gave a mirthless laugh. 'There's no such thing,' she replied. 'And he's a grown-up. He doesn't need you minding him.'

He does, thought Vince, as he opened the door and ushered the girl out into the warm night air.

He shut the door and turned back to Murphy, who was looking the worse for wear, slumped on the banquette.

'What are you playing at, mate?'

'Ah, nothing. She was nothing.' But his expression was dark.

'Do you know if Anna got back OK?'

Murphy didn't reply for a moment. 'Probably,' he said eventually. He didn't seem to care. Vince didn't push it.

'It was a good night,' he said.

Murphy shook himself out of his gloom and grinned.

'We're going to clean up,' he said. 'Hey, that artist from the hut next to yours is definitely after you.'

'You reckon?'

'She couldn't keep her eyes off you all night.'

'I didn't notice.'

'No, I know you didn't, Vince. That's the infuriating thing about you. You haven't a clue. Sometimes I wonder what's the matter with you.'

You don't want to know, mate, thought Vince. You don't want to know.

PIP AND EDIE

The girl was wearing a green silk dress. A deep, bright green. Almost iridescent. She reminded Pip of an exotic parakeet as she flittered about the bookshelves. It was very plain, a shift dress, and it outlined how very tiny she was. Her hair was bleached white and cut in a very short crop. Her eyes were huge and wide with spidery lashes that must be false – no one could have lashes like that in real life – her face pale and otherwise un-made-up.

He wondered what she was doing in the library. She didn't seem to have a great deal of concentration. She would find a book, sit down and read for a while, then sigh, then close whatever she was reading, look up at the ceiling, then open a notebook and scratch away in it with a stubby old pencil, scribbling and crossing things out. Then she would stare around at the other people in the library. She didn't seem to mind them noticing her staring; she smiled back, not disconcerted in the least.

One woman couldn't take it. She stood up and marched over to her. 'Could you stop staring?'

The girl pouted. 'A cat can look at a king.'

'I don't care. It's bloody rude. If you don't stop it, I'll call Security.'

The woman stomped back to her place. Pip smothered

a smile and the girl caught his eye. She seemed to notice him as if for the first time, which didn't surprise him. Pip was used to not being noticed. He looked away, hoping she didn't think he was leering. But she put her head to one side and stared at him, as carefully as a customs officer screening an X-ray machine.

A moment later, she got up and came and sat next to him. Pip felt himself go rather warm. He wasn't used to female attention, and he got a sense that this creature didn't quite follow the same rules as everyone else. Exactly the opposite of him. Pip was big on following rules. He had done all his life. He didn't think he'd ever stepped out of line. He was the model of propriety.

She leaned over to him. 'I didn't think,' she said in a stage whisper 'people really had leather elbow patches, except in movies and books.'

Pip looked down at his corduroy jacket, which did indeed have leather elbow patches. He'd had it so long he couldn't remember where it had come from. He'd had it all throughout university, he was pretty sure. Perhaps his mother had sent him up with it? He certainly couldn't remember going and buying it.

'Well,' he replied. 'I guess they do. Unless we *are* in a movie, in some parallel universe.'

She looked delighted with his reply.

'What are you doing?' she asked him. He was surprised by how forthright she was, but pleased to find it didn't bother him in the least.

'I'm trying to write a review for an anthology of poetry.'

She clapped her hands. 'Of course you are! That is *exactly* what you would be doing in the movie!'

Pip smiled and looked down at the three paltry

sentences he had managed to write. When he'd offered to do the review at the meeting, the editor had been keen for him to have a go, but now he was trying to pin it down in black and white, it was proving devilishly elusive. So he'd decided to take the morning off and seek inspiration at the library. The office was open-plan, and too noisy for the kind of thought the task needed.

'What sort of poetry?'

'Oh, love poetry,' he said, with a sigh. 'Is there any other kind, really? Any other kind that matters, anyway?'

Her proximity was making his heart skitter and lollop. He remembered, when he was small, his rabbit's heart beating at the same rate whenever he scooped him out of his hutch. He used to worry the little creature wouldn't survive the anxiety.

'Well,' she replied. 'There's war poetry. That's kind of important.'

'It is,' he agreed.

She ran her thumb over the edges of her notebook with a sigh. 'I'm trying to write a song. But I know it's not going to happen today. Sometimes you just know.'

'Yeah.' Pip stared at his insufficient contribution. He could sit here all day and it wouldn't get any longer. 'I've got that feeling too. You can't just *make* it happen.'

'Sometimes it's best to give in. When the muse doesn't strike.'

'I feel as if it's all been said before.'

'It probably has. The trick is to fool people.' She waggled her fingers as if she was about to perform magic.

He frowned. 'It seemed like such a good idea when it was in my head. It was all so clear.'

She leaned in close. 'You need a distraction. If you

think too hard about it, it will never work. But if you concentrate on something else ...'

Her eyes were dancing.

Pip felt strange. His heart was still tripping over itself, his head felt light, his palms were slightly clammy; his mouth dry. Once, at university, someone had put something in his drink and the sensation was not dissimilar. Some wag had thought it hilarious to spike the square. He'd stumbled about spouting nonsense before wandering off back to his digs. No great spectacle. Even on drugs, it seemed, he was boring.

He breathed in, but that made his symptoms worse, as he inhaled her scent. Honeysuckle: suddenly he was sitting in a garden on a summer's day. Pip suspected he didn't have long. His instinct told him this girl's attention span was minuscule. Something else would capture her attention if he didn't move fast.

Pip wasn't used to acting on instinct or impulse. He certainly wasn't the kind of person to hit on women in libraries. But he told himself if he didn't, he was going to stay exactly who he was for the rest of his life: square, staid, dull, bookish, stolid Pip, remarkable only for his photographic memory and his beautiful handwriting. Yet in less than a minute, this girl had unlocked something in him: the desire to be spontaneous and take a risk.

It was thrilling.

'In that case, do you want to go for lunch?' he asked.

The words were out. He could hardly believe it. He tensed himself for a rebuff. Ridicule at worst; polite rejection at best.

She put her hands on the table, straightened her back and widened her eyes. She looked pleased. 'Really?'

'Why not? It's nearly one o'clock. Neither of us are getting anything done.'

The angry woman looked over at them, scowling at their sotto voce conversation. Pip looked back at her, defiant, and felt a curious tingle: a mini wave of euphoria at his rebelliousness. The girl scrabbled for her things, gathering them up and stuffing them into a sparkly drawstring bag that looked more suited to a nightclub.

'Come on then.'

The woman looked sour as they walked past. The girl threw her the sweetest of smiles. Normally Pip would be cringing if he was with someone making a scene or an exhibition of themselves, but he found this rather funny.

Outside, the sun bounced off the Bloomsbury pavements. Pip took off his jacket and slung it over one shoulder, pleased he had put a decent shirt on that morning: unironed, but clean. He led her to his favourite café, which had a tiny courtyard garden, with whitewashed walls and pots of pelargoniums. They ordered ciabatta stuffed with salami and mozzarella and avocado and tomatoes and basil, and cans of lemon San Pellegrino to wash it down.

'I want you to tell me everything about you,' his new friend demanded, picking the avocado out of her sandwich and eating it first.

'There's not really a great deal to tell. I'm astonishingly dull.'

'It might seem dull to you.'

'No, really.'

'Try me.'

Pip didn't usually like talking about himself, as he could see people glaze over before he even started. But in the warmth of the sunshine, under her inquisitive gaze, he began to unfold himself.

'I work for a literary magazine. I'm a sort of general dogsbody. I look after all the contracts for the contributors, post the books out to the reviewers, organize the interviews, catalogue everything that comes in – anything anyone else doesn't want to do, really.'

'That's pretty cool.'

Pip braced himself. Usually at this point, people told him they were writing a book, or were going to write a book. He always felt they expected him to say: 'Send it to me; I've got contacts. I'll get you a deal'. As if he was going to recognize their undiscovered genius on the spot and change their lives. As if he even had that power! But she didn't. Thank goodness.

'By the way,' he said. 'I don't know your name.'

'Edie,' she told him. 'After Edie Sedgwick. My mother is a Warhol fan.'

'Pip,' he told her with a rueful grin. 'Mine's a Dickens fan.'

'Pip's sweet. It suits you.'

Pip blushed, not sure how she knew or what that meant, but he felt it was probably a compliment. Edie was looking at him.

'So where are you from?' she asked. 'I can tell you're not from London.'

His accent always gave him away.

'I grew up in a village in the Peak District. With my mum. I never knew my dad. He left when I was eighteen months old. So she had to work to support me – she was an English teacher.'

138

Edie nibbled on a sun-dried tomato. 'That must have been tough for her.'

'Well, I suppose so. But she always seemed quite happy. We were quite happy.'

Pip turned his can of drink round and round. Edie had a curious energy about her – she almost fizzed.

'I was a bit of a swot,' he went on. 'I wasn't really any trouble.'

'No getting drunk and throwing up in the hedge? No snogging unsuitable girls on the doorstep?'

Pip smiled. 'No. As I said, deadly dull really.'

'I'm sure not. Just not the same as everyone else.'

That was true. Pip had never felt like anyone else. He'd always felt an outsider. Never one of the gang. But now was not the time to go into that.

'Anyway, when it came to going to university, I didn't want to leave her on her own. But I got into Cambridge. She insisted I had to go.'

'Of course you had to go. You couldn't stay at home with your mum for ever. That would be weird.'

'I know. And she was so proud.'

Pip remembered his mum standing in his room on his first day at Cambridge and crying with the joy of it. The bloke he was sharing with looked at them both a bit oddly. *His* mum had kissed him goodbye and floated off in a cloud of perfume – all jeans and high heels with a huge handbag and lots of jewellery. Pip's mum was more like a nan in comparison, with her sensible shoes and cardigan and her grey, undone hair. He remembered not wanting her to leave. Wanting to run from the room and get back on the train home with her. He wasn't a mummy's boy. He really wasn't. He was just shy. He hated talking to new people, and he knew he was going to have to do it over and over again in the next few weeks.

He'd survived. Of course he had. His mum had gone back home and left him to it. But even now he was still a bit awkward and socially inept. He hated meetings, phone calls, parties … any social interaction, really. It was funny, he thought, how Edie had managed to draw him out. He didn't feel awkward in her company at all. She made him feel totally comfortable.

She leaned back in her chair, and Pip could see how fragile she was, her collarbone jutting out from behind the green silk, her arms skinny. Despite her childlike frame, though, she had a force and a strength he found reassuring.

'Listen,' she said. 'It's Friday. Can you have the rest of the afternoon off? There's somewhere I'd like to take you.'

Pip thought about it. He had plenty of leave owing to him. He never took unnecessary time off. He never had days off sick. If he phoned in and said he wasn't coming back this afternoon, he didn't think anyone would mind. Or possibly even notice. But he was supposed to be going back home this weekend to see his mum. He'd already got his train ticket. He was looking forward to it. Being able to relax in the comfort of his own home, knowing he wasn't going to have to force himself to be polite and socialize. They wouldn't do much. Watch a bit of telly. Play Scrabble.

Yet somehow Edie's invitation intrigued him. Something told him he shouldn't turn it down. For the first time in his life, he wanted to do something spontaneous.

'Why not?' he said, and he felt as if he was standing on the edge of a cliff about to free-fall, but as if there was deep water beneath that would make his landing safe in the end. A risk. An exhilarating risk.

Edie jumped up, her chair scraping over the gravel.

'We'll take the train,' she said. 'We'll be staying overnight.'

'Won't I need to pack something?'

'We'll get you a toothbrush at the station.'

She was gone, in a blur of green, and he followed her. He couldn't believe what he was doing. Following a strange girl who knows where with nothing but his wallet. Luckily he had plenty of money on him. Cash and credit cards.

He called his mum in the taxi.

'Mum. I hope you don't mind. I can't come home this weekend after all.'

He felt terrible, letting her down. He imagined her, in their little kitchen. She would have made a cake. It would be in the flowery tin on the blue melamine table, waiting for him. There was always cake in that flowery tin. He could remember prising the lid off as a child, the smell of sugar and vanilla. The comfort.

'That's OK, love.' He couldn't tell if she was hiding her disappointment, or if she really didn't mind. 'There'll be another weekend. You have fun, now.'

'Take care, Mum.'

He hung up. Edie looked at him. 'It's your life,' she told him.

'I know,' he said, and was surprised that he didn't feel as guilty as he thought he might.

At Paddington, Edie told him to wait for her on the concourse.

'I won't be long.'

Pip watched her head off amidst the throng and disappear

141

into the first-class lounge. He was standing next to a florist, surrounded by buckets of bright blooms, waiting for the Friday afternoon travellers to make romantic gestures and impulse purchases. When she didn't reappear, he wondered with a hot prickle of anxiety if perhaps she'd played some sort of trick in an effort to get rid of him, but then why bother dragging him here in the first place? She was a curiosity, he thought.

Eventually he saw her white-blonde head weave its way amidst the commuters. She held two first-class tickets.

'How did you get those?' he asked, suspicious.

She laughed. 'The Artful Dodger's got nothing on me.'

'Did you steal them?' Pip was horrified. 'I could have paid.'

She just looked at him, her eyes wide. She was the picture of innocence.

'Come on,' she said. 'We'll go to the champagne bar. The train doesn't leave for another half an hour. We've got time for at least two glasses.'

In the end they drank a bottle. Pip paid up front, because he was terrified she would suggest doing a runner and he definitely couldn't have coped with that. The train arrived and they went to take their seats and any fear they might be apprehended by the guard was blotted out by the champagne. He was getting used to Edie's way.

They were heading for the West Country. They changed trains at Exeter onto a tiny branch line and headed out over the moors towards the coast.

'We'll have to get a taxi at the other end,' said Edie, tipping out the contents of her purse and extracting a crumpled tenner.

'I've got plenty of cash,' said Pip, before she got any ideas about stealing a car. 'Where are we going?'

His geography was terrible, and his eyesight even worse – he couldn't glimpse the names of the stations as they flashed past.

'That's for me to know and you to find out.' Edie smiled and stretched her arms out over her head, yawning. 'But you're going to love it.'

She shut her eyes. Pip wanted to shut his too – he felt sleepy and dry-mouthed after the champagne – but adrenaline kept him awake. He was on a train with a girl he'd only just met, hurtling towards an unknown destination. He didn't care if it was reckless. It was the most exciting thing that had ever happened to him in his life.

The seaside. They were going to the seaside.

Pip had finally fallen asleep in the back of the cab, but felt a sharp elbow in his rib and opened his eyes to see the road snaking down through emerald hills, at the bottom of which he could spy a vast expanse of twinkling turquoise.

'This is always my favourite moment,' sighed Edie. 'The magic never goes away.'

'Where are we?'

'Everdene. Everdene Sands.'

The cab pulled up at a slipway that led down between a cluster of shops and cafés and kiosks to the beach. Pip picked up the tab without being asked and scrambled out onto the pavement. The fresh saltiness of the air flung itself into his lungs. He stood next to Edie, who was taking off her shoes.

'I can't remember the last time I went to the seaside.' His mother and he had rarely gone on holiday.

'Take your shoes off,' Edie ordered him. 'We've got a bit of a walk.'

Pip obeyed, removing his shoes and socks and rolling up his trousers to follow her across the warm sand. They were at the start of a long line of beach huts. As the sun set, the inhabitants were winding down: lighting barbecues, pouring wine or flipping open a beer, hanging out damp towels, brushing down sandy children. It was like another world to him, warm and bright and colourful. He spent so much time indoors, he realized. In his office or in his lodgings or on the Tube. Now he relished the last of the evening sun on his face, the sea breeze ruffling his curls, and the soft grains of sand between his toes.

They walked three-quarters of the way along until Edie stopped outside a cream-coloured hut. It was battered and faded compared to some of the others, but in a style even unaware Pip recognized as shabby chic. Painted metal letters on the door spelled out 'she sells seashells', and a wind chime made of mother-of-pearl tinkled in the breeze.

Edie disappeared around the back and reappeared with a key.

'It belongs to a friend. I can use it whenever I like.'

'How wonderful.'

'It absolutely is.'

She opened the door and stood to one side to let him in.

An hour later, they were sitting on two deckchairs at the front of the hut, eating steaming hot fish and chips from the wrappers, watching the sun edge downwards and plop into the sea. Neither of them had really finished their lunch, so they were both ravenous.

Pip scrumpled up his wrapper and groaned with satisfaction, licking the last of the salty grease from his fingers. He was amazed that Edie had finished hers too – she was so tiny, there didn't seem room inside her for the enormous portions.

'So what do you do?' he asked her, curious to know about her background. He realized he knew nothing much about her except her name.

'I'm between jobs.' She didn't look at him, or indicate what either of those might be. Something told him not to press. 'Sometimes I write songs, but I don't do anything with them.'

She was a curious creature, he thought. Nothing like the girls he had gone to university with, or the girls he came into contact with through work. He felt as if he would never know her, yet he had let her know more about him than anyone ever in his life.

They drank a bottle of red wine she found in the kitchen cupboard, and he told her more about his work, which seemed to fascinate her, although he suspected her fascination was just deflection; a way to ensure he didn't ask her any searching questions. She wouldn't even divulge where she lived – just gave an airy, 'Oh, north London. One of the bits that isn't fashionable.'

Pip wouldn't have had an idea of which bits were or weren't fashionable, so that didn't narrow it down for him. He was living in digs on the top floor of a house in Southfields. Renting out attic conversions had become the new way to plug the financial gap when middle-class people lost their jobs in the city: a couple of hundred quid cash in the back pocket went a long way in Waitrose, and if you found a tenant like Pip it was easy money. He was no trouble. He always put his porridge bowl in the dishwasher before he left for work. He even put out the recycling without being asked. His landlords often said they didn't know he was there.

Pip often felt as if he wasn't there. As if he moved through life making little or no impact on other people. If he disappeared, it would be a minor irritation at worst, not a drama. But sitting on the beach with Edie, just sipping wine and feeling the kiss of night settle on his skin, he felt as if he mattered, just a tiny bit. Even though he wasn't entirely sure what he was doing here, in this rather magical place. He decided he wasn't going to question it. He was going to enjoy the moment.

Wow, he thought. He was being positively existential.

As it crept towards midnight, the huts on the beach fell quiet. Lights were turned out, music dimmed, and all that could be heard was the murmur of the waves rocking themselves to sleep.

Edie stood up. 'Let's go for a swim.'

'We can't.' Pip looked alarmed. 'We've had far too much to drink.'

'Don't be silly. Not that much. And we won't go out deep. The tide's coming in. We'll be fine.'

Pip felt even more alarmed as she pulled off her dress and flung it onto the deck chair. Absolutely no way was he going skinny-dipping. Yet he wanted to follow her. He wanted just an ounce of her abandon. He watched as she peeled off her underwear and set off towards the water.

'Man up,' he told himself. He would, he realized, look more of a fool if he dithered. He began to unbutton his shirt, wishing he had the courage to follow her in naked, but he had neither the physique nor the bravado to carry it off. All he could be thankful for was the timely purchase a couple of months earlier of some decent Marks & Spencer boxer shorts.

Edie's body was as pale as a pearl in the moonlight. She rushed into the water, whooping with delight, throwing herself without hesitation under the surface. Pip edged in more cautiously behind her.

'Come on!' urged Edie, flicking water at him. He flinched as the icy droplets hit his torso, then thought to hell with it as he flung himself under. His breath left him for just a moment, then he rather relished the silky-soft cool of the ocean as it wrapped itself around his limbs.

They lay on their backs looking up at the stars.

'Isn't it amazing?' Edie breathed.

Pip pointed out all the constellations, though it was hard to float and point at the same time, so in the end he gave up and they simply stargazed.

He wondered what his mum would think, if she knew what he was doing, floating in the sea with a naked girl. He didn't think she'd be cross. Or perhaps not even shocked. Perhaps just surprised. Maybe even pleased.

He let himself melt into the water, feeling the tension that had been holding him together for so long diffuse. Relaxation had become so alien to him. Grief and guilt had kept him on high alert; nothing had protected him from the nightmares. There had been times when he had wondered if it was worth the effort of staying alive, so pernicious had been his misery.

Edie stood up in the water suddenly. He could see her

in the moonlight, her breasts covered in goosebumps, her hair slicked back, and he shivered.

'It's cold,' said Edie. 'Let's go in.'

They waded through the water, then raced back up the beach. Edie, unselfconscious, ran like the wind, laughing and whirling her arms with the glorious freedom of it all, unperturbed by the possibility of someone from a neighbouring hut seeing her. Pip, who hadn't done much exercise since compulsory gym in the sixth form, lumbered up behind her, panting and breathless. By the time he got to the hut, she had dried herself off and wrapped herself up in a huge tartan blanket.

'Here.' She threw a matching one at him. He folded himself up in its softness and hung his wet boxers on the back of a chair.

She lit a portable barbecue, then split open the skins of two bananas, pushed squares of chocolate inside and wrapped them in foil. They sat and warmed themselves on the step while the packages cooked, then gorged on the oozing sweetness.

Edie put an arm round him and pulled him to her.

'I've had a brilliant evening,' she whispered in his ear.

She dropped a kiss on his shoulder. Pip felt the warmth of it burn his skin. He was all too aware of their nakedness underneath the blankets.

What was supposed to happen now? He wasn't sure of the rules, or of the state of their relationship. What on earth was this all about? She had a kittenish flirtatiousness about her, but he didn't think that was reserved for him; he thought it was her default setting. They hadn't touched in a particularly intimate way. She hadn't come on to him, but why else would she lure a man down to the seaside if not to indulge in some sexual exploit or other?

Would she expect him to be an attentive and expert lover? Surely she could surmise from everything he'd told her that he was far from experienced? He didn't want to disappoint her. Yet if it wasn't expected of him at all, he wished he had some way of knowing so he could stop worrying. It was the kissing that terrified him more than anything. It seemed more intimate than any of the rest of it. If you got that wrong, you were doomed. And it was all in the timing; the moment.

Before he had time to strategize his next move, Edie stood up.

'We should go to bed,' she said.

Pip quailed. He pulled the blanket more tightly around him, went to speak, but Edie patted him on the shoulder before he could vocalize anything.

'I'll take the top bunk.'

Pip let out a sigh, realizing he'd been holding his breath. He didn't know whether to be relieved or disappointed, but at least this outcome meant him not having to make the first move. He knew he wouldn't have been able to take the humiliation of rejection.

As he snuggled into the bottom bunk, he was still mystified as to why Edie had brought him here. Not for hot, unconditional sex, that was obvious. Which didn't really surprise him. Nevertheless, he felt they had connected in some way. He felt lighter of heart than he had done for months. Maybe even a little more confident.

In the bunk above him, Edie's breathing, deep and regular, told him she was already fast asleep.

*

Pip slept the sweetest and longest sleep he had slept for a long time. Maybe it was the sea air, or the late-night swim, or the unaccustomed alcohol, but he was still comatose at ten o'clock, even though the sun was sneaking in through the cracks in the curtains, as if to remind him that he was missing a beautiful day.

It was someone opening the door that woke him. Swiftly followed by an angry voice.

'What the hell are you doing here?' It was a female voice, high and indignant. 'Who are you?'

Pip sat up, still fuddled by sleep, to find a freckled, bespectacled face surrounded by a cloud of fine curls glaring at him.

'Seriously. What's going on?' The angry girl – woman? Pip couldn't put an age on her – whipped a phone out of her jeans pocket and waved it at him. 'I'm going to call the police.'

'I'm awfully sorry. I'm here with Edie.'

He pointed to the top bunk, presuming Edie would give him back-up.

But she wasn't there. The bunk where she should have been was empty.

'Who the bloody hell is Edie?' The girl stepped forward, one hand on her hip.

Pip felt very vulnerable. He was naked, for a start, he realized with horror. He couldn't hop out of bed to explain himself. He pulled the blanket up around him.

'We came down last night. She said the hut belonged to friends of hers and they wouldn't mind—'

'This hut belongs to my family. We don't just let randomers in, willy-nilly.'

'Honestly! I mean, I wouldn't just break in. I'm not

that sort of person.' Pip looked pained. 'Look – would you mind awfully if I got dressed so we can sort this out?'

'I should call the police.'

'Please don't. I mean, do if you have to. I understand. You must feel ... violated.'

'No. Just pissed off.'

She scowled. She might be small but she was fierce. Pip pointed to his pile of clothes at the foot of the bed. She gave a heavy sigh with a roll of her eyes and tossed them over to him.

'It's OK,' she said. 'I won't look.'

She turned her back to him and crossed her arms. He tried to get dressed under the blankets as quickly as he could, then emerged, sheepish.

'I'm all decent.'

She turned back around.

'So. Where is this mystery girl?'

'Perhaps she's gone to the shops? She'll be back in a minute to explain.'

But even as he said it, he didn't believe it.

And then a horrible thought occurred to him.

'My wallet!'

His wallet. Oh hell – where was his wallet? It had a couple of hundred pounds in it, and his credit cards, his identification – everything. His heart started hammering and he felt sick as he looked wildly around.

He turned to the girl, hoping to appeal to her.

'Look, it's obvious. I've been stitched up. I've been lured here and ... whoever she was has made off with all my cash. Oh shit – and she'll have got my address. She's probably back in London now, pinching the rest of my stuff—'

The girl was looking at him stonily, eyebrows raised. She

clearly wasn't buying any of it. She pointed to the floor behind him.

'Is that it?'

He looked down and saw his wallet. He grabbed it, hot with relief. Everything was still intact.

'Nice try,' said the girl. 'Now, how did you get in?'

Pip swallowed and tried to remember.

'There was a key. Round the back. On a hook.'

Something registered in the girl's face. The merest flicker of a realization.

'What did she look like, this Edie?'

Pip paused to think for a moment.

'About your size. Very … slight. Short blonde hair.'

'Was she a bit … manic?'

'Manic?' Had she been manic? She'd been different, certainly. If anything, she'd reminded him of Tinkerbell in *Peter Pan*. Feisty and busy and slightly unpredictable. 'Maybe …'

The girl gave a heavy sigh and ran her hands through her hair. 'OK. This is all starting to make sense.'

'Is it?' asked Pip, mystified. And as he looked at her, he felt unsettled, for now he was focusing on her, he could spot similarities. The small, neat nose, the slight figure; a timbre in the voice. Just take away the cloud of curls … A slow realization began to dawn.

'Is she … your sister?'

'Yes. Except her name's not Edie.' The girl rolled her eyes. 'It's Fran. But that wouldn't be glamorous enough. Not when she's off on one of her …'

She waved her hands in the air, lost for a word to describe what she meant.

'Her …?'

'Look. Fran has ... issues. She has episodes. When she goes off into the realms of total fantasy. I'm afraid you got swept up in one of her dramas. What did she tell you?'

Pip frowned. 'Actually, not a lot. Not a lot at all. It was me who did most of the talking.'

'That makes a change.'

'She was very kind to me. Actually.' Pip felt the need to defend Edie. Fran. Whoever she was. Even if she had done a runner and left him looking a fool. Luckily he was used to that.

Her sister smiled a weary, long-suffering smile. 'God, I'm really sorry. You must think we're both mad.' She stepped forward and held out her hand. 'I'm Mary. This is our family hut but we're all kind of estranged from Fran. She can be really difficult. There was an incident last summer ...'

'An incident?' Pip looked alarmed. He didn't much want to think about it.

'We haven't heard from her since.' Mary looked around the hut. 'What time did you last see her?'

'We went to bed about ... two?' Pip was flustered. 'Not that kind of bed. Sleep bed. We didn't ... I didn't ...'

'It's OK,' said Mary. 'You're both grown-ups. You can do what you like.'

Pip went pink at the thought that Mary might consider they'd had a night of torrid passion.

'I met her in the library. We went for lunch. And she brought me here. It was a spur of the moment thing.' A thought occurred to him. 'I've never done anything like that before.'

'That's Fran for you. She can talk anyone into anything when she's on a mission. She's very persuasive.'

'Yes. I didn't really get much say. But it was wonderful. In a strange way.'

Mary gave a dismissive snort. She didn't seem very impressed. Now he was properly awake, Pip could see how very like Edie she was. It was the mass of hair that disguised it, and the glasses, and the hoodie and jeans. He couldn't help laughing.

'This is crazy. Twenty-four hours ago I was sitting in the library minding my own business. Now I don't even know where I am. It's crazy. No one would believe it if I told them.'

Mary interrupted, crisp, 'Well, I hate to break it to you, but you're not in some kooky Richard Curtis film with a happy ending. You got away lightly, before she got her claws into you and then had a meltdown.'

Pip grimaced. 'Oh.'

'Yes. It's never pretty.' Mary looked at her watch. 'I need to contact my parents. Get them to track her down. Make sure she's OK.' She tilted her chin upwards. 'I don't have anything to do with her any more. But it's not as if I don't care.'

'No, I'm sure you care. Is there anything I can do?'

It was in Pip's nature to be helpful. Mary looked at him steadily, wrong-footed by his apparent concern.

'Just count yourself lucky and get a cab to the station.'

'Of course.' Pip realized that making himself scarce was the wisest course. This kind of thing didn't happen to him, ever. He wasn't sure how to handle it. 'Um – would you mind if I used the bathroom first?'

A flicker of irritation passed over Mary's face. Of course she wanted him gone as quickly as possible. 'Yes, yes. Hurry up.'

'Thanks.' Pip scuttled into the tiny bathroom and shut the door. He flipped up the loo seat and began to pee, staring at himself in the shell-encrusted mirror on the wall. The reflection that stared back at him was completely baffled. He didn't know what to make of the situation at all.

On the other side of the door, Mary prowled the hut in fury. Bloody Fran. It was typical of her. Toying with people. Playing with them. Not giving a thought to the consequences. Whoever her latest victim was, he seemed sweet – and absolutely not Fran's usual type. He was genuinely mortified at being caught and couldn't wait to get away.

Just like Sven last summer. The memory still made Mary weak with fury.

The trouble with Fran was she felt she had the right to judge, and that she knew better than everyone else about most things. That she was tuned in to something that no one else was. That she was special. Which wasn't surprising, given that their parents had always made her feel that way. They had long given up any hope of taming her, or expecting her to follow any conventional path. They veered between benign bemusement and outright amusement at her antics, only occasionally tipping over into genuine concern when Fran went a step too far. But then they didn't know the half of it. It was Mary who was usually party to the fallout from Fran's games and escapades and covered up for her. Dramas in pubs and at parties; showdowns and confrontations. Mary was never quite sure why she always felt the need to protect her, but she had a sisterly loyalty she couldn't ignore. It was exhausting.

She had once sat her parents down and told them she thought Fran should go to a psychiatrist.

'I think she's bi-polar,' she told them. 'Or manic-depressive. I've looked into it. There are patterns to her behaviour. Cycles.'

They couldn't see it. Because Fran was beautiful and beguiling and charming, they thought she was 'spirited', or 'eccentric'.

'Frances is her own person,' her mother always said. As if Mary herself wasn't, Mary thought, exasperated.

'How can somebody who is perfectly intelligent, but can't pass an exam, or hold down a job, or a relationship, not have something wrong with them?' she demanded.

'She'll settle down eventually,' her father said.

'Yes, but how many people will get hurt along the way?' asked Mary.

They didn't see the damage Fran did, the havoc she wreaked. The incident with Sven was the first real evidence they'd had, and even then they chose to swallow Frances' implausible story: that she was saving Mary.

Sven and Mary met at a Shakespeare summer school she was teaching at just after leaving university. She was besotted; he seemed to be so. They agreed to spend the second half of the summer in England at the beach hut, then head off to Sweden.

Fran took an instant dislike to Sven, and made her mistrust as clear as a cat, skirting round him with distaste.

'He's tight,' she complained to Mary. 'He never puts his hand in his pocket for anything. He's taking you for a ride. Why wouldn't he? The chance of a summer by the seaside in England, all expenses paid?'

'He's a poor student, like me,' protested Mary. 'I'm sure he'll repay the hospitality once we're in Sweden.'

'And he's not interested in anyone but himself,' Fran went on. 'He drones on and on and doesn't ask any questions or interact.'

'He's shy. And he doesn't feel his English is that good.'

'Rubbish. He's fluent. All Swedes are. And he's lazy. He'd stay in bed all day given half the chance.'

'So what? It's the holidays!'

'He just lets you get up and do all the skivvying and the shopping while he sits on his arse.'

Mary ignored her. Yet Fran's observations began to niggle at her. She did notice Sven holding court while people glazed over slightly. She observed how adept he was at avoiding a round when they went to the Ship Aground for a few drinks. And he never cleared away the breakfast things, or set the table for lunch, or helped wash up.

Then Fran showed her what she'd found on Facebook. She had trawled religiously through every one of Sven's friends, and found a girl whose information read 'In a relationship with Sven Jansson'. And the girl's Facebook status she had run through Google Translate which effectively read: 'Only twelve more sleeps until Sven Jansson comes home'.

'Maybe she's just a friend!' shouted Mary.

'Maybe you're just an idiot!' Fran shouted back.

'Maybe you're just jealous?' Sven, for all his possible faults, was blond and tanned and better looking than Mary felt she deserved.

Fran gave a dismissive snort and slammed the lid of the laptop down as Sven came in.

'Oh, how kind, Sven, you shouldn't have,' she said sweetly.

'Shouldn't have what?' he asked.

'Exactly.' She swept out of the hut.

Mary gave an apologetic shrug.

'What's the matter with your sister?' asked Sven.

'We've been trying to figure that out for years.'

Two days later, Mary came back from a shopping trip to find Fran in flagrante delicto on the bottom bunk with Sven.

'Wow,' gasped Fran. 'I can see why you put up with him.'

Mary dropped her shopping and fled.

Twenty-four hours later, Sven was on a plane back to Sweden and Mary had thrown Fran out of the beach hut.

'I wanted you to see what he was.' Fran was defiant.

'You wanted him for yourself. You couldn't bear the fact that I finally had a good-looking boyfriend, and you were jealous.'

Frances went white. 'Why doesn't anyone understand me?'

'Because you're a fuck-up.'

'Do you really want a boyfriend who is happy to get it on with your sister? He didn't take much persuading.'

'I don't want a sister who is happy to let my boyfriend "get it on" with her.' Mary could hardly bear to say it.

'You don't get it, do you?'

'I get that you are a crazy, destructive lunatic.'

'I saved you from him. If it hadn't been me, it would have been someone else. Lots of someone elses, probably. I can't bear to see you being made to look a fool.'

'You can't bear to see me happy.'

Fran stared at her, fists clenched. 'Why does no one ever understand me?' Her voice was barely above a whisper.

Mary put her face up close. 'I totally understand you. Now get out. Before I kill you.'

Fran's face crumpled. There was distress and grief and despair etched in every line. Mary's face, by contrast, was made of stone. Smooth and expressionless.

'Stop with the stage school act,' she said. 'You've finally been exposed for what you are.'

'And Sven. What about him? What's he?'

Mary held her head high. 'Another victim. Another one of your pawns.'

Fran pointed at her as she left. 'You'll figure it out. You'll think about it and you'll realize I'm right and that I was trying to protect you.'

'Fran,' said Mary. 'Fuck off.'

Even now, she could feel Fran's presence in the hut; a ghostly shadow looking over her shoulder. She could smell her perfume in the air. If she listened hard enough she felt sure she would be able to hear her laughing. She shivered and brushed at her arms, as if to sweep her away.

Yet a year later on, she had to admit to herself that Fran had been right. She herself had trawled the Facebook photos. Seen pictures of Sven pop up week after week of him with a girl. She couldn't speak a word of Swedish, but she could see they were deeply in love. The realization had made her doubly sick. Sick that she had been betrayed by Sven, and that she had mistrusted her sister. Yet why had Fran chosen such a cruel way to prove her point?

Because it was typical of Fran, to prove that she was irresistible. Even though she was proving to Mary Sven was a cheat, she had to prove that he would be powerless if she chose to lure him. It was so, so subtle, Fran's one-upmanship of Mary. It exhausted her.

She didn't know who this latest victim was, or what role he was playing in Fran's fantasy life, but he was certainly taking a long time in the bathroom.

It was then she saw the note on the table. Propped up against the blue spotted vase that was empty of flowers. She walked over and picked it up. It was written in brown ink in Fran's wild and erratic writing – the writing that suited her personality so well; all swirls and dashes and ellipses.

I knew ... I knew as soon as I saw him – just as I knew about Sven. But this one is right for you – I promise. Treasure him ...
F xxxxxx

Mary took in a breath. The paper shook in her hand as things started falling into place. The unexpected visitor certainly wasn't the type she would expect Fran to drag back to her cave to devour. He was far too gentle. Too polite. Fran favoured men with tattoos and piercings and attitude. Not rather cuddly teddy bears with lovely smiles and even lovelier manners.

Pip came out of the bathroom looking rather abashed.

'I'll shoot off then. Although I'm not even sure where we are. I didn't take much notice yesterday.'

'Everdene. The nearest train's at Bamford. You'll have to get a cab.' Mary was curt, still trying to process Fran's letter.

'Right.' He clapped his hand to his pocket to make sure his wallet was still there. 'Well – it was very nice to meet you. Despite the circumstances. And I apologize again ...'

He held out his hand. Mary looked at his gentle brown eyes that turned down at the corners, his shy smile, his rumpled curls, and felt her heart give a thump. What if Fran, bloody freak that she was, *was* right?

Because really what Mary hadn't forgiven Fran for was being right about Sven. For being able to see through him in a split second, while Mary had floundered about in his thrall, making a fool of herself, unable to see that she was being used. Of course she hated her sister for her perspicacity. Yet she loved her for it too. It was just that the wounds were taking a long time to heal. Being made to feel a fool is never comfortable.

This was Fran's way of saying please forgive me. This was Fran's way of saying I love you and I will protect you for ever even though you hate me for it.

She didn't have time to think about it. In two moments he would be gone. She needed to employ her sister's impulsivity. And she needed to trust her.

'Listen,' she managed. 'Stay and have some breakfast at least. I can do you coffee and eggs and toast.'

'Oh no – I couldn't put you to any trouble.' Fran's gift to her was putting on his jacket, eager to get away.

'It's not any trouble.' Mary began unpacking the bag of groceries she'd brought with her and held out a box of eggs. 'Please. You can't go off on an empty stomach.'

'Well, that's very kind.' Pip looked hesitant.

'Honestly. You won't be able to get anything at the station and it's a long way back to London.'

Their eyes met, and he smiled. 'OK.'

He began to help her unpack and carry stuff over to the fridge. 'Where's your sister gone, do you think?'

He looked mystified. Mary wasn't quite sure how she was supposed to explain. How did you tell someone that they had been picked out as some sort of blind date, as atonement for a wrong that had been done with good intent? He'd run a mile, probably.

In the end, she decided not to even go there. She just gave a rueful 'who knows' shrug.

'I'm Pip, by the way,' he said.

She smiled. 'Pip – from *Great Expectations*?'

'Exactly that.'

Then Mary noticed the leather patches on his corduroy jacket. Funny, she thought, she didn't think anyone ever wore those in real life, but somehow, they made her warm to him even more.

'Scrambled or poached?' she asked.

'Scrambled. Please.'

'Right answer,' she said. 'Saturdays are made for scrambled eggs.'

They smiled at each other, their first agreement on something, and it felt right. And somewhere, who knew where, Mary felt Fran give a little air punch, and she forgave her sister; her crazy sister, who saw the world in a different way from everyone else, but who always saw the important things.

ELODIE

*'Light, airy room available in return for light housekeeping
duties. Lady Bellnapp, Kensington 453'*

*T*here was something about the succinctness of the advert
that appealed to Elodie. It was straightforward with no
euphemisms, and sounded just what she needed. A roof over
her head while she took stock.

Lady Bellnap was direct on the telephone. *'I don't want a
fuss or anyone getting under my feet. But I want everything
done without having to ask twice. Come and see me and I'll
see if I like the cut of your jib. I'll know immediately.'*

'So will I,' said Elodie, with spirit, and the old girl chuckled.

Lady Bellnap lived in a garden flat off Kensington High
Street. She'd spent her married life in the Far East, with her
husband, a military doctor. They'd had no children.

*'Darling Bill was bitten by a tsetse fly and that was the end
of it,'* Lady Bellnap told her. She had tiny, spindly legs and
arms, a stout bosom, a hooked nose and piercing eyes. *'No role
for me out there so I had to come back. Heartbroken, of course.
Now I just rattle about playing bridge. Do you like dusting?'*

The flat was crammed with mementoes of the Bellnaps' life
together: enormous stone vases, carved wooden chests, a tiger's
head on a rug, china dragons. There wasn't a square inch of

free space, and the room smelled of sandalwood. Elodie loved it the moment she saw it.

'Not particularly,' Elodie told her.

'Good. I wouldn't want to spend any more time than necessary with someone who cared for dusting. I'd be very suspicious. But it needs doing, as you can see. So if you can see your way to taking care of this lot—' she waved a hand around her artefacts – 'and perhaps push the Ewbank around, and make sure we don't run out of milk, then the spare room is a very nice one. You'll be looking for a proper job, I suppose?'

'Well, yes. Although I'm not sure quite what yet.'

'Well, a girl must do something. There's more to life than bloody flower arranging.'

She pulled a face, as if to equate the pastime with something far more nefarious. An image of Lillie tweaking a vase of flowers in the drawing room popped into Elodie's head. She felt uneasy. As if herein lay a clue. She wasn't going to dwell on it. That had been her promise to herself.

Forwards, not backwards.

She moved in the next day.

The arrangement was perfect. Elodie quickly became fond of Lady Bellnap. Despite her forthright manner, and her occasional querulousness if she became tired, she was a source of inspiration, dauntless and full of energy despite her age. They spent a great deal of their time laughing, which was healing for Elodie.

She didn't want to rush into gainful employment; she wanted to be sure of finding the right job, now she had a roof over her head. Luckily she had plenty of savings. That was one of the benefits of working for your father and living at home: there'd not been much to spend her wages on, as

164

unlike Lillie she wasn't much of a clothes person. She didn't tell Lady Bellnap the truth about why she was there. She just said she'd had a disagreement with her parents and wanted a change. She sensed the old lady suspected there was more to it, but she wasn't one to pry. And if she told her what had happened, then she would have to discuss it. All she wanted to do was bury the memory.

The one thing Elodie did find was the shock of everything – the upheaval, the new surroundings and getting used to London when she was used to either the country or the seaside – made her very tired. She couldn't stop sleeping. And then one lunchtime, when she looked at the tinned peaches and evaporated milk she had prepared for their pudding, she had an overwhelming desire to be sick.

'I'm sorry,' she gasped, and ran from the room.

When she came back, pale-faced, she apologized again and sat down at the table. Lady Bellnap leaned forward.

'My dear,' she said. 'I think you might be having a baby.'

Elodie saw the kindly wisdom in the old woman's eyes and felt her heart lurch. Her mind was racing as she thought back to the memories she had tried to suppress as they were too painful, those clandestine encounters between her and Jolyon in the beach hut, their secret hideaway. Once or twice, as the wedding loomed, she thought they might not have been as careful as they should. She hadn't panicked at the time, because she had thought 'honeymoon baby. Nobody minds a honeymoon baby'.

But, of course, there hadn't been a honeymoon.

And a baby, when you were on your own, with no husband, no job, no roof of your own, in a strange city, was a very different kettle of fish indeed.

'Oh hell,' she said.

Lady Bellnap put a freckled hand over hers. 'There are far worse things in life to cope with,' she said, 'than an unexpected baby.'

Elodie felt nausea rise up again, but this time it was fear. 'What am I going to do?'

'Well,' said Lady Bellnap. 'You're a bright girl. You've got a roof over your head. And I won't see you starve.'

Elodie met the old lady's perspicacious gaze. She saw nothing but kindly concern in her eyes.

'I would have thought you'd be horrified.' She had a vision of being thrown out into the street. But Lady Bellnap didn't turn a hair.

'My dear, not at all.' She put down her spoon. 'Now, we need to make an appointment for you. My doctor is excellent. Once we've got it confirmed, then we can decide what to do.'

Elodie wondered how on earth she could have got so far away from herself in such a short space of time. If it hadn't been for coming back to The Grey House early that afternoon, she would be safely married to Jolyon, and this news would be mildly alarming, but not disastrous. She would have had Jolyon to share it with. They would be starting to make plans, deciding where to raise their family.

She remembered her mother's prophetic words to Jolyon that afternoon: 'Elodie will have a baby. She will be as happy as can be.'

It was then the grief finally hit her. This should be momentous, the revelation that she was going to bring another life into the world. She should be sharing the joy with her husband. Her mother should be her greatest support. Instead, the realization brought home her plight. Pregnant and unmarried at twenty? It was a scandal. She put her hands to *her face and began to weep, shoulders juddering, as all the pent-up tears finally fell.*

'I think,' said Lady Bellnap, 'that it's time to tell me what's been going on.'

Time and again Elodie thanked her lucky stars for her guardian angel, whose kindness and practicality never ceased to amaze her. But as Lady Bellnap pointed out, when you'd been out in the Far East, dealing with the victims of tropical disease, drought, famine – whatever the elements chose to throw at them – the arrival of a baby in leafy Kensington really didn't constitute a crisis.

Although the flat itself wasn't huge, thanks to the ephemera packed inside, Elodie's room was light and bright and there would be plenty of room for a cot once the baby arrived. She worked out that she had enough money to stay lodging with Lady Bellnap until the baby was six months. Then she would have to think about gainful employment.

In the meantime, she walked every morning to the greengrocer and the butcher to buy their daily food. Lady Bellnap was disinterested in cooking, so Elodie tried to make their meals as interesting as their combined budget would allow. She carried on doing the housework, as she wanted to keep as active as possible throughout her pregnancy.

In the afternoons, she worked her way through Lady Bellnap's library. One entire wall of the drawing room was taken up with shelves, which were crammed with books. It was sheer bliss, curled up reading, then having a little snooze. Tolstoy, Dickens, Agatha Christie, Sherlock Holmes – her literary diet was varied and nourishing and a constant source of delight. Her mind was expanding as fast as her middle. She felt as content as she possibly could be.

It was the middle of March when the baby was born. A little boy, weighing seven pounds.

'I think,' said Elodie, 'I will call him Otto.'

The name pleased her, because it had no connotations and reminded her of no one.

Lady Bellnap was the most wonderful guide. Although she'd had no children of her own, she had been a very hands-on doctor's wife. She was practical, strict and no-nonsense.

'The important thing is for a baby to be adaptable,' she would tell Elodie. 'You don't want to make a rod for your own back by having too much of a routine. Lug it with you wherever you're going. Don't pander to it. Makes sure he's adaptable and biddable. No one likes a spoilt little beast.'

As Otto got plumper and more jolly and more interesting, Elodie realized with a sinking heart that the day was getting closer for her to find a job. Her savings were dwindling. And while she knew Lady Bellnap wouldn't see her want for anything, she couldn't rely on her generosity for ever. She needed to be independent, and to find a home for Otto and herself.

In the post office up the road, she saw an advert for a childminder who lived a few streets away. She contacted her to make a visit. In her mind's eye, she built up an image of some sort of Dickensian baby farm, little bodies all swaddled and left to fend for themselves while the childminder drank gin and counted her money. The reality was a pleasant surprise. Bernie had a light and airy room leading out into a sunny garden where she supervised a maximum of four little ones, and she had space.

'It will do Otto good,' said Lady Bellnap, 'to mix with other children. And it will do you good to use your brain.

*You're far too bright to do nothing, and the longer you leave
it the harder it will be to get back to work.'*

*Half of Elodie agreed; the other half absolutely dreaded
leaving Otto, but the truth was she desperately needed money,
and she knew she would find no nicer person than Bernie to
look after him, so she snapped the place up straight away and
resolved to use the time while Otto was with Bernie to look
for work.*

*When Elodie told Lady Bellnap she was applying for a job
in the Millinery Department at Harrods, she was furious.*

'A shop girl? Don't be ludicrous. Try the BBC.'

*It was why Elodie adored Lady Bellnap. Everything was
so simple and straightforward for her. She spoke as if Elodie
should just get the BBC on the phone and demand a job on
the spot. At first, Elodie ignored her advice. What experience
did she have of broadcasting, or anything to do with it? But
then she decided to employ some of Lady Bellnap's gumption,
so she phoned the Personnel Department and spoke to a very
nice woman who asked her about herself, and then suggested
she pop in for an interview the very next day.*

*'I have a radio drama producer who is looking for a produc-
tion secretary. You sound very much up his street. I presume
you can type?'*

*'Absolutely,' Elodie assured her. She hadn't touched a type-
writer for ages. She'd had a girl to do all that for her at the
jam factory. If she got the job, she'd worry about the typing
afterwards. And radio drama sounded far more interesting
than selling hats in Harrods.*

*Elodie hadn't really any time to prepare for the interview,
apart from Lady Bellnap grilling her over breakfast, firing*

questions at her while she tried to shovel mashed banana into a disinterested Otto.

In at the deep end, thought Elodie, who was wearing her going-away outfit, the smartest thing she had: a turquoise linen suit from Jaeger her mother had chosen for her. It felt odd, putting it on now, over a year after she should have worn it. She looked in the mirror and didn't really recognize herself. She looked older, and thinner, rather surprisingly – well, her face certainly was – and her hair was past her shoulders so she'd tied it up in a low bun.

She looked, she realized, like a grown-up.

She made her way from Kensington into the West End on the bus, to Broadcasting House. As the bus made its way up Regent Street, she tried not to think about all the times she and her mother had gone up there, weaving in and out of the shops, buying whatever they wanted, knowing that Desmond would pick up the bill. Not that Elodie had ever been that interested. She had always shopped under sufferance, dragged along in Lillie's wake. It seemed a million years ago. Now she was just another girl swallowed up by the big city. A girl trying to make her way in the world with more than her fair share of encumbrances. How did life do that: turn your world upside down in a trice and take away your anchors?

She was surviving, though. She had found new anchors. And a new side to her: her love for Otto was the most profound and perfect thing she had ever felt. Motherhood made her feel complete. Now she was just going to have to find a way to protect and keep her tiny little family – her family of two. She couldn't rely on Lady Bellnap's benevolence indefinitely. She had to be independent. It was terrifying, but Elodie had discovered of late that she was stronger than she ever thought she'd need to be.

In Broadcasting House, she found herself led down endless dingy corridors, then was left to sit in a plastic chair outside a door alongside two other women obviously being interviewed for the same role. They were both older than she, quietly confident, and looked her up and down. They were both in drab skirts and cardigans without a trace of lipstick. Her mother's grooming habits had been drilled into her, so by contrast Elodie felt overdressed and over made-up. She felt her mouth go dry and her mind go blank. What on earth was she going to say at the interview? She knew nothing about radio, or drama, let alone the two together. She hadn't an earthly how a programme was put together or what her role in that might be. She held tight onto her handbag until she was finally called in, the last candidate.

Edmund Smithers, her prospective employer, looked at her with slight bemusement all the way through the interview as if he wasn't quite sure what she, or indeed he, was doing there. He frowned down at her details, which were sadly lacking due to the short notice, and ran his fingers through his flyaway curls, as if hoping they might be persuaded to stay put. She couldn't put an age on him. He had a baby face yet his hair was greying. He could be anywhere between thirty and fifty, she thought.

'Jam,' he said, staring at her. 'Jam. How fascinating.'

'Well,' said Elodie. 'Not really. But it was my job to make everyone want it.'

'Who doesn't like jam?' He seemed to give this great thought.

'Oh everyone loves jam. But I had to make them want our jam. That was the trick.'

She told him about Sammy and Sally Strawberry, and he seemed tickled by the notion.

'Were they your idea?' he asked.

'Oh, absolutely. No one else would have come up with anything so ridiculous.' Elodie made a self-deprecating face. 'But you'd be amazed how many children sent off for the badges.'

Edmund nodded. He was staring at her again, almost puzzled.

'What do you think the most important part of this job is?' He spoke the question as a sort of sigh, as if the question was rather unsavoury but he felt he had to say it.

Elodie wondered if perhaps he didn't want a secretary at all, but was being forced into it. She felt as if she was supposed to say something frightfully clever and intellectual at this point, to pique his interest. But in the end, she could only come up with one answer.

'Well,' she replied. 'I suppose it's to make sure you're happy. Otherwise there doesn't seem to be much point at all.'

To her astonishment this answer seemed to please him greatly, and he positively beamed. Then laughed. She blushed a little, wondering if her reply had been pert or unseemly.

There was an awkward silence.

'That's all,' he said. 'I can't think of anything else to ask.'

'Oh,' said Elodie. 'Well, thank you.'

She went to shake his hand. He looked perturbed, but took it nevertheless. She felt crushed with disappointment that she was being dismissed so quickly. The other two women had been interviewed for at least quarter of an hour. She'd only been in there five minutes.

She left the building as quickly as she could. Hats in Harrods it was.

She rushed to Bernie's to collect Otto, who had been utterly contented all afternoon. It was the longest she had left him, *and Elodie wasn't sure whether to be offended or relieved, but it certainly boded well for the future. She scooped him up in her arms, hugging his warm little body to her.*

'I'm sorry I had to leave you,' she whispered into his ear. 'But this is how it's going to have to be. Else we'll starve.' By way of reply, he squirmed and giggled, seemingly unperturbed by his ordeal, going limp in her arms and spreading himself out like a starfish, looking up at her with love and absolute forgiveness, his head flung back. For one fleeting moment she thought of Jolyon, and felt a squeeze of guilt that he would never know the sheer joy of his son, but then she hardened her heart. He'd relinquished any right to Otto the day he had succumbed to her mother. She quickened her step so as to get back home quickly, to immerse herself in the evening ritual of tea, bath, bedtime. Anything to stop her thinking of her past.

As soon she got back to the flat, Lady Bellnap was holding out the telephone for her. It rang only rarely, and hardly ever for Elodie, so she was puzzled.

It was the personnel officer at the BBC. Elodie couldn't really take in what she was saying.

'We'd like you to start as soon as possible,' she finished. 'Would a fortnight be enough time?'

'Sorry?' said Elodie, confused.

'The job? You came in this afternoon? Mr Smithers made his mind up straight away it was you he wanted. When would you be able to start?'

Elodie looked at Otto in his high chair. Her heart gave a lurch. She had absolutely no choice in the matter. She needed to work. She had to leave him. From across the room, Lady Bellnap gave her an encouraging nod.

'Well,' she said. 'A fortnight sounds fine.'

That would give her enough time to get organized, buy some

173

new work clothes – and spend her last few days with Otto, spoiling him rotten.

She put the phone down rather dazed.

'Splendid!' said Lady Bellnap. 'There we are. Shop girl indeed. You mark my words, you'll be Director-General before we know it.'

Within a week of starting work, Elodie realized she had strayed rather by default into a rather magical world.

The job itself was complicated, varied and required immense concentration and attention to detail. As well as the usual secretarial duties – answering the telephone and taking dictation– she was to type scripts and fill out the seemingly endless forms that went with recording a drama. At first it all made her head spin as there seemed to be no rhyme or reason to any of it and Edmund seemed rather baffled by it himself, but she quickly made friends with some of the other staff in the canteen and worked out the logic.

'Wait until you go into the studio!' one girl told her. 'Then the fun will really start.'

Gradually she got her typing up to speed and began to make less mistakes. As the weeks went by, she became more absorbed in the content she was typing up. Edmund engaged her in conversation, asking her what she thought about characters and how the plots developed, and she began to think about how each play was structured, and understand the scribbles he put in the margin, and the cuts he made to up the tension.

When they went into the studio, her job was to time each segment they recorded with a stopwatch and mark up the script, so that when Edmund went to edit the material, he could get the programme to run to time – the slots were very specific and there was no margin for error. Elodie was spellbound by the whole process – how a sixty-page script could turn into something that transported you to another world. She had nothing but admiration for the actors who brought the scripts to life, and the soundmen whose ingenuity created a soundscape. There was an immense library of sound effects which meant anything could be recreated: a medieval battle, a car crash, a football match . . .

It was a truly happy time for her. It was tough, of course it was, with a small baby, but by being very organized she managed it. She got up very early, at six o'clock, and had an hour of playtime with Otto before they both got dressed and had breakfast. Then she pushed him in his pram down to Bernie's before running to catch the bus to be at work by nine. She left on the dot of five and was usually back home by six. She crawled into bed not long after Otto, barely reading two paragraphs of her book before falling asleep.

And at the weekend, she had two full days to spend with her boy. She usually packed a picnic and they walked up through Kensington to Hyde Park, and he learned to take tentative steps on the paths that wound alongside the Serpentine.

And if sometimes, she thought about The Grey House, and how much Otto would enjoy being on the beach, and splashing about in the shallows, and digging in the sand, she soon banished the thought. This was her new life. She wasn't going to reflect on her old life. Or anyone in it. Not for a moment longer than necessary.

After a year, she had saved enough to move to her own little flat – not in grand Kensington, which she couldn't afford, but in Ealing. She still had to share a bedroom with Otto, but she didn't mind, and she need no longer worry about getting in Lady Bellnap's way or disturbing her. She cried copiously the day she left.

'You've been like a mother to me,' she sniffed, thinking that actually Lady Bellnap had been far more. And, for the first time ever, she found herself folded in Lady Bellnap's arms, as the old lady squeezed her to her ample bosom with what Elodie thought was probably the most impulsive gesture she had made for years.

'I'm only a bus ride away,' said Lady Bellnap in a voice gruff with unshed tears. 'I'll be livid if you don't call in with Otto at least once a fortnight.'

She sent Elodie off with a stack of linen sheets and pillow-cases, a set of coffee cups and some silver teaspoons for her new flat.

In the meantime, Elodie became more and more absorbed by her job. Edmund didn't treat her like a secretary, more an assistant. He valued her opinion. Demanded it, even. He took her out to lunch with any writers he was working with, expecting her to stay drinking wine with them rather than return to her desk at two o'clock, and she loved listening to them discussing the plays they were working on, and dissect-ing other people's work. She loved being part of the fictional world Edmund created for the listener.

'It's an escape,' he told her. 'Everyone needs to escape.'

She didn't tell him how very well she knew that.

And on Friday afternoons, more often than not, he told her to slip off a couple of hours early.

'I'll tell Personnel I've sent you off to get something I need for next week's sound effects,' he told her. 'Should anyone ask.'

She appreciated his kindness, and the truth of it was she worked twice as hard for him as she would otherwise.

*

Two years puttered by, and Otto grew strong and confident and brought her more joy than she could imagine. At work, she became more involved in the productions than any of the other secretaries she knew. She talked at length about the plays Edmund was producing, made suggestions, even came to him with ideas for adaptations. And he entrusted her with his slush pile – the dozens of unsolicited scripts that came his way for consideration. She compiled a detailed report on each, and was thrilled to bits when one of her recommendations went into production. It might never have seen the light of day otherwise.

Of course, all of this was beyond the duty of a mere production secretary, but Elodie didn't mind that she wasn't being paid for what she was doing. She loved it, and that was all that mattered, and she didn't feel exploited, or as if Edmund was using her to his own end. He always gave her credit for what she had done, and praised her work. She felt they were a team, and nothing gave her more joy than the afternoons they played back the programmes they had recorded in their entirety. It was so satisfying listening to what they had shaped; to hear the pages leap from the script and into life. Often the actors and writer would come in to listen too, and they would end up drinking wine in a celebratory fashion.

One particular lunchtime, after the playback of a new detective drama serial, Edmund and Elodie sat down to finish the last of the wine once the actors had gone. They were in a self-congratulatory mood, because the head of drama had commissioned another five episodes, and the writer had been a recent discovery of theirs, so they felt particularly jubilant.

Edmund cleared his throat as he topped up her wine. He looked awkward.

'There's something I need to talk to you about,' he said.

Elodie's heart hammered. He was going to tell her he was moving on. He was always being offered jobs in television or theatre. It was inevitable that one day he would take up one of those offers. But where would that leave her? She couldn't bear to think of his replacement, who might relegate her back down to her official duties, and might not appreciate her input.

She sighed. Nothing stayed the same for ever.

'I suppose,' Edmund carried on, 'that I should have bought a ring...'

'A ring?' Elodie tried to recalibrate her brain to take in what he was saying.

He was blushing. Right to the tips of his ears.

'I wanted to ask you ... if you would marry me.'

Blood pounded in her ears as she realized just what he had asked. She'd had no inkling whatsoever that he might. She was astonished. She stared at him, unable to answer.

He backed up his proposal.

'I think the world of you. I think you are astonishingly talented and I want to help you make the most of that talent. And I want to look after you. And Otto.'

She'd brought Otto into the office quite a few times. Edmund had always shown a kindly interest and let him play with his headphones.

Elodie felt shock and panic in equal measure. She put down her glass, suddenly unable to stomach any more of the warm, indifferent wine that Hospitality provided.

What on earth was she going to say? She liked Edmund. More than liked him: she nurtured a warm fondness for him that had depth and breadth and would endure. She respected him and valued his opinion and admired him possibly more than anyone else she had ever met. She was in awe of his intellect; touched by his kindness. His friendship and guidance meant more to her than anything in the world.

But marry him? No. She just couldn't imagine it. She couldn't put her finger on why. It was excruciating. She wished she were anywhere else in the world. She wished he had never asked, because she didn't want to say no to him: dear, kind, precious Edmund, whom she knew had agonized over this question. He hadn't asked her lightly.

She picked up her glass again and took a gulp of wine, to moisten her dry mouth. How could she find the right words? She couldn't find a single syllable that seemed appropriate. Her mouth opened and closed once, twice. She felt hot with panic and fear and misery. This was the most awful situation she had ever found herself in.

Then Edmund reached across and put his hand on hers. Inwardly she begged him not to put her under more pressure. Instead, he looked at her and smiled sadly.

'It's all right,' he said. 'I understand. Please, don't upset yourself. I wanted to ask, but I ... entirely appreciate ... it's ... not what you want.'

Elodie's face crumpled.

'It's not that I don't love you,' she finally managed. 'I do. Very much. Just ... not in that way.'

He picked up the bottle of wine and refilled their glasses.

'No,' he said. 'I know. I suppose I'd hoped that—' He broke off with a shake of his head. 'Never mind. I'm not going to go all self-pitying and mawkish. I don't want to make it any more difficult for you.'

She thought she was going to cry. Why did his kindness make her feel so sad?

'I'd do anything to help you,' he went on. 'You do know

that? School fees for Otto, maybe? Or a holiday? When did you last have a holiday?'

Her mind flickered back to the beach at Everdene. It was the only place she'd ever been on holiday. The only place she'd ever wanted to go. It seemed a million miles away now.

'I'm fine, Edmund,' she told him. 'I want for nothing. And if I ever do need anything, I know you're there.'

Was that enough, to let him know that she knew if she needed him, he was there? Was that simply exploiting him? After all, what was she giving him in return?

'It's all right,' he smiled, as if reading her mind. 'You're not using me.'

Her heart contracted with love, but the wrong kind of love. She knew she would never meet anyone as devoted or kind as long as she lived. But to tie herself to him when she knew, deep down, that she didn't feel about him the way he felt about her was wrong. It would be cruel. It would end in her disappointment and his disillusionment. She would feel trapped and he would feel betrayed. They would live out their days in a grindingly soulless union, each resenting the other for what they couldn't provide.

And then Edmund's fingers stroked her hand gently and she realized why it was She could never give herself to him the way she had Jolyon. She didn't feel for him, physically; not in the same way. The realisation made her pity him, and she didn't want him to see that pity. She never wanted to humiliate him that much.

She spent the rest of the afternoon in the Xeroxing room, her head dull with too much wine. The noxious chemical smell of the copying fluid did nothing to help, as she ran off copy after copy of the latest script, the letters bleeding into the cheap paper they used for early drafts. She thought she would go mad with the noise.

At the end of the day, Edmund scooped his jacket off the coat stand as he always did and bade her good night. He was no more stiff than usual. Elodie wondered just how much of their conversation he had taken to heart. If once she had rejected him he had pushed the matter to one side, or if he was going home to reflect on how he might have done things differently, what it was about him that had made her say no? We rarely know the full impact our actions have on others, she thought. She realized she didn't even know what his house was like: whether he just had a room in a boarding house, or his own flat, or lived with his parents, or had a four-storey townhouse to call his own. How very self-centred she was, she chided herself. She had never bothered to find out much about him. Their relationship had always been about his interest in and concern over her.

More shame burned in her gullet. She really didn't like herself very much today. She grabbed her own coat, pulled it on along with her gloves, and hurried down the stairs to the ground floor and out onto the street to catch the bus home. She wanted Otto. To hold him to her and squeeze him tight. He was the only human she wanted to be emotionally responsible for.

That night she couldn't sleep. She lay listening to Otto snuffling in his cot. What if she were wrong to turn down Edmund's proposal? What if their marriage just happened to work? That they might happily coexist, bumbling along in harmony rather than united in passion, rather neatly balanced? Without the huge expectations that came with a more hot-blooded coupling, that began on a huge high and could only go downhill? What if they found something rich and fulfilling and satisfying that nourished their souls?

She was looking for a fairy-tale ending, she realized. She was looking for what she had once had: a glittering, handsome prince who made her heart pound. But where had that got her?

As dawn began to creep into the bedroom, she finally fell to sleep. And when she woke to find Otto standing in his cot, beaming at her, she decided she would accept Edmund's offer. It would be a very different kind of marriage to the one she had thought she would end up with. But it would be a good one. Of that she was sure.

She spent all morning trying to pluck up the courage to approach him. He had been perfectly polite and kind to her – there was no evidence that his proposal had been rejected. He was too much of a gentleman to make her feel bad about it. Finally, just before lunchtime, she came and stood by his desk.

'I think ... you rather took me by surprise yesterday. I hadn't time to think things through properly. I panicked a little. And the offer might not still be open, but I've had a chance to think about what you said, and if it's not too late ...'

He was staring at her. She floundered on.

'If it's not too late, I would like to marry you. Very much.'

For a moment he said nothing. He screwed the lid back on his fountain pen and put it down. Then he stood up and opened his arms.

'I will look after you,' he said, 'until the end of time.'

Elodie stepped into his embrace. He wrapped his arms around her. She felt dazed, unsure if she had made the right decision. But, most of all, she realized, she felt safe.

Lady Bellnap assured her that she had made a very sensible choice.

'It's a choice you have made with your head, and not your heart,' she observed. 'Sometimes that's the wisest course. Our hearts can be broken, after all.'

Hers already had been, Elodie thought. Yet she had survived.

To say the wedding was quiet was an understatement. Just Elodie, in a yellow dress the colour of sunshine, and Edmund, in his usual jacket and trousers, and Lady Bellnap as their witness along with Edmund's brother. Lady Bellnap took them for lunch at the Capital Hotel afterwards, and gave them Elodie's favourite painting from her flat, a vibrant oil of two parrots on a branch.

There was to be no honeymoon, as they were going into the studio the following day to record a play. But instead of going home to the flat in Ealing, Elodie and Otto were going to Twickenham, where it turned out Edmund had a small three-bedroomed terraced house. He'd painted the smallest room for a nursery, and bought a new cot, and put up jolly red curtains.

'I've got my old train set ready for him, for when he's big enough,' he told her shyly, showing her the boxes containing his Hornby waiting on the shelf.

She threw her arms around his neck. 'It's the most wonderful wedding present,' she told him, and she meant it. His thought, his care, the time he'd put in; it all meant more than she could say.

And that night, she discovered there was a different kind of love. Something gentle and tender and meaningful. There might not be the ecstasy or the thrill, but it left her feeling more satisfied. And at peace with herself. She lay in Edmund's arms. She had, she decided, done the right thing.

*

Later that summer, Edmund asked her where she would like to go for a belated honeymoon.

'Oh, nowhere,' she said. 'I'm quite happy.'

But he insisted. 'I know we'll have Otto with us,' he said. 'But it would be nice to mark the wedding with a few days somewhere. So we have a memory.'

Elodie thought about it for a moment. 'Everdene,' she told him. 'I used to go to the seaside there as a child. I think Otto would like it.'

Since Otto had grown bigger, she had thought more and more about the place where she had been so happy, and how he would love it. Now she had the security of marriage, she thought she felt ready to go back. She had no idea how she would feel, or what she might find there, but the place had meant so much to her as a child and she wanted to pass that carefree happiness on to her son. She could picture him on the sand, his fat little feet pottering about, the waves ticking his skin, the sun kissing him. The urge to return there was primal.

Edmund duly booked them into a bed and breakfast. They set off in his A35 at the crack of dawn early one Saturday. Elodie had packed a picnic basket with hard-boiled eggs and ham sandwiches and flapjacks and a flask of tea. It seemed to take forever to get there, but after hours of tedium suddenly they turned a corner and there it was in front of her, her Everdene. Her heart leaped with the joy, and she pulled Otto onto her lap to show him his very first glimpse of sea.

'Look, darling,' she said. 'That's my sea, and I'm giving it to you.'

'Fish,' said Otto solemnly.

'Fish and crabs and sea urchins,' agreed Elodie, remembering the rock pools: she could barely wait to sit with Otto

184

and scoop out the watery treasures. A brand-new bucket was waiting on the back seat for that very purpose.

Edmund looked sideways at her. 'This place means a lot to you, doesn't it?' he asked.

She didn't reply. She had never told him the truth about her past. Like Otto when he hid under a blanket and thought he couldn't be seen, if she didn't tell anyone then it had never happened.

They had a blissful few days. The sun was obliging: warm but not fierce. The bed and breakfast was in a farmhouse half a mile from the coast, and Otto was spoilt rotten by the farmer's wife, who took him to collect eggs and watch the cows being milked. And every day they went to the beach. Elodie made sure they stayed at the far end, nearest the village, away from The Grey House. But she could feel its pull, and she knew she had to go back there. Whatever it was that drew her back was as strong as the urge to protect her child. Yet her parents hadn't protected her. Far from it. Now she had Otto, she was even more bewildered by their treatment of her. It went against all instinct.

She left her visit until the very last day. Edmund took Otto off for a walk while she packed everything up. The packing took her all of five minutes, and then she hurried down to the beach, walking along the bottom of the dunes until she reached the hut belonging to The Grey House. She felt as if she could open the door and find herself in there.

She stood at the bottom of the cliff looking up at the house. In two minutes, she could climb the path and be in the garden. Would they still be there? Her mother and father? Could she wander into the house? What would they say if they saw her?

And then she saw him. Desmond. Flanked by a couple of what she presumed were guests. She saw him gesticulate, *pointing out the view, Lundy Island, with that familiar proprietorial sweep of his hand. Nothing had changed for him, she thought. He wasn't standing there wondering where she was or how she was, his only daughter. He was gloating, showing off his achievements and his possessions. And no doubt Lillie would be sitting in the shade, plotting and scheming. Or maybe she had been banished? Maybe there was someone else sitting in her place?*

The sun went in behind a cloud and Elodie shivered. She pulled her cardigan round her as if to protect herself. She must be mad to even consider returning or making contact. Apart from anything, it wouldn't be fair on Edmund and Otto to dig up her skeletons. They had a perfect life: calm and ordered and secure. They were her future.

The past, Elodie decided, belonged just there.

An hour later, they set off for home, Elodie in the back of the car with Otto wrapped in her arms, safe and secure, a bucket full of shells at their feet. Her little family was all she needed.

CHLOE

Driving at night with the roof down felt a little reckless, somehow. And very intimate, as the sky itself wrapped itself round her, deep Quinky blue. The motorway was empty, and Chloe felt as if she was the last person in the world, driving over the horizon. The stars spread themselves out in front of her, and she felt as if she should be using them to guide her, rather than her prosaic sat nav, which told her she had another thirty-four miles to go.

She couldn't get there fast enough. She couldn't wait to leave it all behind her: today, her wretched job, her flat. The past two years of stress and sleeplessness and toil which had led to bitter disappointment. And injustice.

The anger boiled up inside her and she tried some deep yoga breathing to try and dispel it, but she knew it wouldn't work. It was going to take a bit more than a bit of hippy-dippy claptrap to eradicate the rage. Her fists balled up on the steering wheel even now. How could something like that be allowed to happen, in the twenty-first century? The patriarchy, it seemed, was alive and kicking in the streets of Soho. And she didn't even work in the 'entertainment' industry. The girls she knew who worked in the lap-dancing club over the road had more enlightened bosses than she did. Her stomach churned at the memory. But then, while there were girls like Jasmine in the world, being rewarded for your looks rather than your endeavours was going to carry on.

And to prove it, Chloe had had to suffer the ignominy of Jasmine's smug presence in the office while she worked out her notice. Maybe she should have worn a see-through white lace shirt to the interview? The job might be hers now.

Well, the summer was hers now instead, while she decided what to do with the rest of her life. She was going to have a clean break and six weeks of total freedom while she took stock. There would be no one to answer to. She could do what she liked, thanks to a timely stroke of luck. Swapping her one-bedroom flat in Peckham for a beach hut in Everdene? It was a no-brainer.

She'd gone onto the house-swap site tentatively, not expecting to find anyone wanting to spend the summer in an inner-city high rise. But the email had reached her almost straight away: it was from an older couple who wanted to spend time near their daughter, in Dulwich, as she'd had a premature baby and was struggling for help.

She had looked at the details of the hut with glee, unable to believe her luck. It was about the same size as her flat, with a living area, a sleeping platform, a fully equipped but compact kitchen and a tiny bathroom, but instead of looking out over a school playground, it was about twenty yards from the sea. She could almost smell the ozone and hear the waves crashing onto the sand as she replied to their email confirming the swap.

Now, in her boot, she had a wetsuit, a pile of the books she hadn't ever had time to read, and an empty notebook from Muji for brainstorming what she might do with her life. She wanted to rediscover her brain, retrain it to think for itself instead of spoon-feeding it bytes of information gleaned from Facebook and Twitter and Gawker and Buzzfeed.

Already, she could feel bits of her brain that had lain dormant reigniting. Before, she would have looked at the stars and not seen them. Now, she began to pick out the constellations she remembered from her childhood. She would buy herself a telescope, she decided. And a book, a proper book, to help her decipher the cosmos.

Excitement fizzed through her, and for the first time she felt grateful that she hadn't got the promotion. Otherwise she would still be at her desk, compiling notes for the next pitch, going over it and over it until it was word perfect, trying to second guess what would make the client pick them over any other agency. She never had to do that again if she didn't want to …

Although a small voice inside her told her she did want to. She had loved her job. The campaign director's role would have been a dream come true for the girl who had started out in Admin only five years ago, making tea and binding documents. Howard had picked her out, told her she was going places, encouraged her, promoted her. Only to choose that talentless airhead over her just as she had nearly reached the pinnacle. Why had she trusted him? She hadn't expected any favouritism. Just recognition.

Forget it forget it forget it, Chloe told herself. But the nagging doubt still nibbled away at her. If she'd slept with him, like he'd wanted her to, would the job be hers now? Surely that wasn't how the world worked any more? Surely that wasn't how he worked? She'd admired and trusted him, right up to that night at the dreamy Cotswold hotel where they'd had their annual Christmas getaway because the company had done so well.

His eyes had been wide with Merlot and sincerity when he'd told her, at two o'clock in the morning in the bar, when everyone else had finally trailed away, that he loved her. That he always had, since the day she'd walked in wearing her crop top and her combat trousers, with the pink streak in her hair. Now, of course, she was groomed and polished and Zara-ed up to the nines.

She'd jumped up, away from him, spilling her wine all over the table.

'You're married!' she cried, and he laughed at her.

'When's that ever stopped anyone?' he asked, and in that moment she saw him for what he was, and all her admiration for him crumbled to dust, and she felt a bitter disappointment combined with a crushing sadness. By that time he'd stumbled towards her and grabbed her clumsily, pulling her to him and whispering in her ear, stroking her hair.

'You know you want to,' he mumbled. 'I've seen the way you look at me.'

And she'd wriggled away from him and pulled her arm back and given him the biggest crack across the side of his head that she could manage. The barman had looked over in alarm, putting down the glasses he was wiping.

'You all right, love?'

Chloe couldn't speak. Howard was looking at her with a glare of such malevolence it made her stomach turn.

'You stupid cow,' he told her.

'Yep,' she replied. 'Very stupid. Very stupid indeed.'

She gathered up her bag with as much dignity as she could muster. She knew she'd had too much to drink, and that her words would probably slur, so she chose them carefully.

'I respected and admired you,' she told him. 'You gave me ambition. I wanted to be like you.'

He was lying back on the sofa, legs slightly apart, an arm along the back, smirking up at her. The rest of her words stuck in her throat, and she realized it was because the words had melted into tears.

She wasn't going to let him see her cry.

It was all behind her now, she kept telling herself. She wasn't being manipulated any longer. She turned off the motorway and along the road that would lead to Everdene. It would be late when she got there, but it didn't matter. She could have the biggest lie-in ever tomorrow, and she would be waking up by the sea, with the rest of her life in front of her.

She woke at dawn, as she hadn't bothered to draw the curtains in the beach hut when she crashed into her bed at nearly midnight the night before. As she stepped out of the door onto the sand, the scenery outside took her breath away. The pearliest dawn was creeping over the bay, drawing a veil of early morning mist over the sea. A pale yellow sun hovered on the skyline, tentative at first, but after an hour it had found the confidence to shine as brightly as a buttercup. The air was sweetness and light and danced on Chloe's skin. She breathed it in, feeling the thrill of the new, barefoot in her nightdress on the sand. She wanted to run to the water's edge, and turn cartwheels. The nightmare was behind her.

For five days, she barely moved from the hut, except for the occasional swim. Her skin lost its London pallor and her freckles came out. She read a book a day, and the stories pushed away the memories of the stress and the frustration.

On her first weekend, she walked into Everdene. She went to collect a seafood take-away from The Lobster Shack – a dressed crab, half a dozen langoustines and a handful of prawns. While she waited at the hatch where the takeaways were dispatched, she saw an advert:

'Seasonal staff wanted:
waiters/kitchen porter/bartenders.'

Why not? she thought. She loved the feel of the place; its casual buzziness, and it would be the perfect way to get to know a few people. It would give her some cash, and some structure to her day. And if she didn't like it, she could walk away. She went in and asked for an interview. She had plenty of experience – she'd done her fair share of waitressing at uni.

She was just what they were looking for. Someone bright and informed who could interact with the customers and contribute to the general feel-good vibe.

'You don't think you're a bit overqualified?' the owner, Murphy, asked her. He interviewed her over a heart-stopping Americano in the restaurant window.

'Totally,' she told him. 'But I don't care.'

She didn't. She longed to work here. Every two minutes somebody stopped and spoke to him. She got the feeling that The Lobster Shack was already the place to be, the beating heart of Everdene, even though it had not long opened.

'As long as you don't do an amazing job, then walk off

because you're bored,' Murphy warned her. 'I can see you've got talent. You're not really waitress material.'

'I won't,' she promised. 'But if you want any PR doing, I'm your girl.'

He pointed a warning finger at her. 'You won't be here long. I know you won't. But I'm going to take a risk, because you're just the kind of person we need.'

Chloe put on her Lobster Shack apron on with a frisson of excitement the morning of her first shift, not quite able to believe she had gone from frazzled and burned-out to chilled in such a short space of time. But Everdene had worked its magic. She knew it was a bubble, and that this life couldn't last forever, but she was determined to make the most of it while it lasted.

And her life got even better. Waitressing was hard work. The Lobster Shack was crammed from midday till midnight, turning tables as quickly as was humanly possible. Rave reviews in the Saturday papers only pumped up the waiting list, making it the must-go-to eating venue of the summer. And Chloe found herself with a new crowd of friends, youngsters who dragged her to Tallulah's, the local nightclub that had been in Everdene since the dawn of time. There, she danced till dawn, grabbing a few hours sleep before her next shift, but somehow she never felt tired. The air and the sea gave her energy.

And one day she took a delivery from the fisherman who supplied the lobsters. As she took the huge blue crate from him, crammed with the latest catch, she felt a jolt as she looked into his eyes, admiring his rumpled hair, the tattoo on his arm, his shy smile.

'So who is he?' she asked Jenna, the girl with the ice-cream van, who gave her a knowing grin.

'That's Chris. The boss's brother.'

'Murphy's?'

'No, Vince. His partner. They've got a fishing boat in Tawcombe and they supply all the seafood. Vince keeps a low profile, though.'

'He's cute.'

Jenna nodded. 'He is.'

Something in her tone made Chloe suspicious.

'But?'

'He's absolutely lovely. But he was a drinker until recently. He's on the wagon. So you need to be careful. That's all.'

'Oh.'

'His dad drowned at sea and he never got over it. He was drinking himself into a stupor. But he's a top bloke. He renovated my van for me.' Jenna looked at her. 'I just thought you should know the truth, that's all.'

Chloe took on board what Jenna had told her. For the next few days, she observed Chris from a distance. She didn't want to throw herself into a relationship that was fraught with problems, after all. But he seemed together. The next time Chris came in to make a delivery, Chloe engaged him in conversation.

'So, how many of these guys do you catch a day?'

He told her all about how they caught them, regaling her for a good ten minutes with his anecdotes, and she watched him go with interest. He was cute, and funny, and he had made her laugh.

Before she had the chance to take things any further, though, she had an email from Howard. She picked it up at two o'clock one morning, after dancing the night away, and suddenly the past seemed as if it was not so far away after all. She felt sick as she opened it. He still had the power to unsettle her, it seemed.

Dear Chloe

This is a very difficult email for me to write. I hope you will take it in the spirit in which it is meant, although I wouldn't blame you if you pressed delete. But please take the time to consider my words, and think about what I am going to say.

I think you are extraordinary. I think you are an enormously talented person, and a fantastic human being. I realize that admiration took a wrong turn that night in the Cotswolds, and I did a very stupid thing. I blame the red wine and my stupidity for making the biggest mistake of my life.

Or maybe the second biggest. Giving the creative director's job to Jasmine instead of you was an immense error of judgment. At the time I convinced myself that you didn't have the experience. That you weren't mature enough to handle the job. I realize now that I was wrong.

I want you to know that if you want to come back, there will be a role for you. And if, in time, Jasmine moves on – which I am certain she will do – then that job will be yours. Please give this offer a lot of thought. I need you on my team.

I need you in my life. I miss you. I miss your spirit and your laughter and your energy. If you can see your way to forgiving me, I would be the happiest man in the world.

Yours ever,
Howard

Chloe stared at the screen. What on earth was he trying to say? Obviously he was offering her a job, but what else was between the lines? Was he saying that he loved her?

Did she love him? It was the one question she had never dared ask of herself. She suspected she might. That her admiration of him went further than was professional. Was that why his betrayal had hurt so much? She wished he'd never sent it. It made her feel unsettled. It tainted the new life she had made for herself. Bloody Howard, still pulling her strings from hundreds of miles away, when she had worked so hard to erase him. It was scary, knowing that she could send an email and step back into her former life.

She had to take evasive action.

The next day, when Chris came in with his box of lobsters, Chloe signed for them, swallowed, smiled and took a deep breath.

'I wondered,' she said, 'if you'd like to go for a walk one evening.'

She was careful not to ask him for a drink. She didn't want him to feel awkward or too pressured. A walk seemed the perfect compromise.

He looked surprised. He thought for a moment. She panicked she had been too forward and he was groping about for a polite get out.

'When have you got your next evening off?' he asked after what seemed like an endless wait.

She knew without looking at the rota. 'Tonight, actually.'

She gave him a sheepish smile. There was no point in pretending.

He scratched the back of his head, grinning. 'Tonight it is, then.'

'Great.' She nodded. 'I'll see you by the slipway? Six o'clock?'

'Sure.' He walked away, one hand raised in a farewell, but he was smiling.

Chloe wasn't sure how she was going to get through the next few hours. The restaurant was fully booked, so hopefully the time would fly. And that would give her just enough time to rush back to the hut, get changed and prepare herself for her date.

Jenna teased her. 'You haven't stopped smiling all lunch-time.'

'I'm going for a walk with Chris.'

'Seriously?' Jenna punched the air. 'I have such a good feeling about you guys.'

Chloe put her hands in the pocket of her apron. 'I've never asked someone out before.'

The two girls looked at each other.

'Jeans, T-shirt, hair down, barely-there make-up, small piece of statement jewellery,' said Jenna.

Chloe laughed.

'Exactly what I had in mind,' she said. 'Exactly.'

He was waiting by the slipway. As soon as she saw him, Chloe felt her heart lift a little. She knew she had barely anything to base that feeling on; nothing but instinct. Chemistry. Yet she could see something in his eyes too.

'Where do you want to go?' he asked.

'I haven't really explored the area much. So I'm in your hands.'

'Great,' he said. 'Well, if you don't mind a hike, and you're OK with heights …?'

At that moment, Chloe would have followed him anywhere.

He took her along the coast path that went from Everdene to Mariscombe. It was a tough walk, right on the cliff edge; the path was narrow and the drop to their right hand side was vertiginous – but he chivalrously held her hand whenever the going was too rough. Even though he didn't really have to.

Eventually they turned a corner, and there, thirty feet below them was a tiny lagoon. A steep set of rickety wooden steps led down to it.

'Everdene's best-kept secret,' Chris told her. 'Most people can't be bothered to come here because it takes such a lot of effort.'

'It's stunning,' breathed Chloe. 'It's like something out of the Famous Five.'

She took his hand as he helped her down the steps. And at the bottom they sat on the sand and looked out to sea, their arms around their knees. They might as well have been the only people left on the planet. There wasn't another soul to be seen. The sea and the sky seemed to merge into one and the cliffs stretched up around them. They were alone with just their thoughts.

'They never found his body, you know,' said Chris.

Chloe reached out her hand and picked up his. She didn't have to say anything, or do anything.

'I suppose Jenna told you I've got baggage? The good old Everdene tom-toms.'

'We've all got baggage,' said Chloe. 'But it doesn't mean

you have to drag it round with you.' Howard suddenly seemed a million miles away.

Chris turned to look at her. 'I've never thought of it like that,' he said.

They linked fingers, two virtual strangers who had an instinct that they might come to mean something to each other. The tentative start of something special. Something they both needed to help them heal the past.

That night, Chloe sat down in the beach hut with her laptop in front of her. She knew she had a decision to make. Whether to go backwards or look forwards. Just a fortnight ago, she suspected she would not have given the decision a second thought; she would have dropped everything and rushed back to London. But now all that had changed.

It was amazing, the difference in her mindset. She loved the restaurant. She knew she was only earning a pittance, and that eventually she would feel the financial bite, but she was confident that she would work out her future. And she needn't be a waitress forever. She thought she might try setting up her own agency. There were probably plenty of small businesses down here that could benefit from her expertise. She'd start sounding people out tomorrow. Maybe Vince and Murphy would take her on? She could give them a good discount for being a guinea pig. Obviously she'd never be able to command London prices, but then she wouldn't have London overheads. She could sell her flat and buy something down here; use whatever was left over to set herself up a little office ...

Maybe that was a crazy, unrealistic dream. But surely an unrealistic dream was better than walking back into a trap? Here, whatever happened, she was free from the pressure, the deadlines; the politics. Waitressing brought its own stresses, of course it did, because you had to think on your feet, and there were always difficult customers, and mistakes were made. But the buzz she felt at the end of a shift, when the staff all came out into the bar area and had a beer together with the music on and chilled out, was far greater than the buzz at the end of a campaign, when she had felt sucked dry and overwhelmed by anticlimax.

All she knew was that she never wanted to go back to that life, no matter what the rewards.

She typed out a reply, her fingers sure and speedy over the keyboard. Not once did she hesitate about what to say.

Dear Howard

Of course I forgive you. Your email touched me hugely, and I really appreciate everything you said, and your job offer. But I can't come back. It's time for me to move on and find a new path in life. I am very happy where I am at the moment, and I think there are great things just around the corner for me.

I hope you understand, but I want to move forwards, not backwards.

With very best wishes
Chloe

She read the email again before pressing send. It felt good to have the power. She couldn't quite believe she had done it. Once, that email would have been her dream come true, but now she had opened up her world she realized what confinement she had been in: a prison of her own making.

And then she picked up her phone and sent a text to Chris.

That was the loveliest evening I've had for a long time. Thank you.

She only had to wait thirty seconds for a reply.

Me too. Maybe do something at the weekend? A Famous Five picnic? Let me know.

BOB AND ELVIS

Bob strode along the dunes, puce in the mid-afternoon heat, his baseball hat already soaked with sweat. He could feel beads of it start to trickle down his forehead and down the back of his neck. He pulled the hat off and wiped his face with the back of his arm before the sweat got in his eyes, then rammed it back on his head.

'Elvis!' he shouted again, and he felt sure he could hear a nearby group of girls snickering.

It wasn't funny. Wretched animal. He should never have let it off the lead but Janice always liked it to have a decent run. And it had always come back when she called it. It didn't take a blind bit of notice of Bob. It never had. Janice was its mistress, and it had doted on her. As she had on it.

It. Elvis was a he, obviously. But Bob always referred to him as 'it'. And he always felt an utter fool shouting his name. It was a ludicrous name for a dog. But Janice had adored dogs and Elvis Presley in equal measure, so it had seemed logical, when she brought the little terrier back from the rescue centre four years ago, that Elvis would be what she called it.

'You ain't nothing but a hound dog,' she would sing, and Bob would roll his eyes.

'Nothing but a bloody nuisance,' he would correct her.

'Oh, you love him, you know you do,' Janice would reply, and Bob never disabused her of this, because he might not love Elvis but he loved Janice very much, every inch of her jolly fifteen stone.

They went to the same beach hut at Everdene every summer for their holiday. Largely because of Elvis: most hotels and self-catering places didn't take pets, but the battered old hut they rented welcomed dogs, and there were loads of walks for him – them – to enjoy. Besides, it suited them both. Bob would go birdwatching in the burrows, and do a bit of deep-sea fishing – he'd go out on one of the day boats from the harbour in Tawcombe, the little town on the other side of Mariscombe, the next cove. Janice was happy to sit in her deckchair and read – endless historical novels she borrowed from her friends. She could read five in a week. Bob hadn't ever read a book in his life. He couldn't sit still long enough. His eyes would glaze over after the first line. It seemed to keep her happy, though, being immersed in her world of scoundrels and hussies. One hand dipped in and out of a family-sized bag of crisps as she read, and from time to time she would drop one for Elvis, who lay in the shade of her bulk.

Once during the week, they would walk the coast path from Everdene to Mariscombe. It was a tough route, along a rocky clifftop, and Janice had to stop for a rest on nearly every bench, but they both agreed it was the most beautiful walk in England. If they were lucky, they saw seals. In Mariscombe they would go to the pub for scampi and chips and half a pint of Devon cider. They sat outside in the pub garden, Elvis under the table, and Janice would feed him chips, then they would get a taxi back, because she couldn't manage both ways.

'God's own country,' she would always say on the journey home, Elvis wedged between her feet. They always booked up again as soon as they came back for the following year. The hut was popular: if you didn't get in there quick someone else would nab your week.

In the furore after the funeral, Bob had forgotten all about the booking until the reminder email for the final payment arrived. He was tempted to cancel and lose his deposit, but daughter urged him to go.

'It'll do you good, Dad. A change of scene. And I can have a clear-out while you're gone, if you like.'

She was kind, his daughter. She knew he couldn't face it, the clearing out. He felt filled with gratitude and relief when she told him she'd do it. He would be able to walk back into the house after a week away, and not be confronted with Janice's skirts and jumpers when he opened the wardrobe. Not see her powder and face creams in the bathroom. The thing that really crucified him was the half-finished tapestry on the side table in the lounge. He could see the brightly coloured skeins of thread, and imagine her needle whipping in and out of the holes, as she kept up a running commentary on *Downton Abbey*, flipped channels and texted her friends. Janice had always been able to do several things at once.

The thought of making a decision about any of her things gave him an unpleasant hot feeling in his chest. He would never have described himself as a sentimental man. He knew that keeping her things as they were wouldn't bring her back. And the most ironic thing of all was that he had longed to get rid of what he called her dust-gatherers over the years. She loved her 'bits', did Janice – her collection of piggy banks, the dried flower arrangements, the picture frames with every school photo ever taken of their grandchildren, grinning out at them with gap-toothed innocence from every surface. But now he had the chance, Bob couldn't touch any of it. And it *was* gathering dust. He couldn't be bothered to do any housework. His daughter told him off, but he couldn't see the point. You wiped it away, only for more dust to appear the next day.

So he'd agreed to go. He stuck Elvis in his travelling crate in the boot, and off they went.

There had been a long family debate about Elvis after the funeral. None of their children could have him. Bob wasn't sure he could look after himself, let alone the dog. He'd never taken any responsibility for him. He had no idea about worming or vaccinations or how much of the unappetising brick-coloured lumps that came in a sack he was supposed to be given to eat.

'You could always take him back to the rescue centre,' his daughter suggested.

Elvis had eyed him beadily during the conversation. Bob turned away. 'The bloody thing needs walking three times a day. And it shits all over the garden.'

'You're supposed to pick it up. Mum used to.'

'I know. But I've got better things to do.' Bob looked disgusted at the prospect.

In the end, he decided on one last holiday, then he *would* drop Elvis off at the rescue centre. That was, after all, what rescue centres were for – rehoming dogs when there had been a change of circumstance. There was no point in being sentimental. Elvis would be far better off with a family who craved a canine companion than someone who was merely tolerating him in deference to a wife who was no longer there.

Now, as Bob paced desperately up and down the dunes looking for any sign of the wretched beast, he wished he'd dropped him off before he went. He was going to have a heart attack with the stress of it at this rate. Elvis had spotted a rabbit and had bombed off into the bracken like a high-speed train. The dunes stretched for miles, riddled with warrens and all sorts of enticements for a small terrier who knew only too well he was under sufferance. Elvis knew Bob didn't care much for him, even though he did his best to meet his needs. The unconditional love just wasn't there. They hadn't bonded.

Bob even suspected Elvis thought he'd been jealous of him and his relationship with Janice. He wasn't. Of course he wasn't. He was happy the dog had made Janice happy, but it didn't mean he had to like him. Bob wasn't the jealous type.

He looked at his watch. It was nearly an hour since Elvis had gone. How long were you supposed to search for a missing dog? What were the chances of finding him?

'Elvis!' he bellowed again, feeling furious and helpless but also secretly relieved that this might be the last he'd seen of him. Didn't this absolve him from making the decision? He knew he would have felt guilty taking him back where he had come from, as if he'd betrayed Janice in some way.

'Have you lost your dog?' A woman in billowing shorts and stout sandals, her greying hair scraped back in a ponytail, looked at him, concerned.

'He ran off. After a rabbit. Nearly an hour ago.'

The woman screwed her face up in distress. 'Oh dear. Lots of people lose dogs on these burrows.'

'You reckon I should give up, then?' Bob tried not to look hopeful. He tried not to think about the pork pie that was waiting in the fridge for his tea.

'What sort of dog?'

'Little terrier thing. Mongrel.' Bob held his hands apart to indicate Elvis's size.

'Thing is, once they get down those rabbit holes ...'

Maybe Elvis would be happier without him? Maybe he could live for years on the dunes, roaming wild, sleeping in a rabbit hole, munching on whatever he caught, as happy as Larry? Maybe that had been Elvis' plan all along, to do a bunk, knowing he wasn't wanted, knowing Bob had a plan to dump him? Maybe Elvis wanted to be the master of his own fate? Janice had always said he was clever, and had human feelings.

'Maybe give it till sundown?' the woman suggested.

'Sundown?' Bob looked up at the sky. Dusk was a long way off. Was he going to have to stride up and down for another four hours? What was decent?

Janice, he knew, would have stayed until the end of time looking for Elvis. But Elvis wouldn't have run off if she had been there. He'd have been back by now.

'Well,' said the woman. 'I wish you luck.'

Her tone of voice indicated she didn't think he had much hope.

She strode off. Bob sat down on a nearby bench and watched until she disappeared around a corner. Maybe he would go? If Elvis was going to come back, he would have done by now. He felt pretty confident about that.

He stood up. It was like searching for a needle in a

haystack. There was no point in wasting any more time. But as he set off back down the path, his conscience tugged at him. Janice would never forgive him if he didn't do everything in his power to get the dog back.

Janice wouldn't know, he told himself. Bob had no belief in people looking down from heaven at what you were up to. His wife wouldn't have a clue.

He, however, would have to live with the fact he hadn't given it his best shot. With a sigh, he turned and walked back to the spot where he'd last seen Elvis. He called his name. He tried as many different tones as he could. Authoritative, enticing, casual, panic-stricken. He asked every passer-by if they had seen him, but no one had seen a small, scruffy terrier on the loose. As the sun went down, and the air grew cooler, Bob satisfied himself that he had given Elvis as much chance as he could.

As he made his way back along the dunes and down the steep sandy bank to the row of huts, he couldn't help but look back, to see if the little dog was scampering along behind him. But of Elvis there was no sign.

'Sorry, mate,' he said in his head. 'Hope you're all right.'

He genuinely did. He wished the dog no particular ill, but he felt the burden of responsibility had lifted. He no longer had to worry about his canine legacy.

The hut was strangely peaceful that night. He made his tea – the pork pie, a carton of potato salad, and a bread roll, followed by a Mr Kipling treacle tart with the last of a pot of clotted cream bought from the post office. There were no eyes gazing at him, begging for a stray crumb. No irritating scuttering of claws on the wooden floor. No doggy whimpers during the night disturbing his sleep.

Elvis had always had vivid dreams. Well, now perhaps his dreams had come true. He could chase rabbits until the end of time.

When Bob woke up the next morning he was halfway to the hut door, ready to let Elvis out, when he remembered. Tutting, he made his way to the kettle. Elvis's bowls were still on the floor. He lifted them up, emptied them, then put them in the bin. He wouldn't be needing them. Nor his lead. Or his basket. There wasn't room in the bin for that, so he'd have to take it home and get rid of it there.

He wondered how his daughter was getting on with clearing the house. He wondered how ruthless she was being. He wondered if she would keep the piggy banks for the grandchildren, or if they would end up in some charity shop somewhere, with a sticky label on the bottom stating '50p'. It made him feel morose. He didn't want to think about it.

He tidied the rest of the hut as best he could, as was the arrangement at the end of a week's rental. It had always been Janice who had done the cleaning, while he had loaded the car and gone into the village to buy souvenirs to take back home. Sticks of rock and boxes of fudge. He didn't bother this year. He felt rather out of sorts. He hadn't slept well, despite the silence. Or perhaps because of the silence. He'd sat up more than once, straining his ears for the sound of Elvis' breathing. And at three he had woken up, wondering if the little dog had emerged from whichever rabbit hole he had gone down and was now searching desperately for him. He got up to open the door and look out. There was no sign of him, just the sea edging its way in. He shut the door and told himself Elvis was independent and resourceful and the last person he would look for would be Bob. He lay back down and finally went off to sleep.

At eleven, he vacated the hut and made two trips to the car with his stuff. He looked up the bank to the dunes, and wondered if he should have one last look. Of course he should. Even though it would mean he wouldn't be home until late afternoon. Rolling his eyes at his own sense of duty, he retraced his steps of the day before. There was still no sign of him. Of course there wasn't.

He made his way back to the car, feeling rather heavy of heart. He looked back along the row of huts, where he and Janice had spent so many contented summers. He wouldn't rebook this year, he thought. He'd go somewhere that had no memories of Janice. Even now, he could see her wandering across the sand, holding her sandals in one hand, in one of the rather garish flowered sundresses she loved. She never wanted to fade into the background. She wasn't self-conscious about her size. She was large and flamboyant. And happy. Janice was one of the most contented people Bob had ever known.

He did the journey home in record time, because he only had to stop once. Janice liked to stop off at the teddy bear shop on the way home, to get cuddlies for the grandchildren, and there were always at least two service station stops. And of course, he didn't have to stop to let Elvis out for a pee. By three, he was walking back in over the threshold.

What he found inside took his breath away. The chaos and the clutter had all gone. The surfaces were clear of all but the necessary. All Janice's bits and bobs were nowhere to be seen. In the bedroom, everything was in perfect order. Her nightdress case, her slippers, her endless bottles of designer perfume had vanished, as well as her rails of purple, red and pink clothing.

He sat down on the bed. His chest felt tight. He had known it had to be done; that he couldn't carry on living in a shrine. He was grateful to his daughter for doing the job. But he just wanted to lie down on the bed and sleep for ever. He didn't want to live in this soulless, empty box that wasn't filled with Janice's chatter, the smell of her cooking mingled with whichever celebrity scent she had poured down her cleavage, the ting of her phone as someone texted her, the blaring of the telly – she loved all the soaps and the reality shows. The hole she had left in his life was cavernous – how on earth was he supposed to fill it? Sights, sounds, smells – he felt surrounded by emptiness.

The phone rang, echoing through the hollow bedroom. He reached out for the handset that had now been put on his side of the bed. It was probably his daughter, wanting to know if he was home safely, so he'd better answer or she would worry, and he felt he'd put her through enough of that.

'Hello?'

'Hello?' It was a strange voice; a youngish woman. 'This is the veterinary practice in Tawcombe. We've had a dog brought in – a little terrier. He was found on the dunes in Everdene?'

Bob sat up. 'How did you get this number?' He hoped he didn't sound too aggressive.

'He's been microchipped.'

'Oh.' Microchipped. He remembered Janice getting that done now.

'Is this still the right contact number? We can keep him

here for you in our kennels overnight if you want to come and collect him.'

Bob thought. It would be the easiest thing in the world to deny all knowledge. No doubt the vets would be able to find him a good home. They'd make sure he was all right. At least that way he would know Elvis hadn't got stuck in a rabbit hole and starved to death. He could stop wondering; stop feeling guilty.

He looked around the bedroom. Everything stood to attention, shining and gleaming. Everything was as it should be. No clutter. No noise. No chaos.

No Janice. He didn't know how long he'd be able to stand it.

'I'll come and fetch him,' he said down the phone. 'I'll be there as quickly as I can, first thing.'

He set off back down the motorway at eight o'clock the next morning. He wondered what on earth he was doing. It was going to cost him sixty quid in petrol to fetch the wretched animal, plus the vet would sting him. They always did. He almost turned around halfway. He wouldn't fetch him; wouldn't answer the phone for a few days. What could they do? They couldn't force the dog on him. But something made him drive on.

He managed to find the vets quite easily. There was just a young nurse on duty. She made him fill out some paperwork and, as he predicted, there was a charge for Elvis's overnight stay. He grumbled quietly to himself as he pulled the cash out of his wallet.

'I'll just go and fetch him,' the nurse said, and Bob waited on one of the plastic chairs in the waiting area, reading the adverts for wormers.

Elvis waddled out on the surgery lead, looking baleful and defiant. When he saw Bob he sat down squarely in the middle of the surgery and looked away. Bob felt a surge of something. He wasn't sure what. He got up and walked towards him.

'Hello, boy.' His voice was gruff. He realized that Elvis was a living connection between him and Janice; that his hot, square little body would give him comfort. He squatted down and held out his hand. 'Come here.'

Despite his apparent reluctance, Elvis turned his face back to Bob. He reached his chin forward and rested it on his knee. For a moment, he shut his eyes. Bob stroked his head and Elvis burrowed in further. He seemed to be saying sorry: sorry for being a nuisance and for buggering off.

'It's all right, boy,' said Bob, and found his voice wasn't as strong as it could be. 'Come on, then. Let's go, you and me.'

VINCE

Vince stood at the helm of his boat, his arms crossed. The two brothers who crewed for them had a week off, so he and Chris were going out together with a guy who stood in every now and again. In theory. Yet again, here he was, waiting for Chris to turn up.

Only this time, he didn't mind his reason for being late. He could see the two of them from his vantage point, kissing each other on the harbour as if their lives depended on it. The waitress from The Lobster Shack – Chloe. It was astonishing, he thought, how having the right person in your life could turn it around.

He gave a piercing whistle.

'Oi,' he shouted. 'Put her down.'

Chris didn't miss a bit. Just flipped him the finger. Then extricated himself, grinning, and loped towards the boat, jumping on board.

'Sorry. Did I keep you waiting?'

'It's all right. I've got all day.'

'You're just jealous.'

It was only brotherly banter, but Chris's remark hit home. Because actually, thought Vince, he was. He was jealous of the purity and simplicity of Chris's relationship with Chloe. The lack of complication. Not that he begrudged his brother his newfound love. Not one bit. He was glad and grateful, not least because it had spared him the ghastly task of intervening. Possibly dragging Chris off to rehab. Which, given this was Tawcombe and not LA, would have been very counterintuitive.

They were about to set off when Vince's mobile rang.

It was Murphy.

'Hey.'

There was a choking sound on the end of the line.

'Vince. It's me, mate. She's thrown me out.'

'What?'

'Anna's chucked me out of the house. She packed my bag and threw it out of the window. I've never seen her so mad.'

'What happened?'

'She found a text.'

'Oh, Murphy.' Vince threw his eyes to the sky in exasperation. 'Man.'

'I can't help it if some mad, crazy girl texts me in the middle of the night.'

Vince groaned. 'Not that girl from the launch.'

'Yeah.'

'What did the text say?'

There was a guilty pause. 'It was pretty explicit.'

Vince uncoiled the rope with one hand and jumped back onto the boat, letting it slump with a thump onto the deck. There was no need to delay their journey any longer. He strode over to the wheel. They'd have a phone signal until they were quite a way out, so he turned the key in the ignition, then started to back the boat out carefully.

'How many times have I told you? Don't give out your phone number!'

'You saw what she did! I didn't give it to her.'

'You gave her the come on, though.'

'Vince, I didn't. I swear I didn't.'

'Murphy, you're an idiot.'

'Vince, I adore Anna. You know I do. I would never cheat on her. I know you don't think much of me, but honestly …'

There was genuine pain in his voice.

Vince wasn't surprised. Who wouldn't be distraught at the thought of losing Anna?

'So what are you going to do?' he asked Murphy,

'I'm going to have to come down. She's changed the locks.'

'No way! What about the girls? What has she told them?'

Murphy didn't answer. Vince just heard a bit of a choking noise over the thrum of the engine. His mate was crying. Eventually he managed to get the words out. 'I've told them … We've told them I'm going away on business.'

Vince looked at the horizon. If they pushed it, he would be back at six, in time to take Murphy for a pint.

'You better get your arse into gear and get down here, then.'

He hung up and looked at his brother.

'Trouble?'

'It was only a matter of time. You know what Murphy's like.'

'Get in there, then.'

Vince looked at his brother sharply. 'What?'

'Ah, come on, Vince. It's bloody obvious you've got a

thing for Anna. Why else have you lived like a monk for the past ... Well, since forever?'

Vince glowered at the horizon, feeling a fool. If it had been obvious to drunken Chris, who else had cottoned on?

Not Murphy. Because all Murphy wanted to do, once he'd arrived and drunk four pints, was to get Vince to go up and talk sense into his wife.

They sat in front of Vince's beach hut with the remains of a bottle of Havana Club, the cool of the night air settling round them.

'Vince, you know what I'm like better than anyone. And you saw that girl set me up. She's been bombarding me with filth since I let her get my number. But I don't reply to her.'

'Really?'

'Well, only to say it might be a good idea if she stopped.'

'You should have changed your number.'

'It's too bloody inconvenient. And I didn't think Anna was going to find it. I don't understand. She's just not the snooping-about-in-your-phone type.'

'It must have been obvious, Murph.'

Murphy poured out another inch of rum.

'I can't lose her. She's my rock, Vince. We're a great team. We've got our beautiful girls. She can't want to break up over a stupid text, surely?'

'Well, they say sending explicit texts is as bad as being unfaithful nowadays.'

'Thanks for that, Vince. That's great.'

Vince felt conflicted. He hated seeing his mate in such distress, but he did think he'd been an idiot. If he'd really respected Anna, he wouldn't have played into the girl's hands in the first place.

'Do you want me to go up and see her for you? Explain how things are.'

Murphy looked at him, surprised.

'Would you do that for me?'

'Of course.' Vince gazed at the horizon. It was rapidly disappearing from view as the sky joined the sea in submission to the night.

'Explain to her that I'm an idiot. Not a bastard. I'd never be unfaithful to her. Never.'

Vince looked at his mate. Did Murphy protest too much? He couldn't be sure. But he knew it was up to him to try and save his marriage. That was, after all, what friends were for.

ELODIE

A more contented marriage Edmund and Elodie's could not have been. It may not have reached the giddy heights of passion, but it worked. It allowed them both to be the people they needed to be, and to be the parents they wanted to be to Otto.

And Elodie took the plunge: she left her secretarial post and began to write. She had learned so much during her time working with Edmund, and she found she was itching to tell stories herself. She started off small, writing half-hour plays and short stories, submitting them under a pseudonym to his colleagues, for she never wanted to be accused of nepotism. And then, one day, she got her first commission, and confessed to him what she had been doing.

He was delighted, and from that day on gave her his unstinting support, taking Otto out to the park at weekends so she could bash away on her typewriter, reading her work, giving constructive criticism, suggesting books she might like to try and adapt. And then encouraging her to make the leap from writing for radio to writing for television: a former colleague was producing a weekly police drama, and was looking for new writers.

Elodie found that her way of looking at the world was just what television needed. She brought a warmth and sparkle to *scripts without ever sacrificing depth or nuance. She became more and more in demand. Her success meant they moved to a larger house, in Teddington, and were able to employ a nanny. Edmund never begrudged her success or the amount of her time it absorbed. He was delighted and endlessly proud. He was quite happy in his niche. Despite numerous offers, he himself was never tempted to move on career-wise, yet he never felt inferior to her.*

She wrote under her married name – Smithers – because she didn't want to draw attention to herself. Her first name was unusual enough. She didn't want anyone spotting her name in the Radio Times *and getting in touch. She knew if her parents had wanted to find her enough they would have, but nevertheless she wanted to keep a low profile. Even without the past she was so eager to forget, she was a private person who didn't court publicity, despite the world she moved in. And people liked her even more for that: she was modest and self-deprecating about her increased success.*

They had a wide-ranging circle of loyal friends; bohemian intellectuals who loved coming round for the endless Sunday lunches for which they became famous, at which children ran riot and the wine flowed. Elodie had a knack of collecting people, because she was interested in them, fascinated by them, wanted to know what made them tick. Edmund was endlessly charmed by his talented and extravert wife, happy to bob along in her wake, comfortable enough in his skin not to feel overshadowed, even when she went on to win awards for some of her work, because she always, always said she couldn't have done it without him.

And then one day, Edmund had a heart attack. A con-genital fault, said the consultant. He had been sitting on a time bomb. He was three days in a coma before they turned off the life support machine.

The weeks following Edmund's death were a blur, but her friends were incredible. They somehow knew exactly when she needed company and when she needed to be left alone; when she needed a warming casserole brought round and when she just wanted to sit and drink a bottle of wine with someone. The letters of condolence she received brought her the most comfort and yet the most sadness. Edmund had been an even better friend to people than she had realized; always a font of knowledge and advice and quiet support, especially to the writers whom he had worked with. Several of them told her how his wisdom and encouragement had brought them back from the brink of despair. Elodie herself knew how a gift could turn into a curse if the muse didn't materialize. She rarely suffered from writer's block herself, but understood how it could drive someone to the edge of madness. That Edmund had kept his loyalty so quiet made her realize even more keenly what she had lost.

And then an envelope arrived via the undertakers and she recognized the writing immediately, even without the Worcestershire postmark. Her mouth was dry as she opened it.

My darling Elodie,

I read about the death of your dear Edmund in the newspaper.

Of course, I have followed your career and your life from afar. Do not think that I have not thought about you every day, or that I did not care. I have never forgiven myself for what happened, for not intervening sooner. But as no doubt you have realized, life is not always straightforward and we do not always make the decisions that are best for us or the others around us. Regret is the bitterest pill.

But I have taken solace in your success, and the fact that you married a kind and honourable man who I hope gave you everything you deserve. I knew you were strong, my Elodie, and that you would survive, and perhaps be better off without us.

That was probably the hardest decision for me to make, but sometimes it is kindest to let go. I hope you understand that, and can forgive me. Both for that decision and everything that went before.

I am proud of you. More than you can possibly know. And if you need me, you know where I am. But I entirely understand if you don't want to make contact.

Your loving father.

Elodie was still too numb from Edmund's death to take in the implications. Desmond had been watching her all this time. He was holding out an olive branch. Somehow, the purity of her marriage to Edmund highlighted even more the rotten state of her own parents' relationship. She had no desire to go back and revisit it. After all, she had now lived longer without them then she had with, so their influence had faded into the background. They were nothing to her now. A distant memory, that was all.

And the following week there came the news that she was up for a BAFTA for a one-off drama she had written: a gritty, humorous piece about a working girl in Soho who became an artists' model, then a muse, then a madame.

It had turned its previously unknown star into a household name, and became something of a cult hit.

When she won Best Screenplay, a month later, and went up onto the stage to accept her award, she broke down when she thanked Edmund, and the cameras went crazy. And every producer in the country wanted to work with her, every broadcaster wanted her to pen a drama series; she could, it seemed, write whatever she wanted. She was so busy, so in demand, so snowed under, that her father's letter became insignificant; the decision of whether to meet him or not got pushed to the back of her mind.

Besides, carrying on with her work was the best tribute she could think of to Edmund. She made sure she had enough projects on the go to give her life momentum. And meetings. She needed meetings if she wasn't to become reclusive, because that was one of the downsides of being a writer; the fact it was such a solitary occupation. Even though she had technically passed retirement age, she stayed in demand. She had never really gone out of fashion, because she moved with the times and didn't get stuck in a rut. She always had something fresh and irreverent to say; her characters were always relevant and with the times. She could pick and choose whom she worked with and no one had the temerity to interfere with her work. She was respected in the industry as someone who could always deliver.

Her busy social life balanced out the days she spent locked away: she moved from the family house in Teddington into a Thameside apartment by Tower Bridge: she loved to be by the water, by the ever-changing narrative that was the river. She was always at the theatre or cinema or out to dinner; never short of invitations, although she never went out on 'dates'. She didn't feel the need for someone else in her life. Otto lived near enough to visit regularly and eventually she became a grandmother, a role she adored. She was just the right sort of granny – practical and hands-on without being interfering. She always remembered how grateful she had been to Lady Bellnap for being the very same, and tried to emulate her attributes.

Lady Bellnap had passed away years before, but had left Elodie a small sum of money along with the diaries she had kept while out in the Far East. Elodie had found them riveting and unputdownable – the incredible human detail moved her to tears, and she knew one day they would be a source of inspiration. Eventually, she sat down and began to sketch out an idea for a drama series based on the diaries – a young doctor and his wife battling to make a change in tropical climes. All great ideas start with a tiny seed. Some hid for years, waiting to germinate, but this one germinated straight away, blossomed and flourished. It wrote itself, which was always the best way. It was dramatic, romantic, the stakes were high, the setting exotic – it had everything needed for a ratings winner.

She wanted to take the idea to an independent producer whose work she had long admired. Colm Sanderson's dramas were always gentle but thought-provoking. They had both depth and warmth, and left the viewer feeling as if they knew something more about the world. He was the perfect person to handle this material, she felt sure. Not that she was precious about her work – Elodie had long learned not to be precious – but at her age, she was entitled to be choosy. And she was also lucky enough to be able to say no if she thought her work was going to be misrepresented. A luxury, she knew.

She sent Colm a treatment. A two-page document that was enough to tantalize him, with enough detail to make

*sure he couldn't just steal the idea (not that he would; bona
fide producers never stole ideas), but leaving it open-ended
enough to invite discussion. A good pitch for a series was
always a starting point; a good writer always left room for
improvement. It was a draft process.*

He responded almost by return of email.

'I love this. It's just the sort of project I am looking for. Edgy
nostalgia: emotional without being sentimental. Let's meet.'

*It was exactly the response she wanted. Positive. To the point.
She emailed him back and made an appointment. She felt
pleased. Finding the right home for a project was tricky. And
although this was a million miles away from a green light, she
felt in her gut that it was a step in the right direction.*

*There was something else, too, but she tried to hide that from
herself, rather coyly. She had always found Colm Sanderson
intriguing. They had met several times at industry parties. He
was tall, statuesque, with a sweep of steel-grey hair that fell
to his upturned collar, and the most fascinating pair of eyes
she had ever looked into. They were knowing, curious, teasing
and inviting all at once. How did he do that? she wondered.
They'd had a couple of conversations over warm white wine
and forgettable canapés, and each time there was a frisson
between them she worried was inappropriate at their age. The
richness of his voice, the gleam in his eyes that was somewhere
between naughty and teasing, the way his mind worked even
faster than hers did: she couldn't deny that she found him
attractive.*

*And, she told herself, a decent enough period of mourning
had passed. She'd been a widow for some years. It wasn't as if*

she was throwing herself at Colm with Edmund barely cold in his grave. It was OK. It wasn't unseemly.

So when the morning of their meeting arrived, she laughed at herself in the mirror as she dressed. How could a woman of her age, her standing, feel flustered? She was being utterly ridiculous, but still she tried on three jackets before deciding that midnight blue velvet made the most of her grey eyes, and that its luxury could be toned down if she wore jeans with it, and that high-heeled boots would give her stature. Colm, she calculated, must be six foot three.

She knew he was separated. He'd been married to a well-known and respected actress for years but she had left him two years before for a much younger man – she had the kind of cheekbones that enabled her to do that without anyone holding it against her. Colm had taken her departure with an elegant good grace that made him, in Elodie's eyes, even more intriguing. They had three grown-up children. It was all very civilized and sophisticated. Whether he already had someone else was anyone's guess.

They met in his office in Charlotte Street. For two hours they batted ideas backwards and forwards, jotting ideas and straplines down on a white board, thrashing out the story arc of the series, giving it a shape, making sure there was enough content.

She loved the way he worked. He had the utmost respect for her as a writer, for her craft and her skill. He never kidnapped the material and tried to make it his own. Instead, he asked her questions, pushing her to analyse the characters and their individual arcs, enabling her to come up with the answers.

By midday, they had an outline they were both happy with.

'So if I commission you,' he said, 'how long would it take for you to come up with a first draft for episode one and a bible that I can take to the commissioners?'

He would take the project to the BBC or ITV and try and negotiate, but he needed some solid material to convince them: a good script and a document that outlined the series.

'A month,' said Elodie decisively. 'Long enough to do it justice, but short enough to put me under pressure to deliver.'

Colm laughed. 'A month it is then. But there is something else.'

Elodie's heart sank. Here it came. The snag. There would be no budget. He would want her to do it for a pittance. Or he would want to share the credit. Or some other awful condition that would mean her refusing the commission. She could taste disappointment already. She had thought more of him than that.

'What?' she asked him warily.

'You get the commission on condition you come out for lunch with me.'

He was already standing, unhooking his scarf from the hatstand, looking at her with his lopsided smile.

Somehow he had made the words with me sound incredibly intimate. This wasn't an invitation to a working lunch. If she accepted, this would be the start of something.

'I'm starving,' she told him, and locked her eyes on his, and felt a jolt, a spark, a life-affirming tingle that filled her with joy.

He said nothing, just wrapped the scarf around his neck, pulled on his jacket, and she followed him, wordlessly, down the stairs, out of the door, along the street, and into a tiny, bustling brasserie that smelt of sizzling steak and garlic where the maître d' led them, without being asked, to a window table laid for two.

He'd planned it, thought Elodie with a thrill, and she held her menu in front of her face so Colm couldn't see her smile.

From that day on, they were inseparable. And it felt so right. It was so easy. They slotted into each other's lives effortlessly. They didn't even have to discuss it because there was nothing to discuss. They were both free agents. They had so many things in common, and so many things they could share with each other: books, films, food, music. They even read the same newspaper. They were both still utterly absorbed by their work, with no intention of retiring. They were passionate and perfectionist about what they did.

At weekends, they wandered along the South Bank, argued ferociously about art in Tate Modern, bought over-priced cheese at Borough Market and ate it in the front of the telly with heavy red wine that made them both fall asleep. They swapped books and did The Times crossword. They were competitive and symbiotic. They had days out in Whitstable and Woodstock; took a boat up the Thames to Hampton Court. He made chutney and Christmas puddings and she laughed at his domesticity.

And on Valentine's Day – which they both agreed was a ridiculous commercial trap – he nevertheless booked a table at Clos Maggiore, their favourite restaurant in Covent Garden, and, as the waiter took away the plates that had borne the roasted duck breast on a bed of plums, leaned across the table, those eyes that had drawn her in burning with something that told Elodie her life was soon to change.

'After Emma left me I never thought I would get married again,' he said. 'It seemed pointless. Hypocritical, even. To do *it again when you'd fucked it up once. But, right now there is nothing I want more, nothing I would love more, than for you to become my wife. I would be so proud.'*

Elodie put her hands over her face and peered out at him between her fingers. An infantile, girlish gesture that she hated herself for, but it was instinct, to mask the surprise, the delight, the joy for just one moment until she had assimilated what he'd just said.

She didn't need to think about it all. Not really. Yes, it was a risk. He was bound to have flaws. Who didn't? And wouldn't that be part of their future together – discovering each other's weaknesses?

And perhaps one of the nice things about embarking on a relationship when you were older was that you were more aware of your weaknesses, so didn't have to spend so long dwelling on them.

They were sitting on the balcony of her apartment when she saw the advert, in the property section of the Saturday Times. *Her heart turned over once, twice, and her mind started racing. She didn't say anything to Colm, but something came full circle in Elodie's mind. She and Colm had agreed that they would sell her flat and move into his, in Hampstead – although she would miss the water, Hampstead suited their lifestyle far better, with its slightly bohemian café society, and his was much bigger than hers. The sale had been agreed and this was their last Thameside weekend before the contracts were completed.*

And there it was. A quarter-page advert. The Grey House. 'An unmissable maritime opportunity'. It looked just the same. The photo was taken from below, the beach huts in a row beneath the cliff, the house hovering above, nestled amongst the monkey puzzle trees. If she closed her eyes she would be able to smell the sea breeze and feel the warmth of the sun on her face.

Her need to go back was primal. Suddenly, it was the only thing that mattered. It was time. Time to confront her past, so she could have the one thing that had ever really mattered to her. She didn't know what it was she was going to find; who would still be there. How she would feel.

'OK?' Colm was looking over at her with a frown.

'Yes ... ' she nodded, but she thought she was probably far from convincing. She didn't want to tell him the truth. She'd never told anyone her story, except Lady Bellnap. Not even Edmund, who had accepted she was estranged from her parents and seemed to think that it didn't need further qualifying. She had always felt that if she told people, it would define her.

Suddenly, however, the past no longer held any fear for her. She knew who she was, and it wasn't that girl who had been betrayed on her wedding day. She needed to go back, to the time and the place. It wasn't closure she wanted. It was the opposite: the chance to open the past back up. To rediscover the place that had meant so much to her, and to share it with the people who now meant so much to her. And to make her peace with the people who had once mattered.

VINCE

The next day, as Vince drove up the M4 towards Chiswick, he started to question his own motives the nearer he got to London.

Murphy was so grateful that Vince had offered to go and fight his cause. Although Murphy seemed like an open kind of guy, he was in fact intensely private. He liked everything to seem perfect; for people to look at him and think 'that's the kind of life/house/car/wife I want'. The fact that all that was about to come crashing down had made him panic, and he didn't know how to handle it.

So here was Vince, charging to the rescue like the best mate he was. Yet he had to ask himself why he was really doing it. Not just out of friendship. He couldn't fool himself. If Murphy and Anna split up, he was unlikely to see Anna again. So it was in his interests for them to get back together. Although that didn't bring her any closer to him, at least he would get his fix from time to time.

And if he went to plead Murphy's case, he would get a fix straight away. Breathe the same air she was breathing. Feel her eyes on his skin. Know that she had thought of him, because if he was there in front of her she had to think about him, even if it wasn't in the way he wanted to be thought of.

Vince slapped the steering wheel with annoyance. Why couldn't he ever rid himself of this curse? This obsession. Why was he feeding it? It was always the same when he saw her. His longing intensified and tortured him for days, weeks, afterwards. Febrile dreams in which she was just out of reach. He twisted like a kite in the wind. It was exhausting. He sometimes wondered if he could be hypnotized into forgetting her. Then he realized he didn't want to forget her. It was a never-ending loop with no solution and it drove him crazy.

He turned into the wide, leafy street. He'd driven down here so many times, always with his heart in his mouth, his pulse pounding. Today was no different. He pulled into the gravel drive in front of the house. A red-brick Victorian semi he knew was worth over two million because Murphy had told him. Vince thought the house was nice enough, but couldn't get his head around the figure.

He rang the bell and put his hands in his pockets while he waited.

Anna answered eventually. She looked amazing. No make-up, hair loose, dressed in white yoga pants and a grey hooded T-shirt. Bare feet. It was all he could do not to reach out and touch her.

'Vince!' She did a smile/frown – pleasure at seeing him mingled with confusion. 'What are you doing here?' She put her hands up to her hair and ran her fingers through it, pulling it round to one side. He thought of the times he'd wanted to run his fingers through it.

He raised his eyebrow and gave a shrug. 'I came to talk to you about Murphy.'

'I don't know that I want to hear anything that Murphy has to say.'

'He doesn't know I'm here.' Vince had worked out she was more likely to see him if she thought this.

She surveyed him for a moment. Then she looked at her watch. 'I'm supposed to be going out ...'

Vince felt irritated. 'What? To yoga? Or the supermarket? This is important, Anna. There's stuff I think you should know.'

She frowned, then sighed. 'OK. Come in. I'll make us some coffee ...'

He followed her inside. He saw their reflection in the glass of the etched mirror as they walked past and it made his heart judder in his chest. Why couldn't he control himself when he was around her? Get a grip, he told himself.

The kitchen was at the back of the house; an enormous extension with folding glass doors that led out into the garden. Everything was immaculate. Big wicker baskets contained the children's homework. Their paintings were framed on the wall – no Blu-Tak or drawing pins in this house. The island contained baskets of gleaming fruit.

Anna filled the kettle. The water bubbled from the tap like a spume of champagne. Even their water, thought Vince, was better than everyone else's.

She flicked the kettle on and stared at him.

'I'm not having him back,' she said, an edge to her voice.

'You'll never meet anyone who loves you as much as Murphy,' countered Vince.

'I don't need love like that. I read the texts, Vince. They were ...'

She made a face.

233

'They were texts,' said Vince. 'From her to him. He's not interested. I know he isn't.'

'So why give her his number in the first place? Why encourage her?'

'She gave him her number because she wanted a job.'

'You expect me to believe that?'

'I was there, Anna. The worst thing Murphy is guilty of is being a flirt. He's vain. He's a man. We all like to think we're irresistible.'

'You don't behave like that. I know you don't.'

No, thought Vince. Because I'm in love with you and there is no other woman on the planet I'm remotely interested in. He sighed.

'I know it's wrong. But in the grand scheme of things, it's a minor misdemeanour. The punishment doesn't fit the crime, Anna. He's been stupid, yeah. But that's all.'

Anna shook her head. 'I'm sorry, Vince. I can't trust him. I keep wondering what else is going on behind my back? What aren't I giving him that makes him let that go on? That's no basis for a happy marriage.'

'I think you're overreacting,' said Vince. 'I understand that it's threatening, to find that kind of thing. But it doesn't mean anything. I promise you. Murphy's distraught.'

Anna's eyes filled with tears. 'I just don't feel the same way about him any more.'

Vince reached out and touched her hand. Her skin was velvet. He wanted to carry on, run the tips of his fingers up her arm, across her collarbone, but instead he squeezed her fingers in a gesture of reassurance.

'It'll take time,' he said. 'But it will be worth it. Look

at what you've got. What you've built together. And the girls. What about the girls?'

'You think I want them to have a dad around who lets women send him filthy texts?' The scorn in Anna's voice made Vince drop her hand. It was searing. He looked down at the floor. Maybe she was right? Maybe Murphy should have done something to stop it.

He walked over to the doors while Anna busied herself with the cafetière, the scent of freshly ground beans soon filling the air. More perfection. Even the garden was like something out of a magazine and contained the essence of Anna: a soft sweep of lawn, beds stuffed with scented roses and a huge oak tree with a curved wooden bench underneath. It was tranquil and feminine; an oasis. Vince could see the gardener's wheelbarrow perched at the side of one of the beds, filled with rich compost. He'd seen the gardener before, a hulking Mills & Boon of a bloke in khaki fatigues and big boots who turned up twice a week and did all the things that Vince would have done, had he been married to Anna, but that Murphy wouldn't do if you'd put a gun to his head.

Something suddenly struck Vince as odd. There'd been no sign of the gardener, although he was clearly around somewhere. His Hilux in the drive and the waiting wheelbarrow indicated that. But since Vince had arrived, he had not materialized. He frowned, and looked round the kitchen. It was then he noticed the two cups in the sink. Nothing wrong with that, he supposed. It was only polite to offer your gardener a coffee when he arrived. He imagined Anna discussing planting plans, looking through seed catalogues, showing him a picture of something she had seen in a magazine.

There were two plates, too, with knives and crumbs. Well, OK. Nothing wrong with offering him a piece of toast to fuel up the day ahead. But somehow the crockery seemed unspeakably intimate.

'Where's the gardener?' asked Vince. 'Don't want him getting the wrong idea.'

It was a joke. Sort of.

Anna looked at him, the kettle in her hands, about to pour.

The whole story was in her eyes. For one second. Like a subliminal advert in the middle of a film. Guilt and defiance and fear. Then the shutters came down and her gaze was wide with baby-blue innocence.

'He does his own thing. I've no idea. Probably gone to the garden centre for something he's forgotten.'

'His truck's still in the drive.'

Anna just wasn't a good enough actress under interrogation. She turned away.

The only way out of the garden was through the house.

The silence that fell was profound. It went on for five, ten seconds while each of them assessed the situation and decided what to say.

'He's upstairs, isn't he?' said Vince finally.

Anna's jagged breath in and out said it all.

'How long?'

She shrugged, but it was defiant. She looked, if anything, rather sulky. Like a stroppy sixth former who has been caught smoking.

'You were going to let Murphy hang for this.' Vince had never felt fury like it. Not for a person. For the sea, yes. But not for another person.

He grabbed her arm and pulled her round. Her face

was almost devoid of expression, a blank mask; her eyes stony.

'You don't believe there was anything wrong with those texts, do you?' he said. 'It was a very convenient way to ship Murphy out. To let him take the blame for the failure of your marriage.'

'No. No, of course not.'

'But why would you attack him for it, when you were doing worse? Unless you wanted it as an excuse.'

Again, the sulky sixth former look. Vince felt a strong urge to shake her. He remembered the last time he had seen her, and how gorgeous he had thought she looked. At the opening. The opening when the girl had taken Murphy's number.

And when Anna had gone back early because Lyra was poorly.

Another penny dropped.

'She wasn't ill at all that night of the opening, was she? Lyra? You got to Everdene and decided to hightail it back to your lover. You couldn't resist the pull of a free night with him.'

'Now you're being ridiculous. I would never use my children like that.'

But she wouldn't look him in the eye.

'I worshipped you,' said Vince, in wonder. 'I worshipped the bloody ground you walked on.'

'More fool you,' said Anna.

'This will kill him.'

She pressed her lips together. Her chin was trembling. But, Vince realized, there wasn't a hint of remorse. She looked angry. Angry that she had let herself be caught out.

'Are you going to tell him?' she asked.

'Yes,' said Vince. 'I am.'

'What about the girls?'

Vince didn't want to think about the girls. Yet they were the only ones that really mattered in this whole sorry mess. He looked away; looked at their matching spotty mackintoshes hanging on the peg by the back door.

Then he looked back at Anna.

'You should have thought about them before you started sleeping with the help.'

Anna gasped. 'What gives you the right to judge?'

'My friendship with Murphy.' Vince stared her out. 'Which goes back further than your marriage.'

Anna put her hands flat on the slate work surface to try and steady them. Her white gold wedding ring and matching solitaire engagement ring sparkled defiantly. The bracelets she'd been playing with at the opening night hung on her wrists. Vince imagined Murphy choosing them, having them wrapped; handing the box to her one Christmas morning.

'What can I do to persuade you not to tell him?' Her voice was low; there was a wheedling note to it that turned his stomach.

'I came here to plead Murphy's case,' said Vince. 'To beg you to have him back because I know that, despite his flaws and faults, he is a good man. A man who would never actually be unfaithful, despite what you might think. Though I think you know that. It's you with the morals of a snake.' He rubbed his chin. He could feel the stubble scrape his fingers. 'You better tell matey to come out of hiding. He's wasting valuable gardening time.'

Anna stood up. She wrapped her arms around herself and stalked to the bottom of the stairs.

'You can come down,' she called up. 'He knows you're here. So you might as well get on with what you've got to do.'

She stalked back into the kitchen and sat down, crossing her arms.

A moment later footsteps came down the stairs and the guy Vince had seen once or twice before walked through the kitchen and out of the door that led to the garden. There was a cocky carelessness to his gait that Vince didn't much like.

'Does he do this with all his clients, do you think?' he asked Anna, and got a filthy glare in return.

Suddenly she didn't seem so ethereal. She was hard. Her white-blonde hair had a flatness to it; her skin was not so pearlescent. And Vince felt sure he could smell fear on her; something rather sharp that was not to his liking. She tucked her hair back behind her ears, a gesture he had once found charming. Now, it indicated nervousness, and he found it irritating.

'I'm sorry,' she said, and now she seemed near tears. Vince suspected they weren't real; just her next ploy. 'It's just hard, you know, being here on my own while he gallivants about the place.'

Vince looked around the kitchen, with its gleaming surfaces, its sleek appliances. 'Not that hard,' he said.

Anna looked defiant. 'He likes getting attention, Murphy. But he's not very good at giving it.'

'Unlike your man out there?'

Silvery tears began trailing down her cheeks, like raindrops down a window.

'Please don't tell him.'

'What was your plan, Anna? To kick him out and take

him for everything? I suppose you thought you'd get the house? At what point were you going to move him in?' He jerked his head towards the garden.

'It's not like that!'

'Course not. It never is.' He stared at her. 'You're not the person I thought.'

Anna stared back. 'None of us is,' she whispered.

Vince sat down on a chrome stool and put his head in his hands for a moment. He wasn't sure what to think. Murphy was no angel, but he would be gutted if his family was torn apart. He was simply a born flirt, and while that wasn't necessarily right, Vince genuinely didn't think Murphy did any more than just that – Anna had hit the nail on the head when she said he needed attention. While Anna – Anna was clearly guilty of something more serious. Vince didn't know what the man in the garden meant to her, or what they had planned between them, if anything, but they hadn't been upstairs playing chess.

Finally, he looked up.

'Get rid of him,' he told her. 'Tell him to get out of your house and never come back.'

She nodded. 'OK.'

'Now.'

Anna shut her eyes for a moment, and took a deep breath, but there was no mistaking the authority in Vince's voice.

She walked out into the garden, over to the bed where her paramour was forking over the earth. Vince watched them talking, saw the bloke gesticulating, objecting; Anna pleading. How could he have got her so wrong? How could he have wasted all those years, worshipping her like a complete idiot?

He stood by the door as the gardener headed back to the house. He wanted to punch him for his swagger. For taking Murphy's money at the same time as shagging his wife. What kind of a bloke did that?

Vince stood up and put a hand on his chest as he passed him.

'Don't you dare touch her again.'

'Or what?' The bloke smirked. He was strong, but Vince knew he could take him on.

He smirked back. 'Or you'll be sleeping with the fishes.'

The bloke turned to Anna. 'I'll come back for my barrow.'

He managed to make it sound smutty. Anna didn't reply. Vince looked at him in distaste. He was the archetypal bit of rough on the surface, easy on the eye, but he was obviously a total dick. What did Anna see in him?

Moments later, the front door slammed and they heard the Hilux start up.

Anna ran her hands through her hair. She looked as if the air had been sucked out of her; drawn and deflated.

'So what now?' she asked.

Vince felt a sick sense of unease in his stomach. He wished fervently he had stayed in Everdene and let Murphy sort his own life out. He had uncovered something far more unsavoury than the initial problem. Which now, on analysis, hadn't really been a problem at all. Not compared to the scenario he was now dealing with. He felt so many things: revulsion for Anna, pity for his friend, shock. Regret that he had opened such an unsightly can of worms.

'I don't know,' he replied. He didn't want responsibility for what happened next. Why should he be the judge and pass sentence? 'I guess you tell Murphy that everything's

OK. That you forgive him.' He couldn't help a cynical laugh.

She shot him a look.

'You're not going to tell him?'

What would his friend want him to do? Vince tried to imagine. Would he want the truth, or would he want a lie? He thought, very probably, that for all Murphy's bravado and ebullience, the truth would kill him. To know that his wife had been cuckolding him with the gardener?

'I can't tell him,' he told Anna. 'I just can't. And your marriage is your responsibility. You'll have to find a way to get through this yourself. It's going to need work.'

Anna shuddered. 'Ugh. Counselling? Such a middle-class cliché.'

'Almost as clichéd as shagging the gardener.'

She sagged, sitting down hard on one of the bar stools.

'Are you going to hold it over me for the rest of my life?' She gave him a sour look.

Vince wondered how he could ever have thought her beautiful. 'You say that like I forced you into it.'

She put her face in her hands. 'Oh God.' She looked up. 'I'm going to have to tell him. Otherwise we'll be living a lie.'

Vince didn't answer for a while, as he turned the dilemma over in his mind.

'Maybe it's better to live a lie?' he said finally. 'I guess it's called damage limitation. I don't know that Murphy would be able to handle it. I really don't. But I suppose it depends how you feel in your heart. Whether you're prepared to put the work in, work out what was missing and why you did it. And do something about it.' He gave a wry grin. 'I sound like some self-help manual. I don't know, Anna, to be honest. It's a mess, I know that.'

She chewed on the edge of her thumbnail. 'I still love him. I know that.'

'And matey? Do you love him?' Vince nodded to the barrow outside.

Anna scoffed. 'No. No of course I don't. That was about … sex. Sex and attention and … danger?' She laughed, but it was mirthless.

Vince stood up. 'I'm going to go. I'm going to leave you to decide what you do. I'll just say we talked, and I managed to convince you there was nothing to those texts.' He looked at her. 'Because there wasn't. You know that, don't you?'

Anna shrugged. 'It's still not right.'

'But it doesn't give you an excuse to do what you did. Two wrongs don't make a right.'

'I'll call him. When you leave, I'll call him. Get him to come home. We can talk it all through.' She stepped towards him and held out her arms. 'Can I talk to you? If I need to?'

Vince held her, but reluctantly. All those times he had longed to pull her to him, and now he felt awkward. He couldn't wait to let her go.

'Course. Call me whenever you like.'

'Thanks. And I'm sorry …'

'Don't apologize to me.'

'No, I mean I'm sorry you've been dragged into it. It must be difficult for you.'

'Hey. What are friends for?' He supposed he was her friend too. He picked up his keys and walked out of the kitchen. She didn't follow him to the front door, and he was grateful. He couldn't get away fast enough.

In the car on the way home, Vince felt strange. A mix of emotions and questions whirled round. Had he done the right thing? Should he have let Anna get away with it? Should he have told Murphy? Did he really trust her not to cheat on Murphy again? Was her affair a one-off, borne out of a need for attention she wasn't getting, or were the reasons for it darker? And did Murphy's behaviour have some bearing on that?

It wasn't his place to play God, Vince decided. Murphy and Anna would have to sort out their marriage for themselves. He would always be there for his mate. And he would give Anna the benefit of the doubt, for the sake of the children if nothing else. He didn't have the right to be judgmental and tear the family apart. Not really.

Once he came to terms with making the right decision, a huge sense of relief settled on him. Because, he realized, there had been a significant side effect to all of this: the part of his mind that had always been occupied by Anna was free. He no longer worshipped or longed for her. When he thought of her now, he felt a mild distaste. Not the agonizing torment of unrequited love. It was almost as if a curse had been lifted. He could live his life like a normal person now.

He felt slightly elated. He turned up the radio and put his foot down, letting the car eat up the miles. He couldn't wait to get back, sit on the step of the beach hut with a beer, watch the sun go down into the sea knowing that the next day he would wake up with optimism.

As he came back down the hill into Everdene, suddenly the sea looked bluer and the sun looked shinier.

Everything sparkled. He stopped the car for a moment and looked down at the bay. Suddenly, he realized he could now make decisions on behalf of himself. Everything was to play for. He was no longer tied down by his obsession. He was free.

ANGE

Every year, when the day dawned, Ange woke with a horrible stone of dread in the pit of her stomach. She had to go, and she wouldn't dream of not. It was more than Dave's job was worth to miss it. It was a tradition, the Annual Partners' Picnic (their capitals, not hers). They got a proper posh invitation, the kind you were supposed to put on the mantelpiece, but they didn't have one so she stuck theirs on the fridge with a Homer Simpson magnet. Crowfield and Sons hired a beach hut for the day on Everdene Sands, and organized a minibus to take everyone. It was a posh minibus, with leather seats, and it meant everyone could have a drink. When they got there, the men played cricket on the beach while the wives ... Well, the wives sat and gossiped and drank champagne.

Ange found it torture. She really did. She'd far rather be playing cricket with the blokes, but that wasn't done. Oh no. For a start, the wives had to dress up. For a picnic on the beach! The others would all be immaculate in their tiny linen frocks, their make-up perfect and their hair blow-dried to within an inch of their life. Dave had offered to buy her something new if she wanted it, but she didn't. She wasn't bothered about wearing the same dress that she'd worn the year before. She only had one, because she didn't really do dresses – she was a leggings and baggy T-shirt girl. It was all she could do not to rebel and stick on her leggings that morning, but she couldn't let Dave down, so she pulled the dress out of the wardrobe and put it on. Annoyingly, it showed up the burn marks from the afternoon she'd spent in the garden the weekend before, when she'd forgotten to put sun cream on, but she didn't care. Just because the others all had perfect spray tans, didn't mean she had to have one.

The problem was, Ange wasn't Crowfield's idea of a partner's wife. Any more than Dave was their idea of a partner, but they'd had to make him one because he was such a tour de force in the sales department. He had the patter, and he could talk the talk anywhere. Since he'd been in charge, sales of ball bearings had quadrupled, and nobody knew quite how he did it.

Ange knew how. It was because he was a grafter. It was because he did his homework on people, and what they needed, and worked out the best way to woo them. She'd watched him on his laptop late into the night, crunching numbers, working out how to do deals. Caring. Nobody else at Crowfield cared as much as Dave did. They were all too busy choosing their next Range Rovers or booking skiing holidays.

Ange knew she didn't fit in. She didn't do ladies' lunches, or play golf, or have Botox. She was a manageress at the bingo hall. She didn't do it for the money, because Dave brought in a good whack; enough for both of them. She did it because she loved it, and the other wives just didn't get why you would work if you didn't have to. She was only part-time, but she really looked forward to it. She'd go mad if she woke up every morning and didn't know what to do with herself, like them. They were obviously bored out of their brains – you could see it in their eyes – but they'd never admit it.

They obviously thought Ange was a bit common. Well, maybe she was, but at least she knew how to have a good time. That was why Dave loved her. She didn't walk around as if she had a bad smell under her nose. And she liked a laugh, which they didn't, by the look of them. Oh, and she was overweight, which was probably the biggest crime in their book. In Ange's view, they all looked as if they could do with a good meal. They picked at their food, and they all had personal trainers, and went running, and did yoga classes. Torture, if you asked Ange. She liked her grub and she wasn't ashamed to admit it.

Which was why she had been appointed catering monitor at the picnic. She'd done it for the past six years. The other wives all brought hampers, great big wicker things with leather handles, filled with bone china and cut glass to serve the food on. You didn't need proper plates and glasses on a picnic, for heaven's sake. You only had to wash them when you got back. What was the point?

This year, though, she'd decided to do things differently.

When they arrived at the beach hut, Ange was already red-faced and perspiring from the walk. The others were all as cool as cucumbers in their huge black sunglasses. They spread out their tartan picnic rugs and unfolded their deckchairs, then took off their dresses to reveal miniature bikinis, mostly black with big silver buckles. Ange felt awkward, as ever, not sure where to sit or indeed, even how. They all managed to sprawl elegantly. She looked as if she had collapsed in a sweaty heap.

She looked around. The scene looked like an advert – the shabby chic beach hut with the bunting hanging over the front, and half a dozen beautiful women lounging in front of it. Only Ange was out of place; the fly in the ointment. The one the photographer would be waving out of the picture.

She dug her bare toes into the sand, enjoying the feeling of the grains running over her skin. She wished she'd taken time for a pedicure. The others all had immaculate toes, cherry red or dark plum. Yet another fail, she thought. But really, when you thought about it, what was the actual point of painting your toenails?

It was funny, because Dave didn't feel out of place with the other partners in the same way she did. It must be a bloke thing, she decided. They just got on with it; mucked in. She could see them all, engrossed in their game – competitive yes, but in a healthy way. They didn't bully each other, getting one up with their clothes and their thinness and their jewellery. Sometimes she thought she didn't like women very much. There was always some low-lying sense of competition to throw you off kilter.

And it was all too easy to find yourself sucked into the game. She knew she was playing it today by what she had done. But she couldn't bear another year of it. She had to make a statement by getting one up. Did that make her as bad as them? She didn't think so. She wasn't doing it because she felt better than them. She was doing it to feel better about herself.

'New dress?' The MD's wife Rosa looked at her over the top of her Chanel shades.

Why did she even ask when it was obvious it wasn't?

'No,' replied Ange. 'No point, really, when I only wear one once a year. I'm not a dress person.'

Rosa said nothing. She didn't need to. She tried another topic of conversation. At least she was having a go at being polite.

'Have you been away this summer?'

'No,' said Ange. 'I'm not a hot weather person or an abroad person either. Happy pottering about at home, really.'

Dave had offered for her to go wherever she liked. She looked on the Internet but couldn't begin to imagine herself in any of the destinations. They were quite happy firing up the barbecue for themselves and a few friends over the summer, and having the occasional day trip. What was wrong with liking home?

'God, I'd die if I didn't get away. We went to Dubai. The children's club is amaaaazing – didn't see them from dawn till dusk. I just lay on my sun lounger all day, reading, and the waiters bring you whatever you want to drink.' Rosa put a beringed hand up and clicked her fingers to indicate that was all she needed to do to summon the attention of the staff. Her diamonds twinkled in the sunlight.

'Very nice, I'm sure,' said Ange, who couldn't see the point of having children if you were going to bung them in a club all day. She felt bad enough that her two had to go to her mate's today for the picnic.

By one-thirty the sun was still high in the sky, and Ange arranged one of the parasols over a table so they could keep the food in the shade. She could see the other women exchange knowing glances when she took the lid off her cool box. Little smirks, as if to say: 'Here come the pork pies'. She was going to wipe the smile off their faces today.

She spread out a pretty checked tablecloth and began to produce her wares, like a magician pulling rabbits out of a hat.

First, there was a flask of cool, creamy watercress soup, which she poured into little shot glasses and popped on a tray: into each glass she put a tiny slug of truffle oil. Then she laid out a rough game terrine, wrapped in bacon, and a basket of poppy-seed rolls, followed by tomato tartlets criss-crossed with anchovies and scallops on a minted pea puree and chicken coated in breadcrumbs and garlic and parmesan. Then she piled the sweets onto a cake stand she'd brought with her. Macaroons in pastel colours – pale green with pistachio cream, pale pink with rose cream. Strawberry shortcakes, raspberry tartlets, lemon cheesecakes ...

'Where did you get all this?' asked Rosa, in a strangled voice.

'I made it,' Ange replied carelessly. 'I seem to have so much time on my hands now the kids are both at school.'

Rosa and the others gawped at her, then exchanged glances, not sure whether to challenge her. Ange could see they didn't believe her. They thought she'd bought it all in from some smart caterer and put it in her own dishes to make it look as if it was homemade.

Rosa pointed at the macaroons.

'Surely not those?'

'Yes,' Ange nodded. 'Terribly fiddly. And, of course, you have to remember to separate the egg whites two days in advance. It helps give them volume,' she explained airily, picking up her shot glass and hiding her smile behind it.

They were all staring at her food. She could see they were starving. They were practically drooling.

'Go on,' she said. 'Don't let it spoil. One day won't hurt. You can run it off on the beach later.'

They didn't need any second telling. Ange watched in satisfaction as they snatched up delicacy after delicacy, cramming their mouths full and nodding in approval. She passed them a plate of baby chocolate éclairs, the chocolate glaze gleaming.

'Eat them, before they melt,' she urged. They stretched their hands out greedily.

It had taken her a whole year to reach this standard. A year of evening classes at the local college, faffing about with piping bags and bain-maries and sugar thermometers. She could now make choux pastry and béarnaise sauce and fancy fondant potatoes. Of course, she'd had loads of disasters along the way, but she wanted to prove, just for once, that she could do something that would surprise them. That she wasn't just a bingo manageress, to be laughed at. And she could tell she'd impressed them. They were united in their admiration. She felt a glow inside, which was infinitely preferable to the sense of inadequacy she usually had amongst them.

Eventually, the men arrived, hot from their cricket, and hurled themselves down on the rug expectantly. But as they started to look at the food on display, they looked disappointed, somehow.

'Where's the pork pie?' asked Martin, the finance director.

'And the scotch eggs?' demanded Phil, the lawyer.

'And the cold sausages?' finished Ron, the MD. 'A picnic's not a picnic without cold sausages.'

The men all looked at Ange. There was disappointment and confusion etched on all their faces. She laughed, and got up to fetch her second cooler.

'I brought some extra, just in case,' she told them. 'I know how you lot work up an appetite.'

And she started to unload the real food. They all groaned with delight as she chucked them each a packet of cheese and onion crisps to be getting on with.

'Good old Ange!' proclaimed Ron, as Rosa gave him one of her death stares. 'We can always rely on Ange to provide a good spread.'

Ange rewarded him with an old ice-cream tub stuffed with cold bangers.

'I've got a jar of piccalilli if you want to dunk them,' she offered. She could see each of the wives shudder inwardly.

As the sun began to drift downwards, and people began to doze off, soporific and contented, Dave came and lay down beside Ange on the rug.

'Crowfield's just told me I'm in line for vice president,' he whispered.

Ange looked at him. They knew the job was going to be vacant soon, but neither of them had ever dreamed Dave might be in the running.

'How?' she asked.

He shrugged. 'He says I'm a maverick. But I've got the right values. He says it's mine, bar the formalities.'

'Oh.' Ange thought about the news. Of course Dave had the right values. That was why she'd married him. Vice president? She wanted to laugh with glee, but she didn't want to draw attention. What on earth would the other wives say? They'd all be spitting. It was the job they all wanted for their husbands.

She smiled to herself. Fourteen, they'd been when they met. In the youth club in the village hall. They'd never looked back. Never had eyes for anyone but each other, and they were as happy now as they were then.

'I love you,' she said, as quietly as she could. 'And I'm so proud.'

Dave winked at her as he crammed in a piece of pork pie.

Ange wanted to reach over and give him a great big smacker on the cheek, but she didn't think public displays of affection would go down well. That wasn't the role she was playing today.

Today, she was the perfect partner's wife.

The vice president's wife. Maybe.

TIM

Tim didn't tell anyone that his party was basically a farewell party.

As long as he didn't tell anyone, he didn't have to admit it to himself.

As the day dawned, he thought that Everdene was taunting him. Reminding him what he was giving up. Never had it looked more beautiful; the sands pristine, the sky and sea a matching pale turquoise; the occasional puff of cloud dotted overhead to soften the vista; their Daz whiteness matching the lacy surf at the water's edge.

He didn't regret what he was doing, though. He knew it was the right thing. And, he reasoned, he had the rest of the world to explore. He had the freedom and the financial wherewithal to go wherever he pleased, whereas Rachel wouldn't. He felt happy knowing that she would have the beach hut as a refuge and an escape whenever she wanted it.

And if his generosity had come about through guilt, what of it? Was there such a thing as true altruism, he wondered? And actually, he would never stop feeling guilty, no matter how much he tried to atone. Even if what he was guilty of wasn't even his fault.

Yes, he would miss Everdene, but it was time for a new

chapter, time to move on from the regret he would never be allowed to forget as long as he remained here. And who knew what tonight would bring?

The girl from the deli was called Lorraine. Tim remembered her name as soon as he got her email saying she would love to come to the party.

'Can I crash?' she'd asked, and he'd taken that as a good sign, her wanting to stay over. There had definitely been a connection between them as they bantered over the counter. She had something about her. He admired her entrepreneurial spirit, her work ethic and her knowledge of food. As he finished his morning coffee, made from the beans she had roasted and ground for him last time he'd been in, he allowed himself a flicker of excitement. Anticipation was a pleasure in itself, he thought. The allure of the unknown.

The party had turned from a bunch of mates, a pound of sausages and a disposable barbecue into something much more elaborate. He seemed to have asked pretty much everyone on Everdene Sands, because that's the sort of place it was – parties went viral. And it was obvious if you left anyone out: in for a penny, in for a pound, he thought. Although everyone would bring a bottle and muck in.

He spent the day stringing up bunting; pegging out a dance floor with flares stuck into the sand; setting up his sound system and fine-tuning the Spotify playlists on his Mac: seventies' funk, nineties' rave, some chill-out tunes for the small hours, when the full moon would hang over the bay and lull everyone to sleep.

He filled several plastic tubs with sea water. Come

evening they would be packed with ice and cans of Red Stripe and pear cider and bottles of Prosecco.

As soon as he realized that the guest list was getting out of hand, he'd decided to delegate the catering. He didn't want to spend the evening hovering over a barbecue poking sausages. So he was getting The Lobster Shack to come in and do the food. They were bringing industrial catering burners and cooking up huge pans full of seafood paella: golden yellow rice studded with peppers and chicken and giant prawns and mussels.

Then Jenna was bringing down her ice-cream van at midnight, when everyone would be ready for something sweet to keep them going

Tim was pleased to be using the locals to make his final fling perfect.

After all, Everdene had been good to him. He'd had some of the best times in his life here.

He wasn't going to think about the worst.

By six o'clock that evening, everything was in place. He had an hour to wait for everyone to arrive. He showered, stuck on his favourite O'Neill shirt and a pair of khaki shorts. He was just pulling the tab on his first can of Red Stripe when there was a tap on the door.

It was Lorraine. She was as cute as he remembered, her copper bob set off by a turquoise shift dress.

'I'm sorry I'm early,' she said, 'but I thought I'd struggle to find it.'

He stepped back to let her in. 'No worries,' he said. 'Come in. Let me get you a drink.'

Freckles. She had hundreds of freckles. And smiling hazel eyes.

'Oh my God, this is just gorgeous,' she said, looking

round the hut, and he didn't tell her this was his last weekend here. It didn't seem to matter.

Two hours later, the party was in full swing. Kid Creole and the Coconuts were blaring out across the evening air. Most of the day trippers had left, leaving the sands clear for the guests to spill out up to the water's edge – the tide was in as far as it would come. As the sun glided gently towards, the silver sea turned to gold.

Vince stood on the edge of the crowds, wondering why he felt so out of place. He thought he was probably in line for the prize of miserable bastard of the year. He should be happy, after all. Everything in his life was falling into place.

His biggest worry, which had been his brother, now wasn't a worry at all. On the contrary. Chris had totally turned the corner. He was even badgering Vince about them getting another boat and expanding even more. His new girlfriend, Chloe, seemed to have kindled some kind of ambition in him. She was still working at The Lobster Shack, which Vince was pleased about, because she was their best waitress, and she'd promised to stay on until the end of the season. The restaurant was a massive success. It was all down to Murphy, thought Vince. It had been him with the vision.

Murphy. He seemed to have come through the recent events unscathed. In fact, if anything, he and Anna seemed closer than ever. They were here tonight. She'd left the girls with her mother. Of course he was pleased for his friend. Of course he was glad it was working out. But something felt sour. He still wondered if he should have told Murphy the truth.

He drank from his can of Red Stripe. He felt maudlin. Maybe he'd finish his drink and go home. He was about to toss the empty can in the bin and make his escape when he felt a hand on his arm.

It was Anna. Looking as if butter wouldn't melt in a white tunic with silver embroidery, a wide leather belt at her waist; endless legs and silver flip-flops. She looked angelic. Only Vince knew the truth.

'I just want to say thank you,' she said to him. 'Thank you so much. You made me see sense. You made me realize what it was I had to lose.'

He looked at her in distaste. He would never be able to trust her. What would she have done, if he hadn't intervened? Would she have run off with her gardener, leaving Murphy to blame himself? Maybe he should have let her?

'Don't think badly of me,' she pleaded.

'Anna,' he said, with brutal honesty. 'I don't think anything of you.'

He might as well have slapped her.

She breathed in, as if to calm herself.

'Please dance with me,' she said. 'I don't want to lose you as a friend.'

'I can't,' said Vince. 'I'm sorry.'

He was damned if he was going to give her absolution. That way she would have got away with everything.

'You're right,' she said, as if she could read his thoughts. 'I don't deserve you.'

Vince shrugged. Maybe one day he'd feel differently, but right now he didn't want to be anywhere near her.

He watched her walk away, into the crowds, to go and find Murphy, who was holding court, looking ridiculously Don Johnson in an unstructured linen suit and mirrored

Ray-Bans. She grabbed his hand and led him towards the dance area which was now lit by flares. She pulled him towards her, her unsuspecting husband, and began to dance.

Vince could see that for Murphy, there was no one else at the party. He was entranced by his wife, gracious and elegant and slinky. She was mesmerizing.

Vince didn't want to look at them a minute longer.

He turned, and walked straight into Kiki.

'Hey,' she said, holding out her arms. She was so open. So full of joy. So absolutely the antithesis of what he was feeling. 'Do you want to dance?'

'Sorry,' he mumbled, and dodged out of her way. He just wanted to be on his own.

Chloe walked with Chris down to the water's edge. The tide had turned, and the sea was nudging its way back out. They stood in the shallows, letting the water swirl around their ankles.

She knew this was probably hard for him. A party, where everyone was drinking hard and losing their inhibitions. She stuck to water too, in solidarity, even though he told her he didn't mind if she drank. But she found she didn't need alcohol. She felt so happy and relaxed with him. She'd slotted seamlessly into seaside life, which surprised her: her life had been so urban until now, apart from the occasional holiday. Although she was rushed off her feet during her shifts at The Lobster Shack, she adored the way of life.

'I've been thinking,' she said.

'Oh, you don't want to do too much of that,' said Chris, turning and stroking her hair.

She smiled, and nestled into him. 'I might sell my flat,' she said. 'And move down here. Permanently.'

He held her at arm's length and looked at her. 'Are you serious?'

She nodded. 'I've been doing some research. Looking at all the local businesses. I think there might be scope for me to set up my own agency. PR and advertising and web content. Specializing in seaside businesses. I've even got a name. SeaPR.' She laughed at her own play on words.

'Well,' said Chris. 'Maskells could be your first clients.'

'I'd give you a discount.'

He kissed her on the nose. 'Mate's rates.'

'Something like that.' She kissed him back. 'I can carry on waitressing, for the time being. It looks as if the restaurant's enough of a success to carry on through the winter. Then if the agency gets big enough, if I get enough clients ...'

'Are you sure you wouldn't get bored? It's pretty deadly down here out of season. There's nothing much to do.'

Chloe pulled him to her. 'I can think of plenty of things to do,' she whispered.

Jenna drove the ice-cream van carefully across the sands and pulled up in front of Tim's hut. She never failed to enjoy this moment, when people's heads turned and they saw her and their faces lit up with joy. No matter what age, the prospect of ice cream from a van seemed to strike a chord with everyone.

She was so lucky, she thought, although as Craig had pointed out to her, she'd made her own luck, by having the idea and being determined and putting in the graft. Although, to be fair, it was Weasel who'd had the inspiration

– weasel he might be, but she couldn't take that away from him.

The weather over the summer had helped, of course – day after day of glorious sunshine. She had got to the point where she couldn't scoop fast enough, and the farmer who supplied her couldn't make the ice cream fast enough.

As she stopped the van, and slid open her window, and waited for the first of the guests to crowd round and make their choice, she looked out at the beach, the beach where she had first met Craig. That meeting could have taken another turn entirely, she thought, as she remembered the dark place she had been in, and the wrong choices she had made.

Until he had stepped in and come to her rescue. Thank God he had seen the good in her, she thought. If he hadn't, if he'd decided to do his duty and turn her in, she wouldn't be here now. She could see him, through the crowds, sipping his beer, chatting easily. Her hero. Her saviour.

She smiled, slid back the lid of the freezer, revealing a rainbow of ice cream flavours, and began to scoop.

Kiki didn't take Vince's rejection personally. If being in prison taught you anything, it was not to judge anyone. She went back over to the bar to get herself another drink. It was good to let her hair down. She spent most days on show to the general public so she was going to make the most of her chance to relax. Being artist-in-residence was a dream come true, but it was hard work: her beach hut had basically been open to all and sundry throughout the summer, while they watched her paint. But she had an amazing body of work to show for it, and was looking forward to putting together an exhibition when her residency came to an end.

She was pouring herself a glass of wine when one of the other guests came up to her. She recognized him as the boyfriend of the girl with the ice-cream van. He was a copper, but she didn't hold that against him. Just because she'd been inside didn't mean she had an irrational hatred of the law.

'I want to ask you a favour,' he said.

'Sure,' she said. He probably wanted a portrait painting.

'I've got this mad, crazy idea,' he said. 'But I don't think I'm up to the job. I thought you might be able to help.'

'If I can. I like a challenge.'

'It will mean getting up really early in the morning.' He looked at her full glass. 'Tomorrow.'

Kiki was intrigued. 'OK,' she said. 'I'll make this my last drink, in that case. But only if you fill me in.'

Craig looked embarrassed. 'You're going to think I'm mad.'

'Mate, you forget. I've done time. Nothing surprises me. Go on, tell me.'

Vince was skulking about on the edges of the party, watching Kiki talk to Craig. He felt self-conscious, even though no one could have any idea what he was thinking or planning, but he felt as if his intentions were obvious. Although, to be truthful, everyone was probably oblivious by now, judging by the empty bottles.

He didn't know how to go about approaching her. If he hadn't been such an ungracious and curmudgeonly bastard, it wouldn't matter so much. Turning on the charm now was asking for a slap in the face. And he wouldn't blame her. She had done her very best to be nice to him and he'd cut her dead.

He'd been a rotten neighbour, too. He'd watched her painting earlier, peering over the windbreak. She'd taken to putting one up every day now, whether there was a breeze or not, and it was hardly surprising. She wouldn't want a miserable bugger like him gawping at her while she worked. It was the equivalent of a cold shoulder.

She'd had a large canvas on an easel, and a palette of a very few colours – blue, red and black. Thick, treacly paint that she dipped into with a fat brush, daubing the strokes seemingly at random. He'd wondered about her thought process, or if there even was one, as the brush danced over the canvas, too quickly for him to keep up. Was there any logic to it, or was she just doing what something inside her commanded? It seemed entirely abstract to him. He thought he could probably do it himself, slosh a load of paint all over the place like that.

But gradually, as he watched, something definite began to emerge. It was crude, naive even. A lagoon, an island, and seagulls – big, fat beady-eyed seagulls, each one consisting of barely more than half a dozen lines, but so emphatic in their seagullness that Vince realized he had been watching a real talent at work. The scene was impressionistic, but so vivid you could almost smell it.

He'd watched her back as she worked, her thin shoulder blades, her wiry arms, the tiny wrists. Her hair was piled up, as usual, in a brightly coloured scarf, the honey-coloured strands spilling out over the top. She was wearing a tiny turquoise sundress covered in flamingoes.

A digital radio spilled out Northern soul and her brush seemed to dance in time with the music.

She was an inspiration, a ray of light, and he'd been a fool not to see it.

It was now or never. If he didn't ask her today, his life would never change. He would be stuck as miserable Vince, alone and loveless. He needed to put his Murphy hat on; get some confidence.

'Man up,' he told himself. 'What's the worst that can happen? She can say no, and that would be no more than you deserved. So the only way is up.'

He waited until Kiki finished her conversation with Craig. He tousled his hair a bit, tucked his T-shirt into his jeans then pulled it out again, stuck his hands in pockets. Then he grabbed his wallet and walked to Jenna's ice-cream van – she was still serving, even this late on in the evening

She looked delighted to see him.

'Hey, Vince. What can I get you?'

'Two 99s. With flakes.'

'Two?' She gave him a cheeky grin as she picked up two cones and started to fill them. Vince just kicked the sand with his shoe and didn't reply, but he was smiling. As she handed the ice creams over, he went to give her the money but she waved it away.

'It's on me, darling. Good luck.'

Jenna'd had a good summer, Vince knew. If there was any lesson to be learned from Jenna, it was that although you couldn't control everything that happened in life, you were in charge of your own destiny to a certain point. The decisions you made and the risks you took shaped what happened just as much as fate.

The realization made him resolute. He had to take control of his life.

With an ice cream in each hand, he walked over to Kiki, who was sitting on a bean bag, drinking a glass of wine.

She looked up as he approached. She was singing along to the music. He was struck by how incredibly happy she looked. How did people do that, make themselves so happy? He held out an ice cream without speaking, and she put down her glass and took it from him.

'You're a mind reader,' she told him.

'Years of practice,' he told her. 'Me and Derren Brown ...'

He crossed his fingers to indicate how close they were.

She laughed, and he felt pleased. It gave him courage.

'Listen,' he said. 'Do you fancy a trip out to Lundy?' He pointed out to sea. The island was obscured by darkness, but the moon hovered over where it should be, as if pointing it out.

'I'd love to!' She nodded enthusiastically. 'I've looked at it every day since I've been here, wondering what it's like.'

'Well, there's not much there. A few sheep. But it's pretty special. I can take you over there in the boat tomorrow. If you like.'

She looked pleased.

'That would be amazing.'

'It's going to be good weather, so we could make a day of it.'

'Wow. Cool.'

She was smiling at him but she looked a bit puzzled, as if wondering what had brought about his transformation.

'Listen, I've been an arse,' he said. 'Long story.'

'Hey, we all have stuff that makes us behave badly. No worries.'

He didn't think he needed to go into detail. Not at the moment. She didn't seem the type to bear grudges or need an explanation. There would be plenty of time for him to divulge his anxieties, if they ever got that far.

'Be ready at nine,' he told her. 'Bring your swimming stuff. And your painting stuff. And something warm for the journey back, in case the temperature drops.'

'Sorted.' She beamed at him, her eyes sparkling with mischief.

Vince thought he'd better get there early and tidy the boat up a bit. Something told him she wouldn't care much; that she'd enjoy the experience for what it was, but nevertheless the boat really wasn't in an ideal state for a romantic encounter. He'd better stick some cushions around the place at least.

'It's a date, then,' he said, and she nodded at him, and he felt a little glow inside. All those years wasted on Anna, he thought. All the fun he'd missed. Still, Vince decided, he was going to make up for lost time.

At two in the morning, Tim watched the last of his guests sway back down the beach towards the slipway.

The last of his guests but one, that is.

Lorraine was in the crook of his arm. They were both sitting on the front step as the last of the candles sank down into the bottom of the jam jars he'd wedged in the sand in front of the hut. There was little sign that there'd been a party at all; only the tin foil palm trees he'd stuck to the front of the hut rustling in the evening breeze.

He supposed it was time. Until he slept with another

woman, he wouldn't be able to forget. And he liked Lorraine. He really did. She was bright, funny, interesting. They had lots in common. He liked her copper hair and her pale skin and her freckles. It was clear she liked him, by the way she was running her hand up and down his back. Her intentions were clear.

The only thing wrong with her was that she wasn't Rachel.

But every girl he ever met wasn't going to be Rachel.

'Hey.'

He turned to her, realizing he was being rude, drifting off in his reverie.

She put a hand up his face, stroked his cheek, then pulled his face towards her. His mouth met hers. She tasted sweet, of pineapple and honey. Not like Rachel at all.

Not like Rachel, but delicious. He could do this. Of course he could.

Jenna woke up horribly early the morning after Tim's party. She wasn't sure why. She usually slept in after a party: nothing would wake her, but she thought something had been tickling her face. Now she was awake, she couldn't see anything. She sat up. Craig was nowhere to be seen either, which was odd. She peered at her phone to see what the time was. Barely after seven. All she wanted to do was burrow back under the covers, but she wanted to know where Craig was. Perhaps he had gone for an early morning surf? He hadn't said he was going to. And his wetsuit was still hanging up.

She pushed open the door, letting the early-morning breeze envelop her. She breathed it in. It always smelled of newness, and hope. The sun was only just over the horizon, but she could feel its warmth. Another good day for selling ice creams. Part of her wished she could have the day off, but she knew the deal down here. Make hay while the sun shines. There would be plenty of time off come winter.

She stepped out onto the sand, looking round for Craig. He was nowhere to be seen. She scanned the beach, then frowned.

'Oh my God.' What she saw made her stop in her tracks. Was she still dreaming? Or had she drunk more than she thought the night before?

For there, on the beach, was a picture. A picture drawn on the sand, and decorated with shells. A full-size picture of an ice-cream van. Her ice-cream van. And underneath, written in white pebbles, two words.

This was a joke. Some wags from the night before had obviously thought it would be a hilarious prank. Jenna frowned. Who would be that mean? It must have been someone who knew her. They were probably hiding somewhere, waiting for her reaction. Who would do such a thing? She'd rub it out before someone saw it and took the mickey. No, they were probably waiting for her to do that. She would pretend she hadn't noticed it.

She bit her thumb and turned back to the hut. Idiots. Drink did that to people.

Then she saw Craig, standing in the doorway. She couldn't read the expression on his face.

'They're just idiots,' she said. 'They must have been drunk.'

'Hey?'

She pointed. 'Whoever did that. It's cruel, really. To get a girl's hopes up like that. Luckily I'm not that stupid.'

'Stupid?'

'I'm not going to fall for that, am I?'

'Jenna ...' Craig was looking at her. 'Don't you realize who did it?'

She shrugged. She felt embarrassed. She wondered if he thought she'd thought it was real. She hoped not.

'Jen. It was me. Well, me and Kiki. I can't draw something like that. We got up this morning. At the crack of dawn ...'

Jenna looked at Craig.

She looked at the picture.

She looked at the words again.

Marry Me.

'Are you ... ? Do you mean ...? Is it ... a proposal?'

Craig burst out laughing. 'Yeah. I didn't want to do something ordinary. Because you're not ordinary. Because you're ... amazing, and I really admire you for what you've done this summer. And because I want you to be my wife, and to get a house with you, and maybe start a family ...'

Jenna's mouth fell open. 'You're totally kidding.'

'That first day I saw you on the beach, I knew you were special.'

'That first day you saw me nicking stuff?' She started to laugh.

'I knew I could save you from yourself.' He was laughing too.

Jenna looked again at the picture. It was perfect. There was even a little her in the window; a smiley face and a spotty dress.

'The sea's going to wash it away,' she wailed. 'I need to take a picture.'

'We've taken loads of pictures,' Craig told her.

'It's beautiful.'

'Jenna.'

His voice had a note of desperation in it. She turned to look at him.

'What's your answer?'

She didn't reply for a moment. Just stared into his eyes. Then turned and ran down the beach.

For an awful moment, Craig thought she was going to stamp all over it. Then he watched as she took her finger and started drawing in the sand underneath. And, gradually, as the words emerged, he began to smile.

YES YES YES they read.

ELODIE

*E*lodie was standing on the terrace of *The Grey House,* *looking* out over the sea that looked reassuringly the same as it always had, for although it was constantly on the move, it came always back again. Was that why people loved the sea, for its reassurance? She never felt the same anywhere else, that was certain.

She looked at her watch. She'd made the appointment for two o'clock. She felt nervous of what she might find, and what reception she would get. And the possible consequences. And then she realized that the only consequences could be good ones. That nothing could destroy the love she and Colm had for each other.

The home her mother had moved to was on the outskirts of a small town near Everdene – a conversion of a large Victorian house that would once have been a home, then probably a hotel. It was high-end and luxurious, and tried to look as much like a private house as possible, with just a discreet sign that Elodie nearly missed, but even the most skilful interior designer couldn't mask the fact this was an institution.

Her mother's room was large, facing the sea – no doubt she was paying a premium for the privilege – but the blinds were down, leaving it in a crepuscular gloom.

'She doesn't like the light,' whispered the assistant, who was dressed in the house uniform of navy blue high-collared tunic and trousers, designed to look as little like a uniform as possible while being practical. 'It hurts her eyes.'

Elodie could see Lillie, sitting in a large wing-backed chair she recognized from *The Grey House*. She could pick out other familiar artefacts too, as if Lillie had tried as hard as she could to recreate her home in this room: paintings and china and pieces of furniture that had been part of their lives for so many years, but it didn't quite work. Like a sensitive shrub, the atmosphere couldn't be transplanted.

Elodie felt a wave of something, she wasn't sure what, settle on her shoulders. This place was so far away from everything Lillie represented, despite the superficial luxury. She realized the feeling was guilt – a sense of filial guilt.

How, after everything that her mother had done to her, could that feeling suddenly be so strong? Was it because she herself was staring old age in the face – it was only round the corner – and she was looking at what she feared? Being alone in a place she didn't want to be, with no one to care about her?

'Hello? Who is that?' The voice was unmistakably her mother's. The accent as strong as ever. The assertive tone.

Elodie walked towards her chair. She didn't quite know how to announce herself, or how to address her – Mother, Mummy, Maman, Madame? She decided on nothing, for the moment.

'It's me.'

She wondered if Lillie would recognize her voice. Its timbre must have changed over fifty years.

She heard her mother take in a slow, juddering breath.

'Elodie?'

'Yes.' She was right by her chair now. She felt wrong, towering over her, so she crouched down.

She couldn't believe how tiny Lillie had become. She had never been large – always petite – but now she was a shrunken little woman, no bigger than a six-year-old child. Her hair was wispy and white and barely covered her scalp. Her cheekbones were sharper than ever; her lips cracked; her eyes huge in her face.

She looked pitiful. No matter what her mother had done to her, Elodie wouldn't have wished this on her. She felt revulsion and pity rise up in the throat. She hadn't expected this.

Lillie was reaching out a hand. Spillikin fingers, as cold as ice, clutched Elodie's arm.

'Is it really you? I can't tell.'

Of course she wouldn't recognize her. The last time Lillie had seen her daughter, Elodie had been a bride of twenty. Now she was seventy, albeit well preserved. She could still pass for mid-fifties. She had kept her figure. She dressed well. Her skin was good; her haircut sharp. The importance of those things her mother had drummed into her. Yet age, it seemed, got you in the end, no matter how good your genes or your regime.

'Yes. It's me.'

'My beautiful girl…' Lillie reached out and touched Elodie's face. Her hair. 'What did I do to you?'

Her voice was cracked with sadness. Her face even more so.

'It's OK. It doesn't matter now.' Elodie wanted to reassure her. She couldn't berate this pitiful creature. Not that she had intended to do that. She picked her mother's hands up in hers, stroking them, running her fingertips over the swollen joints, the raised veins.

'What do you want?' Lillie sounded distressed. 'What have you come for, after all this time?'

274

'I wanted to see you, Maman.' Elodie found herself instinctively reverting to the French, which she had used when she was small.

Lillie shook her head. 'I wanted to find you. I wanted to explain. It wasn't meant to happen like that ... But I was too afraid. Too ashamed.'

'I know. I know.' Elodie found herself murmuring empty platitudes. She couldn't bear the thought that she was causing this pitiful creature distress. She was so frail; she didn't think she could take it. 'Please – I didn't come here to upset you.'

There was no point in a confrontation or recriminations. It would be like crushing a beetle with her boot.

'Every day I have thought of you. Every day I have wondered how you are. Do you know what it's like, to lose your daughter?'

'No ...' Elodie couldn't begin to imagine it. 'But I'm here now, Maman.'

'But why?' There were tears in Lillie's eyes.

'Because ... because I wanted to tell you it's OK.'

How bald and insufficient that word seemed. But it was true. There was no point in Lillie seeing her days out in this room, tortured by what she had done. She had suffered enough.

She could feel her mother trembling. Should she notify one of the staff? Did she always tremble, or was the emotion too much for her? She had to admit she felt shaky herself.

'Could I have some water?' Lillie held out an arm to indicate a carafe on the dressing table. Elodie filled a paper cup, then handed it to her mother. She looked like a baby bird as she bent her head to drink: bedraggled, vulnerable.

When she'd finished she looked at Elodie. The water seemed to revive her. She held her head proud, and Elodie saw a vestige of her former beauty.

275

'Your father ... I am not going to blame him, but he was a very cruel man. He wanted to keep me ... in a cage. A beautiful gold cage that only he had the key to. I was so bored, Elodie. I wanted to do so much more with my life, but how could I? I had to be the dutiful wife. He would not let me work. Use my brain. All I had to think about was what I looked like ...'

'I thought ...' Elodie was surprised. 'I thought that was what you wanted?'

'No. To be truthful, I didn't know what I wanted. But I was jealous of you.'

'Jealous?' Elodie felt shocked. Never for a moment would she have imagined the self-assured and glamorous Lillie being jealous of her.

'You had a future. I knew you would be something. You would never just turn into a version of me. You had so much more about you. You were strong.'

She held the cup up to her lips and drank again. Elodie had a flashback of Lillie with a coupe of champagne. Her heart contracted with regret for the lost years.

'I didn't like myself very much, my darling. I felt useless. Pointless. I was just an ornament for your father. Another one of his status symbols.' She shut her eyes. Elodie could see tiny blue veins on the lids. 'I went after Jolyon to hurt them, not you.'

'Them?'

'Your father and Jeanie.'

Elodie blinked. She processed the thought. If anything, she would have suspected her mother and Roger of having an affair. Jeanie had seemed so perfect, so untouchable. Suddenly, everything made more sense.

Desmond and Jeanie.

'They were having an affair?'

'Oh yes. That's why he was so delighted about you and Jolyon. It cemented the partnership. It meant he could always be near her.'

Elodie felt queasy. She had been manipulated by everyone. She had been oblivious. She had been wrapped up in her happy-ever-after without knowing she was a pawn in everyone else's sordid little game. Everyone was complicit except Roger – ironically, the one person who had made her feel suspicious was the only one not implicated.

Lillie carried on talking, her voice an eerie whisper in the gloom, as if it was the ghost of her former self.

'I felt humiliated. They flaunted it, with their trips away, their meetings, their plans. I wanted to prove to myself that I was powerful. That I could have whoever I wanted. Seducing Jolyon was the perfect answer ...'

At this point she gave such a Gallic shrug that Elodie almost laughed. It was such a French solution to the problem; so typical of her mother, now Elodie had the benefit of hindsight and life experience. Of course, at the time, she had been blind to everything.

'Once I had seduced him, I couldn't let go.' There was a flicker of Lillie's old defiance. Elodie flinched at the words. She didn't want to think about it, even now. Her mother closing in on Jolyon, beguiling him with her beauty. How could he have resisted?

'I became addicted to his attention. I wanted to be wanted so much. I didn't care that he wasn't mine to have, that he was yours, that he was your future.'

The hand holding Lillie's cup was trembling so much that she dropped it. Water splashed onto her skirt, but neither of them took any notice.

'It was a terrible thing to do,' whispered Elodie, 'but I think I understand.'

'You weren't supposed to find out.' Lillie's head lolled to one side, as if she was too tired to hold it up. 'I was never going to stop you having your life with him.'

'But he thought it was OK to do that?' Elodie found her voice tightening, with anger and tears.

'Elodie, he had no idea what he was doing. He was young, vulnerable, confused. He didn't feel good about it. He was ... tortured.'

Elodie shut her eyes. She could feel tears coming as she remembered overhearing the conversation that had changed her life. She knew her mother was right: that Jolyon had suffered. That didn't take away from the fact that he had done what he must have known was wrong.

'What happened to him?'

'Jolyon?' Lillie gave a shrug. 'I do not know. There was never any reason for me to find out what happened to him. Maybe he found another girl?'

Elodie chewed her lip. She had always avoided trying to track down Jolyon, although it would have been easy, for she had felt so strongly that Edmund had been Otto's father. She didn't want to confuse her son, although Otto knew Edmund was not of his blood. And Edmund had done such a wonderful job, she felt it would be disrespectful to dig up Jolyon and produce him like a rabbit out of a hat, even after Edmund's death. Anyway, Otto was now a grown man and had children himself. If he'd wanted to find out who his real father was, Elodie wouldn't have stood in his way, but he had never asked her for the information.

Lillie was shifting in her chair. She looked uncomfortable. 'After the wedding, everything fell apart,' she said. 'Your

278

father was furious. Even though he was guilty too, what I had done was so much worse. And it was in public, so everyone knew.'

Elodie couldn't begin to imagine the aftermath. Everyone's life unravelling in full view of friends and relatives. And Jolyon in the middle of it. Hardly an innocent victim – Lillie hadn't held a gun to his head, presumably – but he'd had the most to lose.

'The business partnership collapsed, of course. Your father pulled out his investment. And Roger left Jeanie, but he was no innocent. He was only with her for the money. The rat deserted the sinking ship.'

The bitterness in Lillie's tone told Elodie that Roger must have spurned her advances at some point. But she wasn't going to accuse her mother of anything else. It hardly mattered now. All that was evident is that the situation had been a hotbed of unhappy people in unhappy marriages. Elodie was not going to judge. All she felt was lucky that she had been able to have a happy life after the event, despite everything, and that she thought the best was probably yet to come.

'And … my father?'

'We stayed together for a while. There seemed no point in separating. But eventually we drifted apart. I stayed in The Grey House. He stayed up in Worcestershire. He died … five years ago.'

Elodie took in a breath. Even though they had had no contact for all those years, apart from the olive branch she had chosen to ignore, it was still a shock to hear he was dead. She felt a ripple of regret that it was too late for any sort of reconciliation with him.

Yet not too late for her and Lillie. Her profoundest feeling, as she looked at her mother, was of pity. She doubted Lillie had set out to be cruel. She was selfish, perhaps, and self-centred, but she was certain her intention hadn't been to hurt Elodie. She had thought she would get away with it, no doubt. She'd been insecure, unhappy; lonely too, probably. As a writer, Elodie had spent a long time thinking about human motivation and why people behaved the way they did. It had given her empathy for most things.

Lillie let out a sigh and seemed to crumple before her very eyes, as if talking had sucked the very last of her energy.

'Are you all right?' asked Elodie.

Lillie shut her eyes and shook her head. 'I'm so very tired.'

Her voice was barely there. It faded away to a whisper. Her head fell to one side and a moment later she was asleep, her breathing shallow. Elodie had no idea if this was normal, or what her mother's official state of health was, but in that moment, she made a decision.

She would take her mother back to The Grey House. She could have her old room, with the view she loved so much. She would hire a carer to look after her when she wasn't there. She couldn't bear to see her alone in this place a moment longer, with its sterile, efficient service that had no heart. It was time to forget what had happened and to set things right. To let the house heal the rift.

Lillie opened her eyes.

'I want you to come home with me,' Elodie told her. 'It will be a couple of months, because there's work to be done.'

'Home?' Lillie's eyes clouded with confusion. 'Where is that?'

'The Grey House. I bought The Grey House.'

'You did?' Lillie took in the information, a veil of bewilderment over her face. 'But why?'

'It was the place where I was happiest. It's where I belong. It's where we belong.'

'I don't understand. I don't understand how you could... want me there.'

Elodie sighed.

'Because you're my mother, and what happened doesn't matter any more. And because...' she took in a deep breath for the last revelation. 'Because I am going to marry the love of my life. And I want you to meet him. And I want you to meet my son.'

'Son...' Lillie seemed to be trying the word as if for the first time. 'You have children. I have a grandson.'

'You have a wonderful grandson.' She wasn't going to break the news that Otto was Jolyon's. She thought perhaps her mother had taken on enough that afternoon. She seemed, if it were possible, even frailer than she had when Elodie arrived. 'And great-grandchildren. And all of them are reasons for my coming back here.'

The picture was clear in her head. All of them, her existing family and her new family, on the beach, spilling out of the hut, talking, laughing, eating, arguing, running, making sandcastles, playing rounders. And she and Colm in the centre of it. Their rocks.

Lillie held out a hand – a shrivelled little claw. Elodie grasped it tight.

'I'm sorry,' said Lillie. 'I am so, so sorry.'

A trail of glittery tears seeped out of her eyes and down the paper-thin skin on her face. Elodie reached out and brushed them gently away.

'This is not a day for tears, Maman,' she said.

TIM AND RACHEL

Only a few weeks ago, the midday sun would have made Rachel feel sick. But now she had passed into the middle trimester, the nausea had passed as swiftly as it had arrived. She felt stronger and more full of energy, even though her condition was now apparent to anyone who cared to look closely. She held her shoes in her hand, walking on the damp sand the tide had recently vacated. It was cool on the soles of her feet. The dry sand further up would be scorching: she would walk along the beach as far as she could before venturing onto it, once she became level with the hut.

She didn't know how she was going to approach him. There was no script for what she was about to do, of that she was certain. But she had to ask. She'd be crazy not to ask. Though she felt slightly uncomfortable when she thought of his possible reaction. Her proposition, she thought, could go either way.

It wasn't how she'd planned it. It really wasn't. A suspicious mind might assume it had been premeditated from the word go, but Rachel had honestly thought it was all going to be all right with Lee. He had been shocked when she told him she was pregnant at first, but his shock had quickly turned to pride and excitement. He had wanted to shout the news from the rooftops, but she had urged him to wait until the crucial first three months were over before broadcasting it to all and sundry.

By which time, he had started to get cold feet. The weekend she had got back from the beach hut, the weekend she had confessed her condition to Tim, she could tell by the state of the flat that Lee had been out on the razz. His nights out had become more and more frequent. He ended up sleeping on the sofa – so as not to disturb her, he said, but she sensed a reluctance in him to touch her. A reluctance that almost became a revulsion as her condition became more apparent.

She'd called him on it. This was important to her, this baby. All babies were important, of course, but she felt even more protective than the average first-time mother, given what she had been through.

'You're not happy about this, are you?' she asked him one night while he sat in front of the TV screen, manipulating the handset of some intergalactic computer game – it had seemed to become his escape, this world fraught with danger and noise.

She wasn't being confrontational, just matter-of-fact.

He didn't bluster or protest. He paused his game and looked her straight in the eye. 'I don't think I'm ready.'

She nodded as she considered his reply. 'Fair enough.'

He picked up his bottle of beer and starting picking at the label.

'I'm sorry. I just can't get my head round it. I mean, it's going to be like a prison sentence, isn't it?' He peeled off a long strip and crumpled the paper up in his fingers.

She tried not to show the ice in her eyes. 'The baby's

going to be our priority, yes. If that's what you mean. Of course it is.'

Lee looked awkward. He leaned forward, resting his arms on his thighs, the bottle dangling between the fingers of one hand, staring down at the floor. His long fringe fell forward; his shoulders were slight. He seemed like a boy, although he was thirty-four. Perfectly old enough to take the responsibility. But she wasn't going to force him into it. She wanted the father of her baby to be one hundred percent dedicated. She could sense the tension and the arguments already, and the baby was barely bigger than an orange. Already it had come between them.

'It would be better if we split now, than put the baby through all the arguing.' She couldn't believe how calmly she said it.

He looked up. The relief on his face was palpable. 'I'm really sorry, Rach. I just think I'll be a shit dad. I'll give you money and everything ...'

The baby had been unexpected, but he knew what she'd been through, so they'd agreed to give it a go. Rachel had been so bowled over by being pregnant, she hadn't read the danger signs or picked up on his underlying reluctance. She'd mistakenly expected Lee to be as thrilled as she was, which in retrospect was a huge error of judgment. But her judgment had been skewed – by the drugs, the disappointment, the divorce.

'It wasn't fair of me, to force you into it.'

'You didn't force me.' Lee seemed distressed. 'You so didn't. I wanted it too. At least I thought I did. But now I just don't know ...'

'It's OK,' she said. 'If you want to go, go. I'll be fine. I know I will.'

'But it's a terrible thing to do.'

'No,' said Rachel. 'What would be terrible would be for us to stay together and end up hating each other and splitting up anyway. This way we can stay friends.'

Her clarity astonished her. She found a strength inside she didn't know she had. The choice was up to him, though. She wasn't going to force him into anything. He was the baby's father. It was up to him to decide.

He went. They wept together, and hugged, and he packed up his clothes and his Xbox and his bike and went to stay with his mate. And Rachel glided around her empty flat for three weeks, turning things over in her mind, examining her conscience, reassuring herself that she hadn't used or manipulated Lee. Her fear was that he, or people, might think she had just used him and then thrown him to one side when he had served his purpose, but she genuinely hadn't. She'd gone into their relationship with optimism. She had liked him. His aversion to the situation had come from him, not any particular pressure she had put him under. Of that she was quite sure.

So when she drove down the motorway to Everdene, her conscience was clear. She had no inkling what her reception would be. If this was the craziest idea ever. But she had to give it a go.

She'd tried not to overthink what she was doing. She hadn't run through all the possible scenarios. It was too stressful. She had decided that what would be would be. And anyway, the most likely outcome would be that she would head back home on her own. That she would have the baby on her own. And she would manage.

And now here she was, in front of the beach hut. The beach hut that Tim wanted to be hers. The beach hut that

285

had once been theirs. Even now, she could remember their euphoria as they took possession of it on that first day. It wasn't the most salubrious hut on the beach: it was ramshackle and wonky and really needed knocking down and re-building, but it had been theirs and they had loved it.

The door was shut. There was no way of telling what sort of shut. A just-popped-to-the-shop sort of shut, or something more permanent. She felt wrong-footed. On a glorious Saturday like this, she had felt sure he would be there. She felt the key in her pocket. It would be wrong of her to go in. It would be an invasion of his privacy. And she didn't know what she might find.

But she felt so tired. The drive, the walk, the heat – it overwhelmed her. She needed something to drink. She could walk back up the beach to one of the vans selling cold cans and ice cream. On the other hand, she knew he wouldn't mind. He just wouldn't. That's how well she knew him.

She slid the key into the lock and pushed open the door. Inside, nothing much had changed since she'd left it. She tried very hard not to examine everything for evidence of anyone else. It took a supreme effort of will. But nothing was apparent. No female detritus. No scarves or dinky little size ten wetsuits or lipstick traces.

She filled up a glass of water at the sink and drank. She'd overdone it, she realized. She would have to sit down. She collapsed onto the sofa, remembering the last time the two of them had sat there. When he'd made the incredibly generous offer that had made her realize there was never going to be another man for her. Had that subconsciously made her send off negative signals to Lee, she wondered? Had something deep within her driven him away? She hoped not.

The thoughts spinning round her head became jumbled and she felt herself drifting. She lay her head down on a cushion. Just for a moment, she thought. Just a moment …

'Hey.' The voice was gentle and kind. 'Hey. Goldilocks.'

Rachel started awake. Oh God. She hadn't meant to fall asleep. And now she'd been caught, bang to rights. Tim was standing over her. He was in his wetsuit, his hair still damp and slicked back. He looked concerned.

'Are you OK?'

She sat up, insensible with afternoon sleep. 'Oh my God, I'm so sorry. I just came in for some water. You must think I'm really out of order—'

'Rach …' He put out a hand to touch her shoulder. 'Don't be daft.'

'But it's your month.'

He rolled his eyes and shook his head with a smile. 'You're being silly.'

She felt sticky; her hair had stuck to the side of her head where she'd lain on the pillow.

'What are you doing here?'

She blinked at him. Now she was here, her idea seemed mad. She didn't know what to say.

'Is everything all right?' He looked down at her stomach. There was a noticeable bump; a perfect dome, hard under the soft fabric of her T-shirt. She saw him take in the slightest breath.

'Yes. Yes, everything's fine. Absolutely fine.' She couldn't think what to say.

'So …?'

What should she tell him? She swallowed. Put a hand on her stomach with one hand; brushed her hair back with the other.

'I ...'

She was going to tell him. She was going to tell him about Lee going, and leave it up to him. But before the words came out of her mouth, another figure appeared in the doorway. A slight woman, with equally damp hair and a freckled face, also in a wetsuit. She was carrying two Magnums.

'Quick – before they melt. I got you the dark chocolate one. Better for you than the white ...'

The woman stopped and looked at Rachel.

'This is Rachel,' said Tim.

'Oh,' said the woman, a million meanings in the word.

'She can have my ice cream.' Tim took one of the Magnums and passed it to Rachel. The woman did not look best pleased.

Rachel floundered for an explanation.

'I just called in because ... I was down seeing some friends and it seemed rude not to come and say hello.' It was lame, but it was the best she could come up with.

'Really.' The chill in the woman's tone was arctic. 'I'll go, then, shall I?'

'No!' Rachel panicked. She didn't want to cause trouble. 'Honestly. I was in Everdene and I thought ...'

'Yeah.' The woman marched across the hut to grab what Rachel could now see were her clothes, hanging on the back of a chair – a sweatshirt and jeans she had mistaken for Tim's.

'Honey—' Tim put out a restraining hand.

'Don't call me honey.' She jerked away from him, her face full of fury.

'Please,' said Rachel. 'It's a misunderstanding.'

The woman stood in front of her with her clothes bunched up in a bundle. 'Mystery pregnant woman appears from nowhere? I'm not an idiot.'

Rachel and Tim looked at each other.

'Oh God. It's not mine! If that's what you're thinking,' said Tim.

'You would say that.' The woman shoved her ice cream at him. 'You can have that one. I've lost my appetite all of a sudden.'

She turned and marched out of the hut.

Tim raised his eyebrows and gave a heavy sigh. 'Well.'

'Oh God,' said Rachel. 'I'm so sorry.'

'Don't be,' said Tim. 'She was getting a bit much. Nice girl but a total control freak. Won't even let me choose my own Magnum flavour.'

He started unwrapping the ice cream nevertheless. They ate in silence for a moment, looking at each other. Tim started to laugh. 'Talk about getting the wrong end of the stick.'

Rachel joined in. 'I know. Gotta love irony.'

They carried on laughing, almost until it hurt, the tension and weirdness of the situation fuelling their mirth. Tim had always been able to make her laugh, thought Rachel. And laughing was so important. She realized she hadn't laughed, not properly, for a very long time.

Tim suddenly stopped, and stared at her. She stared back. Time stood still. Should she tell him? Or should she make her escape; face the journey on her own? Pretend she really had just called in to say hello.

'We've split up.'

'What – you and—' He still couldn't remember the bloke's name. Something footballer-y.

'Lee. Yes.'

Tim nodded. Swallowed and nodded, wondering what was coming next.

'I'm sorry. I guess? If you are? I don't know …'

'I'm not sorry. I'm relieved.' The words tumbled out of her.

'Good. I suppose.'

He felt so awkward. He didn't know the rules, or why she was here, or what he was supposed to say. He turned away, because he realized he had the tiniest of hopes and he didn't want her to see it. Just in case.

'Would you like a cup of tea?' God, how banal and English.

'I don't really drink tea at the moment.'

'No. Of course not. What would you like instead?'

She didn't answer. He turned around. 'Rach?'

She was sitting up straight, staring at him. He wanted to touch her hair. Her beautiful hair. He wanted to take her in his arms.

'Is it too late?' she asked.

'For what?'

'Us?'

His heart was hammering. 'I don't know what you mean.'

'I don't want to have this baby on my own. If I have to, I will, of course. But …'

'Oh my God.'

'Or is it just too weird?'

'Weird?' Tim shook his head in disbelief. 'Yes, it's

weird, because it's like a dream come true. I haven't stopped thinking about you since you left. I haven't stopped worrying about you. I haven't stopped wanting you, Rachel – wanting to look after you. Wanting to spend the rest of my life with you ...'

His voice broke. The emotion was too much. He came and knelt in front of her, holding her hands.

'I feel the same,' she whispered.

He pulled her in tight, ran his hands through her hair, that silken hair he had never forgotten.

'I didn't plan it,' said Rachel. 'I didn't use Lee. I honestly didn't. I thought it would work. But it wasn't what he wanted.'

'Shhhh,' said Tim. 'I know. It's OK. You haven't done anything wrong.'

'People will think it's strange.'

'People can think what they like.'

'It's my baby,' said Rachel. 'It's my baby, first and foremost. Isn't it?'

'Of course it is.'

They held each other, as tight as tight could be.

'You can teach the baby to swim,' said Rachel. 'I can watch while you teach the baby to swim.'

Tim buried his face in her neck, breathed in the scent of Rachel that he had never forgotten. He had gone from feeling empty, a shadow of himself, like a very bad actor playing a part in a play he didn't believe in, to feeling invincible. So filled with happiness it hurt.

She held his hands and pulled herself to her feet. 'Let's walk down to the sea,' she said. 'I want to feel the water on my skin.'

They wandered hand in hand down to the sea edge. The

beach was crowded, but they felt as if they were the only people in the world. Rachel rolled up her skirt and they walked into the water. The waves lapped around them, eager, as if welcoming them back after a long time away.

'Cordelia,' said Rachel. 'It means daughter of the sea.'

'Is it a girl, then?'

'I don't know,' said Rachel.

'Well, definitely Cordelia,' said Tim. 'If it's a girl. Obviously.'

She nudged him with her elbow, smiling. 'What if it's a boy?'

They both thought for a moment.

'How about Neptune?' Tim suggested. 'Going with the sea theme.'

She frowned. 'I thought Poisedon.'

They turned to look at each other. They were both trying desperately to keep a straight face. Rachel cracked first. She bent double, laughing, and Tim pretended to look wounded and confused but then he gave in, and they leaned into each other as the water swirled around them, helpless with the kind of laughter that makes you want to live forever and ever.

ELODIE

Elodie stood at the top of the cliff path. It was only just before dawn, and a soft breeze ruffled the marram grass. Pink started to spread across the sky, like paint being squeezed from a tube. It lit up the horizon with a rosiness that lifted her heart. There was nothing more uplifting than daybreak by the sea.

Earlier in the week she and Colm had married, very quietly, in a civil ceremony at a hotel in Hampstead, with afternoon tea afterwards. She had eschewed a reception and a honeymoon; just told him that she had a surprise. She had left him the night before with a white envelope he wasn't to open until the morning, which contained instructions on how to get to Everdene. All their children had a similar envelope, and instructions to pack overnight bags for themselves and the grandchildren.

Fifteen altogether, they would be, their enmeshed family. The bedrooms were all made up and ready. The house had been painted in a pale limewash, the wooden floors stripped; the kitchens and bathrooms replaced with simple white units. The drawing room had lost its formality – now there were low, squashy sofas and sheer curtains in different shades of grey and silver. There was very little else yet – Elodie wanted the house to grow with her and Colm in their new life, rather than inflict what she already had upon it. They would choose books and paintings and ornaments together over the next few years. She wanted the house to be allowed to breathe; to let it evolve.

The pièce de résistance, for the youngest ones, was the beach hut. She'd had it completely renovated, re-using all the old wood, so it still had the feel of having been there decades, yet had all the mod cons needed for an overnight stay. There were curtains and cushions in ice-cream stripes, and bunk beds and built-in cupboards, as snug as a gypsy caravan.

The hut still felt special to her. The memories from her childhood were still good ones; she wouldn't let them be spoiled by what came after. And actually, she wouldn't go back and change anything. She loved who she was, what she had become, the people she had spent her life with, the life she wasn't meant to have had. Lady Bellnap, Edmund, and now Colm – she would never have known their kindness and strength and wisdom had things gone according to plan.

All that was left of that part of her past was Lillie. But they had reforged their bond and it was stronger than ever. Some of her mother's old strength and spirit seemed to have been restored to her since she left the home. She had put on weight and she was a far better colour. Her interest in her appearance had revived – thanks to Elodie, Lillie had discovered the Internet, and there was hardly a day when a new silk scarf or flacon of perfume didn't arrive. Elodie had found a local woman who was happy to come in and keep house while she was in London, so she knew Lillie was looked after properly, and she had been in to see the local GP to make sure that if her mother needed medical attention, they were on hand.

And now she waited for the rest of her family to arrive – her own flesh and blood, and her offspring by marriage. Everdene was the perfect place for the generations to co-exist. She wanted The Grey House to be there for all of them, for them to come and go as they pleased, for them to be able to invite their friends. She wanted security and happiness and a sense of place for all of them, a sense of coming home.

After all, if she could have that feeling, after fifty years, then Everdene would work its magic on them too. She put her face up to the breeze, marvelling at how happy she felt, how contented, how calm.

At half past ten, she heard the crunch of tyres on the new gravel she'd had laid on the drive. She rushed to the front door, flinging it open, and her heart swelled with joy as she saw Colm get out of his car, a smile of bemused wonder on his face.

'Nice gaffe,' he said, with his usual dry understatement.

'Well,' said Elodie. 'It's sort of my wedding present. Not just to you, but to all of us.'

Colm took his overnight bag out of the boot and slammed it shut. 'It's a lovely present. Much nicer than a wedding reception. A family weekend at the seaside.' He breathed in the sea air appreciatively.

'Um. Not just a weekend.'

Colm raised an eyebrow as he grinned at her, and Elodie looked a bit sheepish. But that was what she loved about him – the fact that he wouldn't question what she had done or complain that she had kept a secret from him. They trusted each other so completely. They were as one, yet two distinct individuals.

Elodie drew him inside and walked him through the hall towards the drawing room. She threw open the door. It had never looked more perfect, the sunshine streaming in, turning the grey to silver; the sea a haze of pewter in the distance.

'Wow.' Colm nodded. 'Just … wow.'

'This is ours,' said Elodie. 'It's for you and me, and all the children. All of us. For ever.'

'Really?' Colm looked at her.

'I'm not trying to hijack our life,' Elodie told him, 'but this place means more to me than anywhere on earth, and I want you and I and our families to enjoy it.'

'You've bought it?'

Elodie bit her lip, but she couldn't help smiling as she nodded. 'Brings new meaning to the words impulse purchase.'

'You can say that again.'

'Though it wasn't an impulse purchase, really. It was a … compulsory purchase. I didn't have any choice in the matter.'

'I can imagine. It's a magical place,' said Colm. He took her hand, and together they walked out through the French windows and onto the terrace. The sea breeze rushed forward to caress them. Elodie felt a rush of joy; a huge sense that everything had come full circle after all these years.

'There is a story, of course.'

Colm smiled. 'Of course there is. It wouldn't be you if there wasn't.'

'Do you want to hear it?'

'Does it have a happy ending?'

She smiled. 'This is the ending.'

'Then yes. I'd love to hear it.'

Elodie led him down onto the lawn. She couldn't begin to count the number of times she had walked across it. But this time, she was with the love of her life. The man she wanted to spend the rest of her days with. They reached the top of the dunes and she heard Colm take in a breath of wonder as he took in the full view of the beach below and the sea beyond.

'Once upon a time,' she began, 'there was a girl who spent every summer by the seaside ...'